SGT. THOR

THE DAMNED BK.03

JASON **ANSPACH**
NICK **COLE**

An imprint of Galaxy's Edge Press

PO BOX 534
Puyallup, Washington 98371

Paperback ISBN: 979-8-88922-041-1

www.wargatebooks.com

CHAPTER ONE

BEYOND THE CITIES OF MEN, SERGEANT THOR ventured into the depths of the mysterious Eastern Wastes, seeking an edge against which to test himself. A challenge to be worthy of, and perhaps... an answer for a question he knew not yet the words of.

But any sage or wandering deranged and lotus-addled bard, chanting hypnotic nonsense words from long ago, could have told that fearsome and moody wanderer what lay there among the lost and past mysteries of the Rift and the fractured and time-broken lands encompassed within the barely marked regions on the ancient yellowing maps of the Ruin.

Danger.

Death.

Mysteries to be revealed if only damnation could be cheated in a game of desperate chance.

In those vast and fractured lands whose boundaries were unsure, and depths unknown, lay lost cities from the long-ago-lost fabled Golden Age of the Ruin, when once for a bright and shining moment the upstart civilizations of humanity almost had their chance, fighting great wars and undertaking expansions to drive back the foul and corrupt, ever-insidious Saur, banishing them forever across the cursed boundaries of the River of Night. There were rumors of bizarre wizards of great power and inexplicable schools of sinister magic unknown before, or ever in the times since. And yes... there were the true stories of heroes only known now as recounted myth and half-told legend, writ large in glyph and symbol, or arcanely along the carvings and obelisks half-buried within those vast and sinking sands. And too there were the lost remains of great expeditions that never returned, forever lost within the unknown spreading of the Wastes, and the Rift at their heart...

It was into these strange, fractured lands the Ranger rode his horse, followed by the thief and a serving girl, one horse to each, and a thankless mule for the burden of crossing into the unknown from the comfortable known. There were many adventures in the days of the trio's crossing into the make-a-sign-to-ward-off-evil east, for *east is curst*, as they say true, departing as they did from the Fields of the Dead beyond the fabled City of Thieves, and then onto the high plateaus above the Rift at the heart of the waste itself where once, long ago, it was said a great star of the stars fell and caused the Ruin, and brought the dragons, and the coming of the Nether Sorcerer, and had caused the enigmatic Rift to be.

And all the strangeness that came afterward.

Here, along the southern edge of the Eastern Wastes, the trio hauling their thankless braying mule that Sato had taken to calling Burūto, they passed the ruins of lost and unremembered fortress cities long haunted by ghosts of the past and jackals and vultures who made their home and hunting grounds there now.

"All of these cities, Warrior," cried Sato over the howling desert blasts, "were where great heroes issued forth to battle against gods and demons and dragons. Now they are lonely places no one dares to venture into. What tales and hoards lie within wouldn't tempt even an army of thieves to come forth in such harsh conditions."

But in many cases the sand had consumed these lost cities as it skirled and blasted, howling like a banshee as the night came on, and all that remained were the highest and most ornate towers, or golden domes of renowned temples, rising from the sands like doomed wrecks must in the seas of all the Ruin.

There were brief breaks in the long and relentless days of heat, and the brutal nights of cold, and it was at a crossroads in these silent and sometimes howling desert lands, where once an ancient stone marker pointed toward the great city none could remember the name of, and the distant ruins that were no longer there anymore...

... that is, unless you asked some travelers on strange full-moon nights, passing along in quiet caravan, cloaked and atop high camels laden with exotic spices from the east and the end of the world who indicated that not just three nights ago they'd stopped at the well in the City of the Golden Dome and were welcomed much by the citizens there.

And yet Sato would comment, rubbing his scraggly chin and musing almost aloud, "But, Warrior, that city has not existed for a thousand years. Vampire clans from the Bloody Cliffs were said to have come in hordes one unfortunate night and carried off all the inhabitants back to their red sandstone fortress high in the unscalable walls of that place not even this humble thief would tempt the locks of, not even for the grand treasures it guards deep down in the caves below."

"But they said they had food and shelter from this cursed wind there, Sato. That would be nice," exclaimed the indignant "serving girl" as she petted her creamy skin. "I burn and chafe under the relentless blast. Soon I'll be old and no one will want me, even at half price."

Sato grunted and muttered, eyeing the horizon and the sunken domes behind it turning to little more than shadows in the bloody red glare of the afternoon.

"The place is gone, foolish girl, and has been for many a year now. My fingers still work just a little better than my mind, but a thief never forgets where he might need to steal a pretty gem from on occasion of dire need. And only the silent walls give tell of the people who once called that city a home and gazed with admiration on their fabled Dome of Achillus the Mighty."

The Golden Dome turned to shadow in the dying of the day, falling farther behind them as the horses and the ungrateful mule took them deeper into the haunted wastes the map made no markings within.

"But it was there, so says the traveler," murmured Alluria, and cast her gaze longingly back upon the cursed place.

Then both made signs to ward off evils and curses, for there are many curses in the Eastern Wastes, and more so the closer one gets to the Great Rift itself, or so it is said.

And so they passed on, following the Ranger into the coming purple night.

They met other seeming lost strangers out there in the desert wastes. A caravan they'd intercepted heading off into the direction it must go to sell its goods at whatever city it had long been plodding toward, the direction at the instance of the crossroads. Another, a messenger perhaps, riding hard for the rumors of an oasis further days ahead, or the edge of the wastes, muttering dark and hopeless prayers that they might never come this way again no matter how much time is saved in the crossing.

No matter how many shining gold coins were promised for the crossing and the important message delivered.

"Many a caravanner has muttered such prayers..." said Sato as they rode along, "... and prayed they would never see the Night that Never Ends, which is a rumor of what lies ahead, a story perhaps, a tale, of what sometimes happens in the wastes the farther one goes, Warrior. These things are worth considering the closer one gets to the Rift itself."

But Sergeant Thor the Ranger said nothing and continued ahead, occasionally patting the Pearl of Great Price he kept in the cargo pocket of his CryePrecisions.

It was at such a crossroads, another meaningless marking that seemed to have no rhyme nor reason why it should ever have been erected, as the devil winds had long ago scoured away any markings along the face of the monument, early night having fallen and the sky turned brown and ominous, almost ochre in the failing half-light, that Thor spied the bent and broken shepherd, his crook in hand, a shadow in the last of the day, peering into the twilight, seeking a flock that could not be found.

It was a strange sight, and something about it bothered the Ranger.

He patted the MK48 super SAW slung across his great broad bare shoulders, and pulled back the dust cover as he did so.

He felt something like a trap, an *X*, approaching. And it paid to be ready for such moments. Or at least, as ready as one could be.

CHAPTER TWO

THOR RODE TOWARD THE SHEPHERD IN THE fading twilight as the night grew stronger and darker. Winds howled and moaned like the keening of the ghosts of wronged women. Flying sand came in sudden blasts and there was... something... something dangerous and wrong in this wind and even Thor could taste and feel it like it was something that, had the twilight and the wind not been so thick and distracting, could be seen as real and present, and dangerous.

The Ranger smelled death on the wind. The air was colder than it should have been despite the day's relentless heat only now just fading. But he said nothing to the others just as he had for most of the day, riding point for most of that hot, tense, and silent afternoon as the storm came on before nightfall and it seemed certain some evil trap lay just ahead.

He'd scanned the horizon, watched the shadows, and waited as nothing revealed itself.

Now... there was the bent and crooked shepherd just ahead and things felt off, and somehow wrong.

"Hail... stranger," crooned the old bent and crooked shepherd, his voice feeble and high, long brown fingers and yellowed too-long nails held to his thin cinnamon lips to make his much-unused voice heard over the storm's sudden shriekings and the whiplash blasts of flying grit seeking their eyes as they shielded against it with their hands. "Seek you the village of Um-Mal, wanderers?"

The thin gaunt man spoke the desert patois of Arabic and Chinese, and a smattering of a few other languages, including Gray Speech and even some cruel and hissing orcish from those hordes passing out of the north and coming this way on their raids that had always plagued this region since anyone could remember.

The Ranger had learned much of this language during his time within the streets and alleys of the City of Thieves, in service to the Thieves' Guild. Now he understood it easily, for the most part. And could speak it slowly and purposefully which was in keeping with his grim and stoic nature regardless.

Such is the demeanor of most Rangers, and he was like all his kind as they were like him in this manner.

Thor lowered his shemagh and spit a stream of dip off into the wind as he studied the bent and crooked old shepherd with the singsong dry croak of a voice.

His time with the Rangers back in the world of the Before had seen many deployments, or "pumps" as the Rangers called them, to the various deserts of the world. Hotspots where bad guys needed to be smoked. Places where hurricanes of incoming lead and falling iron were aimed and directed at the Rangers who unlike all involved were only too willing to Ranger Smash, and fade, leaving the dead to be lamented by their mourning women.

But to Sergeant Thor, on this death of an afternoon, the heat fading to cold, the wind coming in carrying all it could pick up off the desert floor, perhaps there was a village with a mean little tavern, and a stable for the horses and ornery mule, which would be a welcome relief. A place the shepherd called home, and that had to be weighed in the balance. Perhaps it was a "wire" to get behind if there was some danger, some X, out there in the desert twilight headed at them.

It had been a week since the last "town."

And that had been a strange affair indeed.

But... there was something about this shepherd. Something that didn't add up. Something that bothered the Ranger like a tickle in the back of his skull that could neither be scratched nor ignored.

Not out here.

Not on this unquiet evening that was promising to get much worse by the second the darker it got.

Where was the shepherd's flock?

Why was he out here all alone with so much death and danger on the wind and in the back of their skulls? Sato had remarked that there was, "some song in this night, Warrior, one I care not to hear while so exposed and without retreat."

Alluria had bundled into her cloaks as her wide watchful eyes darted here and there.

They hadn't seen another soul since a week ago. The Ranger had figured they were passing into a much-uninhabited region and that it would be that way for some time to come.

But the shepherd perhaps promised something else by his very presence out here in the coming storm.

CHAPTER THREE

"COME THEE, WANDERERS... FOR THE VILLAGE of Um-Mal?" crooned the shepherd above the blasting devil winds again.

The horses snorted and stamped, clearly uneasy about some... *thing*.

"There is a scent in the wind tonight, Warrior. We are near the Rift. Where things... are strange. But this scent is not wild magic... it is death, Ranger. I know it well. As do you." Sato had ridden close to the Ranger to give his unasked counsel on the matter at hand.

Sergeant Thor said nothing astride the powerful war horse the thieves of the guild had provided for him. Somewhere, some mercenary commander back in the City of Thieves was wondering what had become of his prized mount.

Thor's horse was chestnut, and it had a fiery temper as indicated by the beast's name: *Stormbringer*. The beast had seemed, in the pull and yank of the well-meaning thieves who'd stolen it, angry and ready to fight all. But it had found a kindred spirit in the Ranger and would not bite and kick as it had done to others along the way to its deliverance, whenever it possibly could. Sato had a dark horse, patchwork and sanguine, and Alluria's mount was its lighter twin in dapple gray. Both horses had been skittish around the stomping and blustering warhorse, but over the days' journey across the sands of the Eastern Wastes, the mounts had calmed and hunkered down to endure the arduousness of the trek higher and higher up onto the desert plateau that guarded this southern edge of the Rift.

"This storm looks like it'll deliver a solid beating tonight. And... we have had predators on our trail since this afternoon," rumbled Thor in a low voice like afternoon thunder rolling out across the valley, low enough that only Sato could hear beneath the blast of the storm.

The older thief grunted at this and switched to the spartan speech of working thieves.

"How did you know this, Warrior?" he asked in the cant.

"The fallen rocks in the pass," replied the Ranger in kind. "In the late afternoon, those who trailed left long shadows cast against the red rocks. They moved slow and they knew what they were doing, but I was able to catch hints of their movement as they followed us."

As a sniper with the Rangers, the NCO was well versed in observation and spotting the creepers and the stalkers who could always be counted on to be there, somewhere where the jackals and vultures of war collected. He'd played a game that long afternoon and counted more than twenty back there behind and following them.

"I have seen signs too," said Sato in the thieves' cant in such a way that no one listening would have even noticed any meaningful communication was actually taking place.

Other than the constant and clever shadowing up among the red rocks along the high canyon walls, the Ranger didn't know their intentions. But... it was best to assume those intentions were ill.

"They are dangerous," signaled Thor with a slight hand gesture. "They know where we're headed and they'll have the perfect place to trap us. We have to throw a wrench into their plans. If we can."

Thor knew horses could pick up on stuff once it started. So in the pass he had said nothing and kept the trio, their horses, and the mule moving farther up the canyon as swiftly as he could without giving the appearance that he was aware of the dangerous shadows. Another high plateau had been just ahead and he had thought that perhaps there they could make a run across open ground and get away from the barely seen predators along their back trail.

Or they could make a stand on some high ground and force them into a direct attack.

If so, Thor had more than enough armaments and munitions to deal with them.

So he said nothing and kept them all moving as the day waned, and then faded.

But he had not known that Sato had seen them also. Like Thor, the crafty old thief had wisely kept the info, sketchy as it was, to himself until he could be certain the predators didn't know they knew what was going down.

For the old thief, the "signs" were mostly just the possibility of a shadow that had suddenly moved too quickly in the fading light, or an accidental skittering stone knocked loose from high above, tumbling and clinking as it fell onto the rocks below the high burnt walls below the plateau.

It could have been the wind, that's all, the thief had made himself think, though he did not for a moment believe it, for predators had sharp eyes and they could read expressions like a skilled player of cards might to his advantage.

That could have been the wind, thought the thief. Even though it wasn't.

And now the two men, Alluria to the rear and holding the braying mule as the scouring wind came on and grew more dire, each agreed with silent signals on what they must do next.

"Come, wanderers... come with me to the village of Um-Mal."

In front of them the old shepherd turned and moved resolutely through the sandstorm as the last of the day and the coming of the night turned a bloody red-and-purple cloak off in the distances.

And so they proceeded, the sand flying and the wind keening of all the wrongs that had been done that day.

Occasionally the crooked old shepherd would, without turning, wave his hand at them that they should follow him, assuming, knowing really, that they were.

They heard snatches of his mutterings and the occasional laugh to himself as the man pulled himself across the hardpack of the waste, the storm increasing and seeming to swallow him at points. Then the brief front of flying sand would pass and there the bent yet tall shepherd would be, hauling at his staff, and waving them forward to where he was leading them.

Shortly the silhouette of a small village revealed itself ahead against all that sandblasted nothingness that the sky and the lands had become.

It seemed an odd place for a village to be, thought Sergeant Thor. In the middle of nothing remarkable. No road. No river. No mountain rock or high hill to hide on.

It was just a weird little odd collection of a place, leaning in the blasting winds coming off the desert.

Sato rode forward from riding herd to the rear for a time, waiting for the predators to attack. And this time his tone was urgent.

Unusual for the veteran thief.

"Ask me not, Warrior, how I know. But there are... vampires here."

Thor lowered his shemagh and eyed the thief, scrutinizing what his companion had just said. He had been through too much with the man to neglect his words, but...

"It is an old and long story, and if we survive this night... I will tell of it. But there is a smell of death that comes at us even now. Can you not smell it from the dark village ahead? The sun is down and it grows."

The Ranger turned and scented the blasts of wind coming from the shadowy leaning huts and larger buildings ahead. In the murderous blood-red half-light, the buildings looked like crooked and unkempt tombstones rising against the thundering sandstorm.

The old shepherd labored into their clutch, farther ahead than he should have been. Moving faster now as they got closer.

Alluria danced her horse alongside the two men, and the mule honked angrily under its considerable load.

Three days ago, the mule's burden had gotten much heavier from an unexpected, and unplanned, gift. Now the cantankerous mule never seemed to mind very much about complaining at all it had to haul.

The warhorse Thor rode snorted and stamped its great hooves against the desert, thumping as though walking thunder were under the soft shifting sands.

"I think we have a pack of wolves on our butts," said Alluria calmly, lowering her veil. Bow already in her hand. "We should get within the village soon... Though..." her beautiful face seemed quizzical for a moment, "... something else bothers me about that. Does it not you, thieves?"

Her delicate eyebrows arched as she asked the question. As though she was mocking them.

Sergeant Thor, still smelling the wind from off the village, now found the odor of bodies gone long foul within the blasts that came at him.

That smell of death...

He knew it well from the various sandboxes and hellholes the army had sent him off to kill in.

But there was something else. Something darker in it. Something colder passing through it. Something older, and dustier, and yes... evil. Like the smell of a book gone damp and moldy.

But with an aching hunger one could almost feel.

Thor reached for the mule, moving the warhorse close to the boorish beast, and of course the idiot mule didn't like that, but Alluria seemed to have a way with the mule, and that way was swatting the thing with a stick she'd found just right for the work. He pulled the canvas cover off a pack, reached in, and hauled out a small ordinary sack. From inside he pulled forth a belt of seven-six-two, ammunition for the squad automatic weapon, and then linked it to the trailing belt he'd already loaded in. He slung it around the piecemeal armor—scale and some leather and including one plate pauldron he'd acquired among the dwarves' forges in the bazaar, having been assured that it was a fine piece both for defense and offense.

It was worked like the head of an angry and tusked boar.

He adjusted the sling, checking the long-slide Glock and the leather mag holsters that the quiet yet furtive desert dwarves had crafted for him.

Satisfied by a tap that the dire battle axe the Northman merchant and his beautiful daughters had gifted him during a desperate moment in the weapons bazaars of the City of Thieves was on his back, Thor nodded.

There were other "supplies" on the mule, courtesy of the Forge back in Sûstagul and recently arrived via speedball. Weapons, including the super SAW, ammunition, explosives, new gear, and an unexpected few "toys."

And of course, about thirty tins of dip.

"What will we do, Warrior, if vampires lie ahead within the squalid village we approach, their dark hounds on our trail even now as the night makes its entrance? It would seem we are boxed in."

"Vampires," exclaimed Alluria the messenger girl and the secret guild master. The Queen of Thieves herself. Guised as a simple serving girl she'd forced on Thor.

"Yes," murmured Sato. "Ahead in the village, girl."

Alluria accepted this in her role of damsel, tied off the mule to her mount, and drew two arrows for her horse archer's bow.

"What plan have you, Warrior?" asked Sato again as Thor studied the layout of the village ahead in the fading light. It was almost dark. They were running out of options. And as if on cue, behind them a wolf, and a large one at that, cried out in the skirling sand. Howling in the night that the prey was near and the hunt... at an end.

And from a crescent of points behind him, others of his kind began that high mournful wail, joining in as wolves do.

Their prey was near.

The hunt was life.

Ahead, the village was all darkness save for one light in the long low flat building at the center. The light was greasy and thin, a dark star in a very dark night.

Perhaps a candle behind a window. A tattered and mean curtain that made it flicker.

"Wolves," muttered Alluria, looking toward the rear.

Shadowy hulks could be seen in the distance as the blasts of the storm came and went, sweeping the terrain.

These were not *ordinary* wolves. Even for wolves... these were very large.

And the old shepherd.

Gone now.

"What is your plan, Warrior? It is now, or it will be never, in mere moments."

Thor patted the warhorse.

He would see now if the horse could stand gunfire. Automatic gunfire in high dosage. They would fight, because that was all there was to do.

"We take the village," he told them, and then the Ranger kicked the warhorse and rode into the storm of undead within the village coming out to greet them.

CHAPTER FOUR

T HE DUST STORM ROSE AND HOWLED IN
A sudden homicidal fury as the trio rode for the weird high
desert lonely village along the edge of the bowl of the waste
that no map any of the three had ever seen had any markings
of.

It was a strange place indeed. The trio could feel that in
the air even as they thundered into its outskirts, the smell of
night feeders already in the wind and even in the bloody
color of the dying day as a long and perhaps last night came
on and the air was a fury of brown dust and bloody light.

The dawn was, in that moment, forever away.

That was when the vampires came hissing like a sizzling
skillet above the blasting fury, reaching and racing out to
meet them. Not for battle...

But for the sure feeding.

Their revenant eyes glowed pure hell's flames even in the apocalypse of searing sand and dying daylight.

"It is as I suspected, Warrior. They are feeders of the night. There is no bargaining with them." The thief shouted this above the fury in the moment before gunfire as though parley had been some unconsidered and unspoken option on the table between them.

"Good," rumbled Thor and cut loose with a sudden bark of fire from the worthy MK48 super SAW on the nearest hoary thing, moving low and close to the ground as it raced for them at an angle, its unreal and unnaturally long claws almost dragging the sand and creating marks even though the creature was tall, despite being a hunched, almost leering gargoyle in nature.

Hot outgoing rounds tore into the undead beast, rocking it hard with kinetic impacts that could not be denied by magic or the fantastic. At least three hits, though the burst had been six or eight in the trigger pull. The creature howled in unrelenting pain, rearing up to the dying light and throwing its inhuman arms wide as though it were some unholy martyr, its claws splayed in the half-light of the becoming dark that would soon consume this cursed patch of land.

It shrieked an animal cry of pain and rage at all that had been done to it.

Thor's powerful warhorse reared at the sudden short staccato of the powerful Super SAW ripping loose its shots in a tight little bark. Thor corralled the steaming warhorse with his combat boots and a tight pull on the reins even as he held the SAW, forcing the horse to regain its footing and remain still as he ordered it to stand its ground with the phrase he'd trained it to obey in the crossing from the City of Thieves to this deadly battleground.

"*Yalzaq!*" the angry Ranger thundered, and the fighting warhorse stamped the ground and held its place, facing head-on into the other dark vampires coming out of the village to make a meal of the trio in the early dark.

Now, satisfied the horse could take the rapid staccato thunder of hot seven-six-two spitting from the short barrel, Thor brought the weapon up, letting go of the reins and directing the fine mount with slight pressure from his knees and a kick from the boots if need be.

There were at least ten night feeders closing fast on them in that first moment of battle. Sato had already thrown the knives he was most fond of, and the serving girl was threading her bow and placing shots in the dark flapping grave-ragged figures. Nothing but the gunfire seemed to ruin them much, but these other wounds were not mere insults and the undead seemed to suffer some from them.

But there were others now coming out, of all shapes and sizes, back there in the deeps of the small village, their glowing red eyes standing out in the failing light as the world became full night almost all at once and there was no sign of the moon tonight, though there should be for it was almost harvest time.

Sergeant Thor efficiently sighted the barrel of the MK48, using the medium-distance engagement ACOG his brother Rangers had made sure the weapon was equipped with, and aimed once more at the hulking long-limbed thing he'd stitched first. He let go of his breath, engaging with that predator's mind of the Ranger even as the other part of his brain, the tactician every one of his kind is, under fire especially so, worked the solution of survival despite being surrounded and more so with each passing second.

Another burst from the MK48 tore the creepy thing to pieces finally and it went down hard in the dirt, ravaged by fast-moving rounds streaking at twenty-four hundred feet per second. It flailed and finally fell still as though some round, like a wooden stake, had found and... torn out its black and twisted hate-filled heart.

The Rangers, after dealing with their first vampire long ago, had discussed, and by discussed I mean argued, that point extensively. Was a round the same as a wooden stake when it came to vampires?

The verdict was still out.

But headshots worked for the undead in general. And center mass switch kills on the vampires because the same principles of a vampire hunter's wooden stake must apply. Force and materiel applied in just the right spot.

Even at twenty-four hundred feet per second instead of a hammered-stake blow.

The Rangers' first vampire, and really one of the first enemies to make their acquaintance in the Ruin, and then promptly pay for it, had been a Navy SEAL who'd arrived in the Ruin long before them and somehow... along the way... became a creature of the night.

The Ruin reveals, as they say.

After that the Rangers were hoping to kill more SEALs that had decided to make enemies of them. Especially if they were vampires. So the discussion of driving fast-moving belt-fed "stakes" straight through their twisted hearts had been much discussed by the Rangers, who were fascinated by the conversation.

But that is their way. Ask anyone who knows.

Now, there was no time to figure if that had been the case with the first of the night feeders engaging in the twisted and mean little high desert village as Thor got underway with the super SAW and began to devastate more of the hungry and hissing shadow fiends with tight controlled bursts, rocking the MK48 and leaning into the gunfire as he targeted the vampires center-mass coming out of the dust-drowned village being consumed by the night and the storm, never mind all that howling and unholy death that was determined to have its way.

One vampire, this one fat and wild-haired, screaming like a raging banshee, came racing from their flank, fangs bared and claws reaching for the over-burdened mule. Alluria fired her nocked arrow and struck the hideous thing in the raging-red-murder eye. It came on anyway, and Sato kicked his mount, flashing a small, this time very prized blade, as he whipped past the hoary old thing and drove the spike of the tip right into the thing's heart, leaving his blade in the target as the screeching horse the thief rode cried out in fear and wanted to race away from the madness at hand.

"Lost my knife, Warrior!" shouted Sato as he moved to take up the line that drew the rebellious old mule along with them. "Aim for their hearts, girl!" he added as he kicked his horse hard to drag the mule away from a group of the hungry things that looked to slake their thirst in the blood of its flanks.

The Ranger was still dosing the incoming crescent of red-eyed murderers coming out of the darkness at them, dropping some into unclean heaps of ragged and torn clothing fluttering in the blasts of the night storm whipping across the sands and causing the old wooden buildings of the village to creak and groan ominously, while others took rounds and came on regardless.

Somewhere a doom bell began ringing out over the storm. And that detail seemed to make the whole situation even more strange and mad than it already was.

Other vampires, struck hard by the fast-moving seven-six-two from the barking MK48, retreated away from its fiery glare, hissing and cowering as they dragged themselves off through the storm missing limbs now, or ruined by shattered bone the super SAW had managed to smash through with its gunfire despite their undead state.

But even with the overwhelming fire from the Ranger's light machine gun, and Alluria's well-placed shots now despite the high winds and scouring dust, they were being quickly surrounded even as they made the outlying shacks of the mean little village.

Thor was in full kill mode, and he felt the pull of wanting to work that gun and kill them all, but the constant chants of survival at all costs and no matter what, that are a Ranger's brain, had him searching for a place where they could hunker, create a kill box, and wear out and ruin their enemies until there was nothing left but the howling and lonely wind.

More craven night feeders came out of the desert behind them. It was clear this was some kind of long-intended and well-laid trap that had been waiting all along for the trio of adventurers to fall into its clawed, and necrotic, grasp.

Vampires hissed.

Wolves howled.

And the Ranger continued killing as though he would never tire, and never, ever, stop.

CHAPTER FIVE

Encircled by vampires within the small desert village blasted by the devil winds of the early night, red-eyed vampires everywhere, shadowy, hoary things coming at them from every direction, the three, warrior, thief, and seeming serving wench, fought a desperate battle in the dark as Sato lit a torch and waved it about wildly to give them some light to fight and shoot by.

The twang of Alluria's bow punctuated the brief interludes between Sergeant Thor's savage roaring bursts of staccato gunfire.

Surrounding them, the leaning twisted wretched wooden and wind-beaten dwellings seemed obscene and unclean in the half-light of the fierce dust storm. From these tomb-like monuments were vomited up more and more of the enemy revenants, gasping and rasping as they came out to kill, and feed.

The Ranger swung down from his horse, planted his boot in a craven vampire that had gotten too close, and then dosed the thing almost point blank with at least a yard from the belt feeding the weapon.

That vampire was good and dead, finally.

Dismounted, Thor unscrewed the suppressor from the barrel of the MK48. It was still hot even through the new assault gloves he'd gotten from the speedball.

The warhorse thundered off into the storm, rearing and wild around the leering hellish-eyed dead things that had not been torn to pieces yet by the thunder of the SAW.

Or savaged by Sato's knives.

Or shot through expertly by the serving girl.

"Warrior!" shouted Sato above the storm's raging thunder, sliding from his mount even as Alluria, holding her bow, did the same with a lithe and impressive gracefulness befitting any temple or tavern dancer. "If there are allies here... it will be in that temple there at the center of this settlement. Listen—the bell tolls, and perhaps it is a signal of some sort. These foul monsters have not taste for such sacred grounds, Warrior. We may give a good account of our last actions there, perhaps."

Thor clocked the location the thief had identified and grunted. What looked like a leaning old wooden church stood at the center of the village, and for all the Ranger's travels in the Ruin he'd never seen a building of its like.

"Alluria!" shouted Thor as he jerked the squad automatic weapon up, flipping the belt wide and straightening it with a practiced move. "Fall back behind us and take to the steps of that church!"

To the Ranger, a man from ten thousand years ago, the building at the center of town did indeed look like an ancient western church from some old cowboy Western. It was tall and narrow, looming almost over the whole strange village. The main floor of the place was above the wind-blasted desert where ragged vampires, their wrecked and dusty tattered forms, fresh from the grave and still streaming grave-dust, surged toward them.

Alluria did not say *"I will stand at the line of battle with any man, Warrior!"* and instead scampered lightly behind the warrior, expertly shooting down a vampire that had just crept from their rear and was making to launch on her even as she did so.

It gasped horribly as the arrow sank into its chest and it seemed to wither all at once. She watched, fascinated, as the thing that had once been some unlucky man... died again, its cruel fanged mouth working silently, its hands clutching at the shaft of the arrow protruding from its drying flesh. Probably once some ancient traveling mercenary, his armor dented and piecemeal and emblazoned with a rampant three-headed lion in bronze, but all covered in dirty grave-dust now.

It turned its head and watched her as though she might comfort it somehow as death opened wide to finally take it.

She'd fired her powerful bow from near point blank at the unclean thing, driving her arrow right through its heart.

It fell over and was gone from this life, and this death, and even as she opened her mouth in some small *O* of stunned disbelief, a new one attacked.

In an instant she ducked away and fired another arrow straight upward almost, and right through its throat, jaw, and into the skull.

Or where the brain should have been.

But it was undead, a revenant of some greater hidden master, and the arrow tip jutting from the top of the skull, dead hair whipping and flying in the breeze, mattered not to the horror in the night.

But the shot had stopped the lunge, and the thing rocked back on the remaining moldy boot it still had as she retrieved another arrow from her steppe-warrior's fur-lined quiver and fired once again, aiming for the thing's black heart now.

The shot was true, and the dead thing clutched at where she'd driven the power shot right through the ancient breastplate like it was made of merest leather, and then died.

This one too had been some lost and wandering warrior of the same type, but different.

Two down, and still more of the high desert vampires were coming from every direction and every leaning hut within the village and even the more well-made buildings from across the way, except... they did not come from, or want to go near, the strange temple at their back with the strange symbol jutting up into the storm from atop its high point at the front of the church's roof.

The stairs leading up to the door would protect her flanks and maybe even her rear if the door stayed barred shut against the hungry fiends. The Ranger had wisely decided this was the only chokepoint he could establish to murder his foes more effectively. He'd ordered her to move there and fight from there while he cleared and backed up more of the fiends with his strange barking *Wand of Small Fireballs and Thunder*.

Which was how she thought of the SAW.

The vampires swarmed as close as they dared, hissing and gnashing, more and more of them pushing up from nearby root cellars, shrieking as the dust they'd buried themselves in flew away in the storm and flayed everything savagely.

It was clear the revenants could not be held back for long. Their hunger was great, and their fury was growing. In time, they would try to break even the holy bonds of the grounds of the temple in order to come for their prey.

So... she thought to herself as she gained the creaking stairs... *we will make our stand here.* She defied the thoughts that began to make it clear this stand would be their last.

CHAPTER SIX

BEFORE...

Before the vampires of the lost high desert village came swarming out of the root cellars and every ruined door and falling-to-pieces hut...

Before...

As they crossed the low desert and journeyed up onto the high plateaus beneath the steep cliffs that ringed that edge of the waste, the Ranger had spotted a large drone high overhead, circling and following the trio as their horses crossed the vast open spaces beneath monumental and spiky ridgelines and crags. Once whoever was piloting it was sure Thor had spotted it, it began its descent and circled over the area it had chosen as its "landing field."

"What is this strange bird, Warrior?" Alluria asked, a slender porcelain hand shielding her eyes as she looked skyward.

"Don't know," grunted the Ranger. "But I'm betting my friends have been looking for me, and now they've found me, and they want to plus me up with a... speedball from home."

He spat the word *speedball* bitterly as though he was disgusted by it somehow.

He was. And this surprised him about himself... that he was insulted by their concern.

And yet... much of his gear had gone pear-shaped in his travels since leaving his friends at dawn along a beach at the edge of what was once the empire of Sût the Undying. Everything, almost except the knives and *Mjölnir*, was gone, or going. New gear would increase his chances of survival.

And survival... was the point. Survive long enough and he'd find that edge he was looking for.

That was the edge too. Mere survival in a world called the Ruin now, filled with dark magic and dire monsters trying their level best to kill him every day and twice on Tuesdays, as Sergeant Joe would have put it.

"What is a... *speed... ball*?" asked Alluria, still shielding her eyes as she watched the flat matte-gray hull of the drone circle lower and lower.

"A gift. Gifts, girl," muttered Sato, studying the drone just as she did, though the hand that shielded his still bright and twinkling eyes was weathered and scarred.

Those eyes told you the thief had seen everything... until today. Today was something new. Something strange.

"Hmmm..." muttered Sato monastically. "*Speedball.*"

The package had come in by drone. A drone piloted by the pretty blond ponytailed copilot back at FOB Hawthorne.

Perhaps by now, wondered Thor, she'd repositioned forward to Sûstagul and the developing base there now that the Air Force special operations unit had brought in their Forge and lost their transport in the process under heavy attack from bat-winged lion-bodied manticores summoned and driven by the Lich Pharaoh himself during the second battle for that city.

The Ranger had left a field of dead orcs beneath the western wall running sniper operations during that battle.

For a moment, as the Ranger watched the Global Hawk drone, a big one, spiraling lazily in the high sunshine above their heads, and as the trio of horses and riders, pulling their cantankerous mule, made for the landing area, Thor tried to count the days since he'd been gone from the Rangers. Since that battle. Since that field of dead spreading off to the misty dunes on the horizon.

They'd tried. They'd died.

How long, he wondered, and how many adventures had he had, since he'd seen his brother Rangers?

Their fellowship.

Time felt... funny.

One time he'd met an old Ranger scout returned for the annual Black and Tan weekend the regiment held. A tough old guy wearing the Vietnam veteran hat and all his medals with a cigarette hanging from the side of his mouth. "Thing I hate about this..." he told Thor in the heat of a long afternoon of displays and demonstrations of Ranger skills and technique, "is in my mind... it's still yesterday in the bush, kid. It's hot and we're young back then, and we got everything in front of us when this is over. But see... even then, kid... part of me never wanted it to be over. And the curse o' that is, I'll tell ya... in my mind, it ain't *never* over. They're still young, the dead. And so am I. Some mornings I just see a broke old man staring back right at me in the bathroom mirror and I don't know who that guy is. I hate that. I hate him. Miss all of us when we was young and we ruled the jungle. And some days... I miss life and death like it's a game I used to be pretty good at. Ain't games like that back in the world. Sometimes... I miss that as much as I miss the dead. And that... probably ain't right."

Thor had listened, escorting the guy between events. Guy was a stone-cold straight-up killer. Or what some call a *hero*.

The Ranger laughed.

The old guy laughed too. "Know where we can get a beer, kid?" he'd asked. Thor did. And then, when it was had and the time to part was at hand, after all the stories were told of a jungle war long ago when the old man who couldn't stand to look at himself and not see who'd once been had still been a young man who couldn't imagine not staying that way, Sergeant Thor looked the old scout in the eyes and rumbled, "Then don't look in the mirror."

Guy laughed.

"Yeah, that's good advice, kid. I like that. Don't look in the mirror." Then he lit another coffin nail and watched the Ranger go. Knowing—because even then the Ranger had it... *caught up in it*, or *fate*, or call it what you will... had it all over him just like that ship's hedge wizard had told him—knowing the old scout wished just for one more time he could play the game.

The game of life and death for keeps.

Now, watching that big Global Hawk circle lower and lower, the pilot, whoever it was but most likely the pretty blond ponytailed co-pilot, who, yes, he'd had a thing with back at the FOB even though she'd seemed put out about it, he felt like that old Ranger scout trying to remember when last he'd seen his own Ranger brothers.

Six months.

In his mind he said some of their names just to remind himself of their faces. And the things they said.

Time had begun to feel... funny. But that was said in the Ruin. *Time grows strange the closer one gets to the Rift at the heart of the waste.*

Yes. Time... was growing strange.

Many adventures had been had since his parting with the detachment. Since that morning on the beach with the smaj telling him he was just on a reconnaissance. Many more than are recorded here.

Had happened since then.

And the pretty blond ponytailed co-pilot. She'd fallen for him hard. But that was her fault and he'd told her so.

And no... she hadn't liked that.

Of course he'd remained true to himself and told her exactly what he was looking for in this life, and it wasn't a relationship.

Edge don't have room for relationships.

She'd answered, "I didn't fall for you because you're a Ranger, you know. My dad was one and I've only got a vague memory of him. Swore I'd never get involved with one of you. And here I am... *involved*."

She swore in the night as they talked quietly.

It was late.

Only the watch was up at the FOB when they'd been together, somewhere out there on the perimeter. The smaj of course.

No one really knew what they were up to. But there was talk...

He'd fought her off. She was, technically, an officer. And she'd fought him off. She was an Air Force officer, and she had a rule.

No Rangers.

"He get killed?" asked Thor in the darkness around them.

She shook her head.

"Disappeared into the... you know, delta, and supposedly... deeper stuff that doesn't officially exist. When I was fourteen, I told my mom I hated him because he abandoned us. I was mad. She said that wasn't what happened at all. She said that someday, someday somehow... I'd find out. But... and I bet no teenage girl running full afterburn on emotions ever got put in her place by this one... but she said his status was... *a national secret*. And that there were stories and rumors I might hear, but none of those were true. Those were lies to hide the truth, which was the world he was in. She'd been in it too. But in a different way. Only thing I needed to know, and that was big with her, she was a Company analyst..."

"Company?" asked Thor but knew already.

"CIA. Bad guys. Everything was *need to know* and had been since I was a little girl. It became a joke between us if only because... well, because it had to because if we just accepted the way it was, that way lies madness. She knew... when she was dying of cancer, she told me it was that way because she... she knew the secrets of the universe. And it was better that way. I know... messed up, huh?" said the pretty blond ponytailed copilot in the darkness.

Thor said nothing. Sometimes you just listen.

"She said the only thing I ever needed to know was... he never abandoned us."

Silence in the night between two lovers in the Ruin. All that... ten thousand years gone.

Secrets from then don't matter anymore, Thor reminded himself. He'd said that before. But this time, it didn't feel right and so... he said nothing.

He held her.

"I tried to find out," she continued later. "But even his official records are all kinds of fake. The truth was impossible for me to find. So, you see, no Rangers. Ever, I told myself. I can't... I don't want that... ever again."

He put a hand on her shoulder, brushed the fallen hair from her face. The ponytail had come undone.

"No," she said to him softly. "You're going. You're a Ranger, that's what you guys do. And... you're *you*. I feel for you because you're a big piece of meat and you're actually... pretty decent, Ranger. That's all. I had a rule. Rules are meant to be broken... sometimes. It's cool. I don't expect my story, my tale of woe, as that Vandahar guy would say..." She laughed a little, but it was dry and hollow. Then grabbed the canteen she'd brought and drank from it, staring off into the dark.

"Rules are made to be broken, Ranger."

Now Thor studied the circling Global Hawk, watching it come close and closer to the high escarpment at the edge of the Eastern Wastes they'd been heading up for two days now. Working their way through dry ravines and up rocky ledges.

Thinking, for just a moment, of her. And knowing if she were piloting it, she was seeing him.

The mule complained.

The warhorse snorted.

The other horses made their sounds in the vast desert silence of the high rock and fields they'd climbed to. It seemed nothing had ever lived here. And never would.

Alluria asked, "What is that strange bird, Warrior? Its wings do not move."

It was a speedball. A special operations form of urgent resupply in a combat zone. They'd been running drones all over this edge of the world, and somehow, using the facial recognition software, the forces back at the FOB had spotted him. Most likely over subsequent flights they'd confirmed it was him before making their plan to resupply him.

Probably the smaj's idea and he could almost hear the old NCO say, *"He may be a lost soul out there, doin' his thing along the edge. But he's one of us and we're gonna resupply him with everything this damn magic box of unending wonders you call a Forge can crank out for him and stuff in a Global Hawk. Get it done, Rangers."*

The smaj would say that, thought Thor.

Ahead, high and above, another few hours' journey, the escarpment topped out before the jagged teeth of some iron-gray cut and cropped peaks. A pass, according to Sato, led through this area of the ridge and down into the bowl of the waste along its southern and eastern edge.

The Global Hawk was heading for this area now that it had Thor's attention. Most likely the Air Force had identified a landing strip they could use there. A relatively clear field they could safely crash the thing down into.

Later, when they finally reached the downed drone, Thor circled it on horseback, studying it as he did so.

The Rangers had drawn various obscene messages to him with permanent markers all over it.

Of course they had.

He laughed, dismounted, and moved to the cargo compartment, prying open the lid with the help of the Ranger shank, and wonders were indeed revealed within.

"These are weapons of the Before, Warrior?" asked Sato at his side as he stared down in stunned awe at what lay in the coffin-sized compartment of the downed drone.

Thor pulled out the Carl Gustaf recoilless rifle launcher. Held it up and inspected it.

Then...

"Like you ain't never seen, my friend," he rumbled. "And then some."

CHAPTER SEVEN

T HERE ON THE HIGH DESERT PLATEAU ON THE edge of a final climb up through strange and foreboding mountains where the wind howled between the vast and deep silences of the long empty places, the trio of thief, warrior, and not-serving-girl Alluria made camp as Thor dealt with the resupply from the speedball near the crash-landed Global Hawk in the high scrub and soft sand that blew down out of the haunted passes above they would soon cross through and over.

After the Carl Gustaf, the Ranger hoisted out the MK48 super SAW. A squad automatic weapon usually carried by the gunner in a line company. Used for suppression of enemy forces and for the output of much-needed overwhelming fire in dire situations ranging from ambush to assault. But that was the standard two-forty-nine. The MK48 was the Special Forces variant that had fixed the feed problems the previous version had been plagued by and then, just for more punch, had been upgraded to fire seven-six-two instead of five-five-six.

This made the cut-down SAW a heavy hitter and game-changer in the direst of desperate situations. Sergeant Thor had worked with this weapons system before, and it was one of his favorites that wasn't a sniper engagement system. He'd been the SAW gunner in his first squad after completing RASP and coming to the Batts as a private.

His squad leader put him on the SAW because the young Ranger was jacked and could carry the weapon system with ease in any situation from steep mountains to mud-sucking swamps. The fact that he was tall kept the gun out of the swamp water, and the solid NCO had felt that was generally good when wanting a working squad automatic weapon system up and dispensing high-volume death in a sudden firefight out in the jungle deeps of South Am.

Truth be told, after the precision and prowess it took to employ the M105 anti-materiel rifle Thor had become renowned for in the sniper section—*Mjölnir*—the MK48 was a personal favorite for the Ranger, and he'd occasionally picked up a patrol with the scouts when manpower was thin just to carry the thing and support the mission.

It was as close as you were going to get to a death machine in a line unit, and some said it was better than most experiences a man could have.

Make of that what you will.

Rangers are different people.

Sato noticed the quiet grin on Thor's face as he handled these weapons and set them aside on a woven mat purchased from the bazaars of the City of Thieves to organize all his new gear on. Clearly the warrior was pleased with the strange weapons sent him, thought the wise thief and merely studied them all to see what he could learn.

To Sato... they were like magic items of great power. So this was indeed a rare treat for a humble thief.

The cargo compartment inside the wrecked Global Hawk had been tightly and efficiently packed, something Rangers were outstanding at given the need to carry everything they'd use on a pump on their backs, and then jump into a combat zone with it which was probably going to be a hostile situation within a matter of time if not outright and immediately.

The Air Force special operations loadmasters had added their expert refinements to the load, and Thor was stunned at how much they'd been able to get into the Global Hawk for the resupply.

There was a lot. And so Sergeant Thor worked his way through the gear and presently, the more he took out, the more he began to grow concerned. There were weapons in abundance, but so far... no ammo.

That could be... a problem.

Surely, he thought, and didn't finish his concern...

Perhaps it was at the bottom, he reasoned, and pulled the M203 rifle up from the Global Hawk's compartment next. It smelled new and glistened in the chamber with a light coat of CLP. This was the outdated grenadier model of the famed M16 used back in the Cold War and all the way up until the end of the GWOT. The Rangers, like most units, had replaced the grenadier rifle with the smaller M320 grenade launcher. A lighter, more versatile system most hated even though it came with an upgraded range-finding system and the ability to dial in airburst munitions.

But here was the brilliance of the Forge. Not only did it contain the recipes for everything from every weapons system, real, conceived, and experimental, it could also make dip and Rip-Its and your least favorite MRE...

Egg Omelette or Spaghetti and Balls... dealer's choice...

But with the right Forge technician, and Penderly back at FOB Hawthorne was that guy, weapons systems could be monkeyed with, especially if some experimental version had been developed by DoD but never really seen anything beyond R&D.

Thor had no idea whether these particular upgrades were due to the Rangers coaxing Penderly and the Baroness, the smoking hot dark-haired scientist who bore more than a slight resemblance to the *G.I. Joe* villainess who'd been attached to the Ranger detachment that got themselves flung forward in time, to extemporize, or whether the DoD had indeed been developing this weapons system as they dev'd the M320 as a variant mod for the M203 grenadier rifle. He just knew this one came with the range-finding system and the ability to dial in special munitions for airburst.

But where were those munitions?

"Nice," grunted Thor as he set the battle rifle aside.

"Warrior, what is nice about this... magic wand?" asked the thief peering into the speedball weapons package.

"Nice? Nothing nice about it for whoever I shoot. But for us... it's like having some magic spell that will release hornets into the enemy's midst. Except these hornets are moving at about three thousand meters per second and are made of steel fragments."

"*Hai*," exclaimed the master thief. "What is a meter, Warrior?"

Next came the replacement G19 Glock. During their scans they must have clocked Thor's remaining weapons, or figured the sidearm would break down anyway given the lingering effects of the nano-plague even now ten thousand years later. This one came with a red dot sight and a streamlight mounted under the threaded barrel. Bundled alongside the grip was another silencer, fat and long.

But still... no munitions.

Below the weapons, instead of ammo cans or even crates, came gear. Two IFAKs. CAT 5 Israeli tourniquets. A small drum of Motrin. A new plate carrier with ammo pouches along the front. A chest rig with more ammo pouches. Three new sets of CryePrecision fatigues and a much-prized Ranger thermal overshirt. Oakley assault boots in his size. Tan Oakley assault gloves. An assault pack. A collapsed old-school ALICE-style ruck, probably from the smaj himself. Inside the assault pack were MREs of varying degrees of Dante's Inferno and lots of five-fifty cord, smoke, flashbangs, CS, fragmentary grenades, breaching charges, ChemLights, and of course, thirty cans of dip.

Again, the Ranger exclaimed, "Nice!" in his signature good-natured deep basso rumble and started stashing the dip tins all over his person and through his packs. And on the mule, thus making the thankless beast a high-priority executive-protection VIP going forward.

After that he started calling the stupid animal "VIP" and had to explain this to Alluria and Sato.

They still didn't understand. And thankfully, neither wanted to try his strange "dip."

He tapped out the first container and dug himself a fat pinch. Then he placed it between his cheek and gum and turned to a small Pelican case that lay at the bottom.

Other than this there was nothing else. No ammunition for the 203, the Carl, the Glock, or even Raufoss rounds for *Mjölnir*, which they knew he had to still be carrying from their high res-scans and images from the Global Hawk that had no doubt been stalking him for days. Knowing exactly where he'd been as the trio trekked up out of the coastal desert from the City of Thieves and into the region the yellowing and ancient maps of the Ruin called the Eastern Wastes.

"Perplexing..." grunted Thor. He spat some dip off into the hard sand and turned to the Pelican case.

"What is the riddle that vexes you, Warrior? I am good with such things, as all thieves must be if they are to survive poison locks and avoid diabolical traps set by those who do not wish their most valued valuables stolen."

Thor picked up the Pelican and turned it over, looking for any markings on it before he did. Traps and chests in the dungeons and fortresses of the Ruin had trained him to do so, even if the package was from a friendly.

His time with the thieves had made him cautious. Even when he didn't need to be.

And in the Ruin... that wasn't a bad thing.

It was a world that tried to kill you with monsters, magic, or outright slaughter at least once or twice a day. But this has been said before.

"And twice on Tuesdays," as perpetual Ranger PFC Tanner would have added, doing his best Joe voice.

Inside, there was a small emergency satellite beacon and text transmitter. He could send them messages. If he needed help or something.

That also would be the smaj's doing.

He stuck it in a pack, at the bottom, and intended never to use it.

Nearby, Alluria turned to making their evening's meal after starting a small wisping fire as the late afternoon winds raced up the escarpment, driving occasional gusts of sand across their small camp.

The cantankerous mule honked its displeasure at the situation and stared about contemptuously at everyone.

The horses ate what they could find.

"The riddle, Sato..." said Thor, studying the small envelope that had been taped to the bottom of the Ppelican, "is that unless there is ammunition for these weapons systems... they're useless to me."

Sato made a small grunt. Then, "I am familiar, Warrior, with the word *aldhakhira*. But not the word you just used. What does... *dhakhiratan* mean? Is is similar to arrows and bolts?"

They were speaking in Arabic and the mixed patois of the City of Thieves for that was all Alluria spoke, and they'd been conversing in such for days.

The Ranger had used the word *dhakhiratan.* Ammunition. The thief was only familiar with *aldhakhira.* Munitions.

"They mean the same thing in this case, my friend. These weapons will need such, or they will be useless. But I highly doubt my brothers sent me these without the means to implement them effectively. Perhaps there's another drone that will come with the ammo. Maybe. But that seems an odd choice. Both would have to get through for either to be effective, and Rangers don't like that many moving parts. Too much room for catastrophic error."

Sato looked into the purple of the coming night. The food Alluria was preparing already smelled good.

"My eyes are keen, Warrior. I see no other strange bird that will visit us this night."

Thor opened the letter. Inside, written in terse handwriting, the script of the pretty blond ponytailed copilot...

She'd written him a letter once telling him she was cool with how things had ended and she didn't want him distracted by her.

She'd written...

Ammo in Bag of Holding.

Be safe.

Rules are made to be broken, Ranger.

CHAPTER EIGHT

EVEN WITH THE SAW CACKLING ON FULL auto, the going was getting worse by the second as they pushed through the unorganized night feeders who'd thought to merely swarm *en masse* and take down their salacious prey.

Then the feasting could begin.

But whoever had organized the ambush had little understood firepower or the applied use of violence excessively in the hands of a confirmed knucklebuster.

For a moment, seemingly without organized leadership, it was clear the ragged vampires who abode here considered their undead lives more precious than throwing themselves in the face of these unknown magical weapons of fire and thunder.

The storm howled psychotically as they pushed, whipping dust and flying grit straight into the eyes of the determined trio as the building at their back creaked and groaned like some sick old giant dying slowly even as its exposed skin was being flayed alive from sudden cutting squalls of wind and random debris coming from up off the high desert floor.

Vampires were being shot to pieces, collapsing like brittle bundles of rag-wrapped sticks as the ancient weapons sent that deafening thunder and cacophonic fire into and then through them.

These were no eloquent and hearty undead night feeders of lore and movies long gone silent. These were ragged, hoary, undead bundles of once-human flesh and dried-out old bone. Only their bright fangs and hellish eyes gave any energy or life to their shadowy dust-covered wraith-like forms. They howled and gnashed their teeth and died under the SAW's relentless glare.

And yet...

The numbers were against the surrounded trio.

Sato protected Thor's flank where he could with sudden precise slashes that severed rotting muscle and ropy tendons and, even with their near-immortal undead life, denied the foul revenants the ability to move now that they'd been slashed and cut so precisely.

But the craven night feeders seemed to rally as one, as though having heard some master's orders, or the lash of a cruel and unseen whip, and came at the Ranger from every angle and piece of concealment they could advantage.

Cover wasn't an option in the mostly dead old wooden stick and tent village. The SAW ruined everything it was pointed at.

Then, having broken through and mostly torn off an old wooden rail from the rotting stairs of the ancient church, just to the side of the death-dealing Ranger, the mob of grinning hissing death surged and got too close. It was clear to Warrior, Thief, and Wench that they were now making their last desperate stand on rickety old stairs climbing to a looming building that seemed easily unbreachable.

Sato, using a sharp piece of the broken stair railing, rammed it down into the closest fiends' hearts, stopping them forever as the veteran tomb raider wielded the weapon as naturally as though he'd been born with it in his hand. And in each savage instant when Sato plunged that wooden stake through a skinny vampire chest, the fiend turned to dust, desiccating even further, though not completely. Until the wind pulled and tugged at them like some debt collector come to call on a bad debt, and they were carried off into the desert wastes, howling in dire and hopeless lament at the unseen horrors waiting for them in the beyond they were hurtling toward.

Their voices seemed to rewind like they'd been recorded and played backward as they were torn away by the storm from this present reality.

Then the sharp stake shattered, and it mattered not that Sato could sweep their legs or savage their muscles. The fiends would overwhelm them in less than a minute if not a few mere seconds.

Sato used the stick now merely to push them away as their ragged and dirty claws reached out to tear the warrior to pieces even as he shot them down at near point-blank range, the barrel of the SAW beginning to turn a soft orange in the brown light of evening.

And that wasn't good.

"Out of arrows!" yelled Alluria, using a stronger voice than her normal seductive and soft playful teasing lilt. "But I think there are... people... inside the building!"

She turned on the door and began to beat at it, telling whoever was in there to let the trio in and that they were friends.

Thor let the SAW dangle on its sling, pulled his tomahawk, and drew the Glock an instant after.

He slammed the tomahawk down into the nearest vampire suddenly, cleaving through the shoulder as the thing reacted in raspy horror, then pointed the long-slide sidearm right in the thing's head. He pulled the trigger and blew its fevered brains to shreds.

The titanic boom of the unsuppressed weapon was swiftly carried off into the squall and scream of the storm even as the shattered vampire fell back lifeless, claws still reaching into the maggot swarm of his brethren.

Then Thor did it again.

"They're unbolting the door!" shouted Alluria, looking over her shoulder and seeing a sea of shadows with red glowing eyes coming for them, and the warrior called Thor hacking and shooting where he could to keep them back as best he could despite the certain tide.

She saw something else, too. Saw it out there in the seemingly endless sea of the dead...

A woman stood above and behind them all, almost floating over the clan of bloodsuckers. A woman bathed in a weird and wan ethereal red hell-light.

Alluria knew exactly who it was.

Madame Hudu.

The wronged cult leader who was really some form of named vampire come for her revenge on the Ranger who'd destroyed all her plots and plans to take the City of Thieves for her own and make it a cemetery she could feed in forever.

Madame Hudu had planned and arranged this trap, laying in wait for them out here on the high desert plateaus where the winds and features had no name. Surrounded and far from the aid of her own guild, Alluria was certain of that fact, as many of the deep intrigues known to few were known well to the clever Queen of Thieves.

The Ranger had informed the guild—and thus her, listening in the role of serving wench and messenger girl—of his final encounter with the mysterious Madame Hudu, and the offer she'd made him, even as the city burned in sections and the final fight was almost begun.

The offer, shall we say, had been definitely... refused.

And then some.

The vampire lady was still butt-hurt about that. Apparently.

Alluria, in disguise as the serving wench, had kept her thoughts to herself, for the Queen of Thieves, as well as the other guild heads, had known how dangerous this growing and arising new death cult was.

And what the dark-skinned gypsy "girl priest" really was.

A night feeder.

The door behind Alluria suddenly swung wide, with spears and hard-eyed killers on the other side.

She pivoted and came face to face with a scarred and muscled armored warrior covered in bandages. He wore a breastplate with ancient markings and a Spartan's helmet with a fine horsehair plume of blue and red, and he pushed past her, speaking a version of the desert trade patois that seemed antique to her and perhaps even unfamiliar to the speaker.

The Spartan raised his shield, deflected a vampire's clawed swipe that had been aimed directly at Alluria's pretty head, and then flung back his spear on his powerful shoulder, his shredded red cape flying at the storm's tempest, and thrust himself into the press, shouting, "Strike hold, Brothers!" in ancient English, a language the secretive Queen of Thieves disguised as a serving girl knew not at all.

Another Spartan quick on the heels of the first, this one smaller and older, pushed past, as did another who was young, slight, and whose armor seemed more ornate than the first two.

To Alluria this one had the air of a priest, and he carried a sturdy if dented mace instead of a spear.

The following Spartans cried out, "And then some!" as they followed the first and began savaging the vampires all around Thor with a flurry of strikes and stabs, driving their spears like jackhammers into the bloodsucking fiends, pulling them savagely away and then thrusting for some new target for all they were worth.

But there were far too many of the creatures for even these grim warriors, long lost to antiquity and tragedy, fabled Karthian Spartans thought slaughtered to the last man long ago.

Legends. Though Thor did not know any of this. Did not know their story any more than he knew their names.

Yet heroes and legends mattered not on this cursed night, surrounded by vampires on the high desert plain...

It was the numbers that would soon prevail.

CHAPTER NINE

THE RANGER WAS IN MURDER MODE EVEN AS the Spartans came to assist him in the frenetic battle along the stairs. Tactically he was still trying to find a way out for all of them, and he wasn't seeing one. More and more of his mind was moving toward the final conclusion that he would kill as many as he could... and that would just have to be enough.

Even Rangers get tired. Even the legendary Sergeant Thor was reaching a limit. It was getting worse by the second, humping the impossible amount of gear he was carrying and swinging that blood-and-gore-covered tomahawk, taking shots with the long-slide Glock while the hot barrel of the MK48 burned him and he put that down as a later problem he probably wasn't gonna have to deal with in a few seconds as the vampires swarmed him and grabbed at his powerful arms to try and stop him from striking them down.

The Ranger's plan before the Spartans had suddenly thrown themselves into the fight had been to let the gun cool down long enough for it to be used for one last high-cyclic dose of death for all who dared form up against him.

After that...

He could chop and hack at them until...

Then he heard something he'd thought he'd never ever hear again.

Time grows strange...

He heard the proper address and response for members of a once-fabled Airborne unit, a unit gone down ten thousand years ago under a world coming apart at the seams from the ravaging nano-plague... right there behind him.

Strike hold.

And then some.

In English, even.

Then dudes straight out of that movie *The 300* suddenly appeared like very angry and avenging angels deftly and savagely jabbing spears right into the vampires at point-blank range where the Ranger wasn't shredding the bloodthirsty fiends with the tomahawk or the sidearm when he could manage a shot.

There was another Spartan behind him he could not see yet...

That strange young ethereal priest who'd followed the other two out of the door the serving wench had coaxed them to open.

Thor chanced a glance and saw some holy light come out from the priest's upraised palm as that Spartan began to mutter arcane words that were more like some prayer than a magic spell.

The growing pure light revealed the mass of vampires nearest the bloody front of the battles the Spartans, Sato, and Thor worked at to hold the line.

It revealed them as mean villagers. Low travelers. Wandering mercenaries. Lost madmen and other strange professions out there in the seething mass of hissing undeath. They'd been collected here by...

Then Thor spotted her. That dark beauty he'd encountered on the way to the tower of a wizard he was gonna murk. The last moments of his plan within the City of Thieves coming together.

She'd made him an offer. A deal. A chance to salvage her long-laid plans for the city.

Join her and become her champion. And her lover too.

A death cult that would consume the Ruin across all the known maps that had been made and inked and could be trusted.

He'd answered her seductive offer with fast gunfire, and she'd turned to mist in the night just as quick, her wicked laugh mocking as she faded into the nether darknesses of that lonely street on the way to the wizard's tower.

But it was clear... the Ranger's actions had destroyed her carefully laid plans.

Now...

Now she would have her final revenge.

That too was clear.

Out there in that seething mass of vampires, ragged and wretched, cursing and hissing like tormented souls all of them... she floated above, serene like some dark fallen angel come to watch the sufferings of Hell, bathed in a diabolic red light that seemed to come from the ragged and blasted sand beneath her, and even from under hard-packed loveless dirt below.

As though some portal to Hell was the stage on which she'd chosen to set her night's performance of *Revenge in Three Acts*.

The red light surrounding her was the opposite of the clean warm light the Spartan priest behind the Ranger shone out over the press of simpering and at the same time angry fiends trying to take them all into their clawed embrace, even as the cutting and stabbing of spears, and the thunder of the sidearm, ruined what could be ruined with what little time and will was left to them.

The young priest suddenly stepped forward, pushing past the Ranger. The sturdy mace in his gloved hand was a forgotten thing as though confirming that even with weapons, Bronze Age and modern, and even with warriors such as the Spartans and the Ranger Sergeant Thor, that little could be done and only a final act of bravery was left them.

How could such a sea of unholy ravening evil at the doorstep ever be turned away?

The numbers...

That damnation vampire lady...

But of course... the numbers didn't add to victory much less escape. It's almost always the numbers, no matter what the bards and generals go on and on about.

Then in a voice that seemed to have a thunder and confidence all its own as if coming from some other better place not this cursed night, a voice the slender priest in armor would not have been thought to possess, he shouted, "Light... Until Dawn!"

A sudden and very powerful flashbang of epic thunder and holy illumination... *shock waved*... out across the dark sea of seething damned blood-drinkers.

They shrank back all at once where they were not suddenly disintegrated. The two bandaged and scarred Spartan warriors, slaying who they could where they could, suddenly switched mission and pulled their new allies back within the vastness of that ancient leaning church they'd been bolt-holed in, slamming a heavy wooden bar, inlaid with warding prayers, across the rotten wooden doors.

And for a moment... the outside horrors seemed so far away, and a vast and quiet silence like a power rumbled beneath their hearing.

Then outside the vampires hissed and screamed, wailing and writhing in pain as the fading holy shock-wave blast tormented them still with promises of all the hells they'd ever been promised, and banishment from all the paradises they'd ever forsaken.

CHAPTER TEN

In the dim of the old church set smack dab in the middle of the night-feeder-haunted ville, the Ranger stared into a gloom of wounded and haunted men who silently watched the new trio like dead men greeting the next batch of corpses to be tossed into an open grave from which no one ever crawled out of.

The place was indeed a long-forgotten church and looked little used of late. Smashed bench seats and boarded-up tall windows where only thin slivers of ancient memorial glass clung where it had not been shattered by time, violence, and long, long neglect.

Along the dirty debris-littered floor and among the rotten ruined fragments were wounded men, and Thor quickly made a count of them.

Seven.

All of the wounded in various states were Spartans like the three that had come out to rescue them in the thick of a battle quickly turning into a last stand just moments ago. Some wore their bright and shining armor, dented and battered finely worked ornate breastplates, but were bandaged expertly underneath. Others had their armor removed to better treat more severe wounds.

These seemed to be tormented, writhing even now in fever dreams despite the raging bloodsuckers outside beating on the doors and shuttered windows as though they were made of invisible steel. These fever-dreaming Spartans' bandages were soaked through with blood and sweat.

To the Ranger, the room reeked of impending defeat.

He swapped mags on his sidearm and checked to make sure the links to the SAW were still feeding into the Bag of Holding the detachment had sent by speedball. Connected, the supply of linked rounds would be near endless, but he still did not trust it completely because there was "magic" involved and it was clear the margin for error here now was slim and getting slimmer by the second.

But what other options did he have...

Thor listened to the desert vampires beat at the door and slam their bloodied claws against the boarded-up windows. His face must have telegraphed to those around him that he wondered why, for all their savagery, the night feeders were unable to break through the rotting and wooden barriers.

"Because this is a holy place," whispered the young priest of fine features who'd just holy-flashbanged them at the most desperate of moments. Giving the trio just enough time to get inside the sanctum. The priest was handsome in a way many men are not. A blond almost ginger with a high-and-tight fade along the sides of his scalp. His features were thin and aquiline and the opposite of all the other rough-hewn Spartans in the room whom Thor easily recognized as soldiers. Thick, hard, scarred, jacked, and angry even wounded. These were just like any soldiers that could have been found back at any hard-charging line unit ten thousand years ago in what was once called the modern US Army.

But the priest... was different than them. Like some shavetail ROTC L-T fresh out of college and Officer Basic with all kinds of good intentions dying a hard death in the face of the grim and often brutal reality that is a fighting line unit. And though the priest's armor was the same at first inspection, his cloak had a white cross across the back of it whereas the other Spartans were wrapped in only red and blue, and the armor contained other markings the regular Spartans' protection did not.

But all their cloaks were blue on the outside. Red on the inside.

Something tickled the back of Thor's skull. But it was... impossible...

And still...

He remembered Talker and Kennedy going on and on about the Ruin... *revealing*.

"I am John of Towle. Jumpmaster for our cohort. Keeper of the sacred PLF. We are Third Stick. Do you speak our language, stranger?"

Thor snorted, thinking to himself, *The Ruin indeed does reveal*.

But that was a tomorrow problem.

The Ranger sniper glanced at all the entrances and saw that despite the blows of the bloody-fisted demons at the doors, the boards held even though they seemed to thunder and reverberate with the myriad of strikes.

"The holy grounds of this place defy their uncleanness," whispered the priest. Then added, "And I have added what little I possess to its fastness."

And then... all of a sudden... they were gone. The sound of the hammering, the hissing, the moaning hunger... it was all gone. And if that might have been a comfort... it wasn't.

The silence that followed was... ominous.

It was as though all of them, all the dirty, sand-covered, raving, blood-sucking wraiths out there in the storm had suddenly, and all at once, withdrawn from the building as one.

One single mind controlling them all and beckoning them to patience and a biding of time.

The Ranger thought of Lady Hudu out there in the dark. Hungering for more than just blood for the gruesome feeding. But more so hungering for her revenge. On him. Hungering to drink his blood if just for spite for the plans he had ruined back there in the City of Thieves.

"Who…" began the Ranger, turning to scan the darkness and the dim shadows for the sudden appearance of their enemies as though they'd magically found some way in…

He would kill them all if that was the case. He patted the SAW to remind himself how he would do it as long as it could be done.

Bleed the belt until it was dry, mag-dump the secondary, see what weapons he could get out of the Bag of Holding to deploy against them.

Then finally the tomahawk off his assault pack.

He might kill them all.

He might kill most. Or even just some.

They might get him… whispered some dark thought.

We'll see, thought Thor and spit dip off onto an unoccupied space along the debris-and-sand-scattered floor.

The priest had extended his hand when he'd introduced himself. Thor had not taken it and had almost not even seen it.

But that word…*Jumpmaster.*

It had jumped out at him. To those of his kind that was a very specific word.

Even though the youth was clearly some kind of *priest...*

"We are Spartans of Karthia," said the priest softly in the gloomy quiet. "We have traveled far to fulfill a debt deep within the Great Rift owed by our forefathers. Three nights ago, in a great sandstorm, we lost contact with our other elements. Two days ago, we found this village. We thought it was deserted."

The priest swallowed thickly.

Elements, noted Thor.

"Obviously it was not," continued the priest. "We set up camp in an old disused stable instead of this church, for our lieutenant did not trust the holy places of other religions. After nightfall they came, and we fought a running battle of not fifty meters, yet in that space we lost twelve men just to make the church's doors. The LT was one of them."

LT.

The priest looked around, casting his ethereal blue eyes across the wounded lying along the floor. The three troopers who'd dared the QRF were still in armor, carrying bloody weapons and leaning on bloody spears. They watched and said nothing from the nearby shadows.

A few lanterns were lit, but they seemed to struggle unnaturally against the darkness.

Thor turned to Sato.

The little thief's face was a mask, but there was some message there the Ranger could not yet read.

Alluria, far from the serving girl Thor took her to be, cautiously watched the men with an almost scheming look in her eyes that she quickly blanked when she caught the Ranger clocking her. Sergeant Thor took that for a comely girl's innate gifts in guile and survival at any cost.

She'd told him little of her life, but what she'd let drop indicated she'd used her wits to climb up and out from some pretty dire circumstances to the life she'd lived as simple messenger girl and clever informer for the Little Guild back in the city.

As a beauty she would have been a prize in any sultan's harem. It was impossible to think of her as a wife, for she seemed too wild and very ambitious.

Thor laughed to himself as he had these thoughts.

And then there was this bunch here, pinned down and using strange, old words... from before the Ruin had become the way it was.

The math the Ranger was doing in his mind... didn't add. But it wasn't important right now. Survival was important. They had to get ready to defend against the next attack, for the air felt heavy and pregnant that such an attack was going to come...

And the Ranger had been in many such situations.

But they would keep the vampires out there at bay until dawn, he thought, making a plan. Then... make a run for it and try to get clear of the coven's reach. Out there on the high desert floor, perhaps there were ancient ruins or some deep cave they could fade into and keep moving out of the net by day when the vampires could not stalk and track them.

It was a plan. And, thought Sergeant Thor, it would have to do for now until new information updated the course of action.

But first he'd need to kill Madame Hudu.

Rangers didn't leave enemies alive on their rear, even if they were already dead.

CHAPTER ELEVEN

"THIS PLACE IS CLEARLY HALLOWED, WARRIOR. Its portals will hold for now. But if we do not leave soon... then they could trap us here forever. And in time, I fear, make us like them. Servants of the dark."

Sato had motioned for Thor to step aside for a moment while the priest had gone off to attend to the wounded. Sato and Thor hunkered together, Alluria hovering and watching the grim-faced killers all about them. The silence beyond the thin wood walls was ominous, and beneath it was some undetectable noise, a chant or a buzz, that could be felt, almost, but not heard.

"Something very strange goes on here, Warrior," Sato began.

That's for true, thought the Ranger as he puzzled over the words, words in English, the priest had used.

The jumpmaster.

The Spartans, Karthian Spartans apparently whatever they were, shouting, *And then some!* in the thick of the battle at the front door.

Yeah, Thor could tell Sato in ways the thief couldn't detect that there was indeed some strangeness going on. But it would be impossible for Sato to appreciate what Thor was sensing, seeing as the thief, his sidekick and friend, hadn't been alive ten thousand years ago.

But Thor had. And he'd been to Bragg.

But his mind, as logical and as cold at killing as it was, grounded in the reality of the math of life and death as a sniper must be, refused to accept, fully accept, what the implications of these half-mentioned riddles implied.

Sato continued.

"Again, Warrior, know that as a thief, a violator of tombs and a robber of ancient lost treasures, it pays to know a little history now and then. I do not know everything, but I know this. *It is impossible for these men to be who they claim to be.*"

Thor raised one of his eyebrows and said nothing.

"How so?" whispered Alluria, bending over Thor's great back, her soft and supple skin carelessly caressing his body with her ample curves.

He was not immune to the girl's obvious charms. But now was definitely not the time.

And now that they were traveling companions, he had set himself to not be overcome by those charms. There was something about the girl he didn't trust, though she'd saved his life on a few occasions and seemed as faithful as any other member of the Little Guild.

Still, she was a lithe young blond with curves, generous ones in places, and a stunner of a face.

Sato gave the girl a look that seemed to indicate he was displeased with her lack of knowledge.

But why would a girl who specialized in jiggle-giggle and coin know anything of history? Or dusty old tombs that thieves set themselves to robbing...

Again, thought Thor, there was much more going on here than any of them knew. But he kept these thoughts to himself for they weren't important right now. Right now their survival was important, and not ensured by anything he could see at this very moment.

Death stalked them like a panther in the night.

Sure, fade at dawn... if they could hold out until then. But *to where* was the next important question. And it was a very important one. There were no cities close by, no walls to get behind, and very little reliable information regarding anything in the Eastern Wastes. Where could they go that the bloodsuckers would not follow them across the trackless wastes and wait until they had no defenses to get behind to make their move and come at them as a thirsty horde?

But the thief was urgent to tell what he knew, and this was unusual for him. And that too... bothered the Ranger.

"The Karthian Spartans were once-legendary warriors who fought impossible odds... and won, Warrior. Known for their deeds all across the ancient Ruin long before I picked my first pocket. Ancient scrolls tell of how they were nomads at first, wandering warriors for pay and plunder, until they took the fabled Rock Fortress of Karthia on the Eastern Slopes at the back end of foul and cursed Umnoth. Lands of the Orc Khans and of course the Nether Sorcerer himself. These brave Spartans waged many brutal wars, and even conquered Skeletos for a time. They set torch to Caspia one night and burned it to the ground. Or so it is said. Many witches died that night and that is not a bad thing. Other tales say they fought dragons and demons and were never bested by a foe until..."

Sato looked around.

The grim-faced warriors, the ones still on their sandals, attended to their weapons and listened to the keening wind that had risen out there in the night, howling across the eaves of the ancient holy place rocking in the blowing tempest.

The wounded remained wounded in various states, either all too aware of their impending fate, or mad and tormented by the strange and raging fever that made them swoon and moan as the night hours passed.

Satisfied no one was listening too closely, Sato continued in a whisper.

"Until... they disappeared, Warrior, into the Eastern Wastes we track through now. They were never heard from again. Rumors abounded as to their fate... but there were no true leads... even among the sages of the Sons of Kelek who are said to know all things dark and mysterious and will tell it for a price few are willing to pay. So it is said, Warrior. But there is more..."

Thor made a face indicating that what the thief said made no sense.

Then the Ranger whispered, using the cant of thieves he'd learned in their city.

"We are in the Eastern Wastes now. The southern edge. They disappeared in the wastes... so what's the mystery, my friend?"

Sato made a face, then smiled knowingly as was sometimes his way.

"Important detail, Warrior. My apologies. They disappeared ages ago, and Karthia remains little more than a pile of tumbled rocks atop a high crag where nothing grows and nothing lives. I have been there. There is nothing. Only singing ruins made so by the lonely wind and thankless goats."

Thor looked around at the Spartans in the besieged church.

And yet... here they were. Warriors calling themselves Spartans of Karthia. Warriors who bore symbols and markings handed down from before the Ruin. Using strange words that were once commonplace ten thousand years ago.

The oldest was at best thirty-five. Most were much younger.

"They say, Warrior, that time goes strange inside the wastes some days. And stranger still the more one gets nearer the Rift itself. I do not know how, or why, Warrior, but either these men are imposters play-acting at some legend from long ago to use to their advantage, or... or some trickster god has decided to bedevil us. It is impossible that these men are fresh from Karthia on a quest, as they indicate."

Sato watched Thor's eyes and said nothing.

But Thor knew what his friend was thinking. That just as the Ranger was a man out of time, then so, perhaps, might these be too?

CHAPTER TWELVE

"T HEY MAY BE ONE OR THE OTHER, SATO," said Thor warily, rising to his feet after the huddle with Sato and the ever-present Alluria. He arched his back and didn't groan. The SAW was getting heavy, as was the rest of his gear. And the night seemed nowhere half-finished.

He checked the Ranger-green Timex he'd strapped on. The one that had come with the rest of the gear in the speedball.

It was the third time he'd checked it since getting inside, and for some reason... it wasn't working, or it was working... *strange.*

First he'd checked it to see how long they had until there was enough daylight to wait out their captors who'd need to seek shelter. Ruin vampires, like "normal" vampires, were night-hunting creatures. If dawn came, that gave Thor and his new allies some maneuver room. He'd checked the Timex again to hack the exact moment the pounding on the outer walls and doors had stopped. That might be important, but he wasn't sure how, so he'd marked the time and noted it seemed longer according to the watch than his inner and constant count. That hack didn't add because the time didn't match what it should have been, to the Ranger. The first check had indicated a little after eighteen thirty. Just after dark. What should have been a few minutes later read as more than an hour.

And now...

His mind told him it had been a mere two hours except both the Timex and the feel of the night said it was...

He tapped the watch...

Through the thin wooden slats of the old structure they were turtled in, Sergeant Thor could see it was still dark outside, and they'd only been inside the church for a couple of hours, three tops, but the air was cooler just like it got before dawn, and there were strange night birds out there making their first calls before dawn.

Time was indeed... getting strange.

And the new watch was already useless.

The Ruin reveals, but it also just ruins. A common Ranger joke back in the detachment each time some new piece of Forge-generated equipment broke down faster than it was thought that it should have. Either the effects of this...

Rift... at the heart of the Eastern Wastes, or... was this just the still-fading effects of the nano-plague breaking down modern tech just like it did rifles and any of their other modern equipment?

More than likely, decided the Ranger, it was just that. Nano-plague wear and tear.

The vampires' hellish menace had a freaky effect, and by their very inhuman nature things seemed... spooky. He needed to remember that. But he could feel fear out there, emanating not like waves but pulses from some dark radar that seemed to wash through the building and break through.

The ancient dry wood of the place creaked and groaned occasionally and, Thor wondered if this was her, Madame Hudu... radiating some kind of fear attack to break down the "holy" and "sacred" defenses of the building. Thwart the powers of the ethereal priest the Spartans called their *jumpmaster*.

The Ranger snorted, hit some dip, and spit it off into the shadows as he watched the night and tried to spot his foes.

Thermal on the SAW seemed useless against them.

Of course... they were dead, snorted Thor and felt himself digging the challenge of doing them anyway. It was just a problem. And all problems had solutions when Rangers were involved.

Solutions that usually involved high-ex.

But he'd have to get them to cluster...

He mused these things, stroked his beard, and spit dip, watching the strange and misty night out there before the coming day.

And he ignored the waves of fear that came and went like radar pulses seeking a target to reveal.

How much of the waste was woo-woo and creepshow, he wondered. And how much was it just the nano-plague and old legends over a long and very long count of years?

And who were these "Spartans" with their strange Before words and things the Ranger knew from long ago?

Were they two-thousand-year-old heartbreakers and lifetakers? Fine. Maybe they were lying about who they were. That was... a tomorrow problem as the D-Boys say, as every Ranger knows.

D-Boys were Delta.

Rangers usually made their way into the Delta troops if they stayed in the game long enough. But there was wisdom in that.

Right now was get off the *X* and kill the head vampire. Even if it was a dusky little jewel of a hottie. She'd made her mistake and come looking for revenge on him because *her* plans got in the way of *his* plans.

Now... she wasn't gonna pay for that. But she was going to need to be taken off the board because he couldn't have her dogging his rear going forward.

"Sorry 'bout that, chick," muttered Thor to himself as he studied the night beyond the dried and dead old wooden slats of the church. "But it's you or me and I vote me. Nothin' personal. You just gotta go. Time for a permanent dirt nap."

So, who the Spartans were, really were, that was a "tomorrow problem." Right now, they can carry and swing weapons. They are allies, if just to get out of here, get off the *X*, and get clear of the damned ville, the Ranger told himself.

Their identity wasn't the biggest problem.

He spit more dip and turned away from the view of the haunted night.

The biggest problem was the horses and the mule that had run off in the battle in the night.

Most of the good equipment was on those horses. *Mjölnir* too. And the Carl G. And their rations and supplies.

The fact that the horses could outrun vampires was a plus... but had they?

Thor and Sato had let them free to fight for themselves as the vampires closed their net about the three and things got hasty.

"What about the horses?" Thor had asked Sato when they'd barely made the safety of the church.

Sato had rubbed his chin.

"They are not all fighters. Ours are fast and my guess is they outran the attack and probably are lost somewhere out there in the storm. Though one always wonders if animals are really ever lost, Warrior, or just done with your general foolishness. *Your* steed on the other hand, Stormbringer… aaahhh, now he is a vain and angry warrior, in ways like his master. He would fight to the death if he had his way. My guess is he trampled many of the fiends out there so that the others, including the pretty pony Alluria rides, could flee, for he is their leader and that is plain to see. He bears the brunt of their responsibility. In that… he is also like his master."

So Thor's mount could be lying dead not too far away. Which, other than transportation, wasn't a critical loss. It was a good horse. A fighter, like the thief said. But the gear was survival. And the gear would still be there, if it could be found. What did Bronze Age vampires care for gear and an M105A anti-materiel rifle that defied the Ruins' deteriorating effects?

Or the Carl for that matter.

But if he could locate the horse… even if it was dead… then he could kill a lot of them.

Sergeant Thor looked out through one of the cracks and saw what he could of the open hard-packed dirt space that passed for the main street of the ville.

Where there should have been the flapping, wind-beaten corpses of those vampires he'd shot to death, straight-up ruined, there was nothing.

Nothing but the drifting banks of mist.

The wind threw sand across the night in great bursts, like the sudden appearance of some mad flock of shadowy night birds racing off somewhere important. Passing over this murder in the making for some place better and not this night. And beyond the passing night birds of sand... far back in the empty black spaces between the shadows of the other strange and twisted buildings that made up the small settlement... were red eyes like small pinpricks of hateful malevolence burning in the night.

Vampires.

Thor spit dip and pushed away more of the cold tingles that seemed to surround all the talk and the mystery of this region called the Eastern Wastes.

He would need a plan to get them all free of this.

Dawn would come soon.

He set down the SAW, shrugged out of his assault pack, retrieved a ChemLight, and broke it, creating a small circle of wan green-blue illumination. Then the Ranger began to arrange found debris in a small cleared space, making a sand table of what he could see of the village.

Making his plan to murder their way free of the trap Madame Hudu had set.

Getting off the *X*.

CHAPTER THIRTEEN

"How do we kill them?" asked Thor of the priest as Sato, Alluria, and the last two Spartans on their feet looked on. "How do we kill those vampires out there?"

On the floor, in the jade-green wash thrown by the ChemLight, a few blocks of wood, rocks, and some rough lines displayed the cursed ville of the night feeders, or what they could see of it from the church or remember from the bare evening gloom as they'd made their approach and then retreat into the building.

Time felt strange. Definitely. As though the night had gone on forever, but when one really thought about it, thought about recent activities... maybe less than three hours had passed.

"Kill them," said the priest. John of Towle he called himself.

And again, the Ranger knew enough unit history of a once-fabled unit from long ago, from the Before as some in the Ruin called ancient history before everything had become the way it had, to find that an odd coincidence in even the man's name, along with everything else about these... Spartans.

Tomorrow problem. As the D-Boys say.

Survival was all that mattered right now.

In time the bloodsuckers would come for them or wait them out until dawn and see if they'd make a run for it. Then they'd stalk them and run them down another night when the defenses weren't as sure. As "holy" and "sacred" to keep them at bay.

And then there was that fear attack the vampire lady was throwing at them. Sergeant Thor was sure that was doing something against the invisible defenses, prayers or whatever it was, that kept them back. Was her power significant enough that she could weaken the defenses and then lesser vampires could breach and attack?

Unknown.

Uncertain.

Suboptimal.

Best to hit them before they hit first. Ranger gonna Ranger, as Talker would've said. Thor smiled and missed the linguist just a little. The kid was good. One day, if he lived, he'd make a great Ranger.

"They've kept us pinned up with the wolves that come with the light," muttered one of the gruffer and grimmer Spartans from the shadows.

A warrior for sure. He'd introduced himself as "Corporal Max of Gavin" with a gravelly voice and few words. He was scarred, dark, and brooding, and Sergeant Thor knew a dedicated infantryman when he met one. He was the highest ranking still on his feet, and probably, thought Thor as he assessed what he had to work with in the night, this night, the highest ranking among their kind still left alive.

Corporal Max's gladius was shattered just above the hilt. His arms were bandaged. His spear was little more than a club now. It was clear the man had fought desperately for his men to just barely survive and make the holdfast of the strange church.

But it was also clear the lead Spartan wasn't very optimistic they'd make it out of this one alive.

The Ranger could see a grim fatalism in the man's eyes that would take little pleasure in slaying those he would slay before being slain. But still, he would make them pay for what they were about to do to his unit, and him, in the end.

Payback burned like a mean little fire in the corporal's eyes. Thor understood exactly the feeling.

"Wolves?" asked Sato.

"Yes," said the priest with a nod, murmuring slightly and deferentially. "In the three days we have been trapped here, they come out of the desert and surround the church before the rising of the sun. They are... big wolves. The biggest I have ever seen. There are too many of them for us to fight our way through, what with the wounded, and..."

The priest trailed off, not finishing his sentence as though the words that would come next were too heavy a burden to bear.

"The brutes would either trail us," grunted Corporal Max in his grave-dust whisper. His dark eyes watching Thor. "Or slay us on open ground. Not as many of them as there are the soul suckers... but enough to keep us pinned here as they have for three days while the fiends stay out of the sun and wait for the dark to come at us."

That last bit was a bolt out of the blue for the Ranger and something he hadn't considered as he'd developed his sand table and tried to figure a way they could fade before the next attack came.

Or now... be pinned until dusk by big wolves out of the desert.

The chances the horses and mule had survived in light of this new information decreased, thought Thor to himself. Still, *Mjölnir* and the rest of his gear would still be out there lying among a pile of bloody horse guts. Wolves had no use for a Carl.

Thor grunted to himself, "That's right... they sleep, don't they? Vampires have to sleep during the day. They need a place to hide..."

The priest opened his mouth and closed it, nodding to himself as though he too was following what this stranger donning strange gear who was clearly a warrior of some sort, was thinking.

"Yes, strange one, so say the legends. The night feeders must return to their graves, or a dark space underground nearest the realms of nether to wait out the brightness and truth of the sun."

Thor pointed to all the buildings on the sand table.

"Here. This is their base. This is where they're safe when they're vulnerable in the day. In daylight."

The Spartan corporal stepped forward and bent down to the map... he rubbed his three days' beard and lantern jaw.

"Yeah..." grunted the corporal. "When ya look at it that way... they need this place as much as we do."

The Spartan was silent and studied the map with his mouth slightly open.

"So we burn them," rumbled the Ranger, standing to his full height, towering over them. "Tonight. We deny them safety. We burn all the houses and structures in the village, so they have no place to go deep when daylight comes. Then... we leave."

The priest added quickly, "If the village burns... then by dawn they must seek other caves farther away from here, and that gives us time to run. But what about the wolves?"

Thor rubbed his beard.

Then he picked up the super SAW.

"They have no chance against this once we decide to leave. They won't follow when I start laying the hate on the pack."

The remaining Spartans nodded and agreed, but they had no idea what the stranger meant by laying the hate.

Still, it was a chance to survive and live, and they were Karthian Spartans after all. They dared where others did not.

CHAPTER FOURTEEN

THE STRANGE NIGHT CONTINUED, SEEMING to slow even as the unseen dawn hinted at its approaching revelation. Still, it remained pitch black, and the winds softened to a low moan.

Going from place to place, checking the drafts and peering through the cracks between the slats in the tall looming windows, Thor felt the time was right to enact his plan to burn the ville and deny the vampires a place to rest.

At times, a few of the bloodsuckers would come from out of the deep shadows in the dead village and stand near the abandoned church like dark sentinels, their red burning eyes hungry and fixed on the Ranger as he peered out at them.

As though they knew he was in there, watching them.

To Thor the feeling was disconcerting, but he would study what he could see of them before continuing with his fatal calculations to flip the tables on them. To give himself and his allies a chance to survive this cursed place. And... this unholy night.

The speedball had come with a number of grenades but only three thermites.

Three would be enough, reasoned the Ranger as he measured the wind and saw which way it was sweeping across the high desert haunted village.

Shortly the Ranger climbed up some back stairs behind the sanctuary of the old church and reached the upper choir loft. There was nothing here but mice bones and dust. Soon Thor found a ladder that led him further up toward a feature in the construction that was perhaps a steeple, but more like a tower than anything else.

The rungs were ancient and dry and one of the first he grasped hold of didn't snap so much as just disintegrate in his assault glove as he held it in order to haul himself into the upper reaches of the building so he could conduct his fiery attack against Lady Hudu's undead army.

Other rungs snapped too, but Thor was a Ranger and climbing was second nature, with or without assistance. A graduate of the combat climb school long ago, Thor got himself up to where he needed to be to launch the attack. Add in the rock climbing and free climbing he did on leave to get his adventure junkie on back in the world ten thousand years ago, always looking for those sharp edges, and the ascent up through the narrow wooden tower that seemed to sway in the bursts of wind of the vast and spreading desert in the night was of little obstacle to him.

The building groaned more and more, creaking as though the strong pulses of the fear waves were slowly tearing it apart. As though the building was a living thing in long-diseased agony.

The Ranger reached the top, found what he thought he would, and smashed an ancient hatch open with a solid crack from his assault glove because the lock was long rusted shut.

The hatch banged open, disintegrated, and flew off in the dawn-dark winds. Sergeant Thor smelled the night and the sage and desert in it.

As the Ranger ascended through the portal, there was nothing around him but the shadowy vampire-haunted realm of the dead village below. The world, the Ruin, beyond the damned village didn't exist and could not be seen.

And to the Ranger, it didn't matter. The world was tomorrow. Tonight all the vampires, and Hudu... they'd die.

The moon was out and the wind was cold. And to the Ranger, having been penned up for hours with the sick and wounded, that felt good for a moment as he made ready his attack.

He scanned the village, checked the winds once more, then popped the spoons on the three thermite grenades and hurled them into the larger buildings below. Buildings that would be turned to fuel by the little M14 incendiary grenades. Buildings upwind and ready to spread fiery destruction.

Within twenty minutes, the entire village was engulfed by a conflagration as the flames generated by the relentless burning thermite spread from building to building.

Within one, a large tavern, vampires were already burning alive, running from the flung-open cellars and wildly rushing out into the hard-packed dirt streets like Roman candles aflame.

Other vampires merely stared into the leaping flames, transfixed by the destruction that had been slowly wrought upon them. The flames would cook the buildings of the village they'd been hiding in while waiting for their mistress to spring the trap for the prey she'd whispered was coming all along...

The Ranger who'd ruined all her pretty plans for the City of Thieves.

Dirt-floor root cellars, open graves carved in the dirt beneath, and pulled-up floor planking in other buildings, all of it was now, or soon would be, denied them as a place of damnation rest.

A few shadowy fiends were already running off into the darkness and the desert, desperate to find some other crevice or lost ancient well to cast themselves down into and flee from the coming rays of the sun.

But most night feeders, among them haunted and hungry wraiths, still gathered near their queen under the largest building that must have been some base to them. It was already catching fire from some flaming brand that had fallen inside. Gray smoke poured out the eyeless windows. But around her, around Madame Hudu, some unholy court of the damned she ruled over collected around her. All of them, all of these she'd gathered to her as she'd raced ahead of the trio, moaned and screamed, begging her for salvation from what was clearly at hand. She'd taken these in recent weeks, scavenging here and there, then flying ahead of the trio with the big, tall warrior who'd ruined her plans back in the City of Thieves...

She found her praetorian guard and made them her sycophantic servants in the drinking of their blood, taking and transforming wandering tradesmen and lost shepherds that had once called this place home... into her willing thralls in this her final revenge.

And other traders along the way.

Lost mercenaries looking for another war.

And even a troupe of performers. Sinister-eyed clowns and evil-eyed mountebanks who'd once made their living playing tricks and doing tumbles for pretty coin... these gathered closest to the raging lady as Madame Hudu screamed curses into the flames and ordered them to take up what brands they could from the conflagration and cast them upon the church where the last of her enemies waited.

Vampires fear flame.

They watched and instead begged like spoiled children denied their toy and their treat, in full tantrum, that they be saved from the inevitable light of the soon-coming day.

And the flames all around them.

Again...

Vampires do not like flames.

Those that tried to do her will got burned up suddenly like cheap bundles of winter-gathered sticks, as others just shirked her commands like beaten dogs who still could not stray from their wicked master, mewling that undeath was cruel and they were weak.

The three ambulatory Spartans had gone out onto the roof of the old church below the tower steeple, making an opening where none had existed, and used blankets to beat out any stray embers that managed to find the church at the center of the buildings as the night winds whipped and whirled sparks and flaming debris and cinders of hell-ash all about.

The dark lady roared in anger.

Lesser vampires screamed and hissed while some burnt to dark and wisping ash.

And the Ranger and his allies continued their work, sensing a chance to survive just ahead with the coming of a day that must, at some point, appear.

All around, the winds spread the flames to other buildings and carried hot sparks off into the hard desert wastes where low scrub and desert brush caught fire, illuminating the night and turning it almost festive like some late bonfire holiday.

Dark figures below, the few that were left, surrounded their raging queen as she made ready to find some final way to have her revenge, or flee for dark caves and forgotten wells to hide and wait for another night when new plans could be laid to kill the one she so wanted dead, and make him her tormented slave... forever and forever and all the hellish forevers that could be imagined.

But the Ranger was not done with Madame Hudu yet. There was no escape for her as far as he was concerned.

Amid the flames and smoke, Thor slipped from a side entrance of the ancient tall and looming old wooden church, carrying his tomahawk and the stout broken spear of Corporal Maximus of Gavin.

CHAPTER FIFTEEN

Among the gathered inner circle of the vengeful and spite-filled vampire lady within the flaming village, the first vampire slave to be returned to final death was a mercenary. Or had been a mercenary. A man of war and combat for pay. He'd fallen prey to what he thought was a waif of a dusky little roadside prostitute eight days ago. Eight days back when the winds howled and the blowing sand seemed so thick it was almost evening, when really it was half the day done.

She offered her charms and a rude little tent to wait out the storm. Her sly smile and knowing look had seemed a thing the tired man of war needed.

So... perhaps just a moment, or a few hours...

He'd been on the march from the city-states of Gozen, a minor alliance east of mystical Uran, headed toward the fabled City of Palms deep in the wastes with rumors of a new war brewing there and easy coin for spilled blood to be had for one willing to swing a sword for pay.

He'd been among a cabal of like-minded veterans. But his companions had given him up as a desperate drunk and one they no longer wanted to league with much less fight back-to-back and in desperate and bad circumstances with as needs often must for mercenaries of this kind.

What kind?

Low and desperate.

Scarred and often haunted by the things potentates and satraps of the east wanted done to hang on to power just a bit longer.

Battles.

Assassinations.

Genocides.

But Madame Hudu was no mean roadside comfort girl who'd take a goat in trade, or perhaps a sack of gold, for her charming favors...

The undead mercenary vampire once known as Jodon of Haldt, who now counted himself in undeath after her feisty bite in the throes of lust, claws like rusty nails leaving their trails on his scarred and tattooed back, and having now gained powers and unholy skills, counted himself lucky and that fortune favored him now, for this new "life" would give him all the drinking and wenching he could take and slake his unquenchable thirst upon.

Now the dead-eyed merc with black circles under his eyes, and first of the Hudu's "praetorians" to die at the hand of Sergeant Thor, on the stalk low and moving through the smoke and ash, crouched and swift for the target he intended to deal with this night was surrounded by dangerous night feeders just like herself... at that moment the unlucky merc felt himself alive with dark and unholy fear. Yes, Jodon thought himself lucky to have discovered the sultry little chocolate-skinned waif dressed like a gypsy and/or fortune teller offering him a chance at her in her tent. He'd not had gold, and of course no goat, but she'd seemed too young and naive at this business of exchange and flesh to know that, and so when the deed was done he'd made up his mind to strangle her, and then rob her there as she seemed to have no guards and only the lonely tent pitched out in the sand at the top of a long-unused pass.

I should have known better, he thought before becoming her slave, when defenseless and distracted he'd felt her bite deep into his neck and begin to suck the life right from him.

But the curse was a blessing in disguise, he'd discovered...

Right up until the moment the Ranger shanked him hard in the black beating twist he'd called a heart.

Thor ran Jodon through with the shank, driving it deep into the vampire mercenary's heart as the Ranger came at him suddenly out of the night like some great hunting cat, hungry, not to be denied its kill.

Straight through the mercenary's chest and right into the heart wasn't the way it was done, for Jodon had paid much of his bloody earnings for a fine shirt of skillfully worked steel-scale that had saved him many a time from deadly injury in the hot thick of desperate battles past. But the Ranger had assessed the armor and the angle in the moment of his attack, coming out of the smoke and dying comet ash drifting across the battlefield. He came for the tall and lanky man who stood in his way as he threaded the ravening vampires of Lady Hudu, screaming as they lost their deranged minds while their graves and hiding places burned with the night soon done.

Surely.

Surely the end of all dark things was at hand...

Jodon of Haldt turned at the blow, his black-rimmed sunken eyes, a fire of jealous green burning undead at their deep and lifeless centers, suddenly seeing Thor, and he reached quickly to draw the nicked old broadsword he'd once swung for pay. He was already run through but in his feral mind he calmly said, *I'll cut him down, then throw myself on this living human and drink.*

Yes.

Drink and feed and live.

He could already feel the slaking relief from the maddening thirst he'd had for days now even though the shank was deep in his dark vampire's heart, ceasing the beat. Ending the shadow.

The Ranger, assessing the armor the man wore, had surged to the right and jammed the shank right through the side of the armor where it was laced up, pushing it deep into the pericardial sac, puncturing there, and then finally, the heart itself.

Jodon opened his mouth to scream as the world changed and his single-minded plan of feeding vanished. Unseen damnations he'd purchased for himself long before he'd become a night feeder were now revealed to be far too close, and far more real, than he'd ever bargained. And in the same instant, like some threshing machine that kills automatically, the Ranger slashed the fiend's long and muscled throat with a sudden savage swipe from the tomahawk and Jodon made no sound of alarm amid the madness and chaos of the vampire clan.

Instead of a cry of alarm, a gurgling groan was all that came as the corpse of the vampire mercenary fell to the sand and started, even at that moment, to just... *come apart*. And soon, over days perhaps, or even by the end of this cursed night ending so soon, too soon, what remained of Jodon would fly off, drifting and becoming one with the strange mystery of the Eastern Wastes which, as they say, no man truly knows.

But in the next instant, the hunting Ranger had the next target in his sights and the way was cleared to Hudu even more as the sands that counted fell faster and faster with each passing second.

The priest, John of Towle... which seemed among the Spartans to be the formal way of introducing and identifying oneself; afterward it was just John, or Max, or the name of the other Spartan, Ajax of DeGlopper...

The priest, John of Towle, had given Thor, Sato, and Alluria a short course in the sacred knowledge of destroying vampires of the undead kind.

"The holy texts of the sacred field manuals made by Major Baer... say we must attack the heart for them to be fully destroyed, and no other wound shall suffice as it does for the living to be maimed and ultimately cut down. So sayeth the major when first we Red Devils came to the Ruin, made war, and heard the lamentations of our foes' women and children."

Again, Thor raised an eyebrow.

Red Devils.

But none of those listening caught the look, and instead listened as though their lives depended on what the priest was telling them.

Because it did. Vampires were as dangerous as it got, and each culture was filled with terror tales of the fiends and the damnation they wrought for themselves.

Priests and clerics were often slain dealing with the constant undead that plagued the living of the Ruin in abundance, often more so than local orcs or ever-troublesome goblins.

Their undead hatred of the Cities of Men was something that could be counted on as sure as the rising of the first star in the evening. Many defenses and many prayers were made against such predators, for to die by a vampire's hand was much worse, much, much worse, than to be slain by raiding orcs, goblins, gnolls, or ogres.

Eternal darkness and the realms of night and nether were promised for those who fed on the blood of the living.

"They can see the living," continued the priest. "Even when we are hidden. But perhaps flame and fire will distract them as the heat of flame is like the heat of life which they hate so..."

Thor had decided he would use that when he ignited the village. He would use the thermal conflagration to mask his attack.

Or what the Green Beret who ran with the Ranger detachment liked to chuckle and call, *"Surprise, Ranger Smash!"*

Now leaving the dead and shanked mercenary, Thor reset his weapons and pushed closer to the huddle that surrounded the head vampire lady who ran this clan of night feeders.

Madame Hudu.

"It was when we first came to these lands from across the end of the old worlds... so say the texts," the priest had continued as they'd huddled over Sergeant Thor's sand table, hatching their plans to escape the village. The Ranger plotting his solution to murder the problem that had dared stalk him away from the City of Thieves.

Just so she could have her revenge because he had refused her offer. And ruined all her petty diabolical plans.

"It was when we first came to these lands that we found the Bloody Cliffs and did battle against their kind. The undead. The bloodsuckers. We still had the ancient weapons of old."

Each Spartan gazed questioningly at Thor's MK48. Then looked to the priest who nodded knowingly.

"Down into the twisting warrens and even to the ancient Night Fortress itself did the first Devils, our fathers, make their way with the strange weapons of old. Surrounded it is written, it looked dire, but Major Baer, first warlord of the Karthians, slew their chief revenant there and suddenly their armies on all sides turned to dust... *and were no more.*"

The priest paused.

"So it must be this night. To evade the vampires and their pursuit, fiends who will lust for revenge as much as they do our blood once we have burned their graves... if we can find their source, the head vampire, their captain as it were... then perhaps that will end this black coven and allow us to cross through the wastes and rejoin our brothers. Perhaps even the wolves will not arrive with the dawn should their leader be slain and the pact between such broken. If their leader is dead then she may fail to summon them forth for the watch."

The young priest seemed hesitant in his manner, but his words were firm as though each and every one of them was as true as the cardinal directions of the compass. His voice was pure and his speech almost heroic as though written for some bardic lay performed long ago. As he spoke, his hesitant manner vanished and he became more and more their fire, their leader.

"So it is written, so it be so. Until dawn, Devils."

The other two Spartans nodded solemnly and stared down at the sand table like the grim-faced killers they were.

Each pulled forth a medal, and Thor recognized the image instantly.

Saint Michael the Archangel medals.

Paratroopers for time immemorial have carried it. Theirs were looped on crude leather bands, and the medals seemed rough and stamped at some forge.

It's... impossible, the Ranger wanted to tell himself. And yet... here it was.

Then he heard the voice of Ranger Wizard PFC Kennedy. Keeper of lore. Player of strange games of dice and paper.

"Embrace the fantasy, Sar'nt. Better that way in the Ruin."

And Tanner, standing right there. Two-DUI two-stripper-ex-wives perpetual private who never should have been on the pump into the future much less been a PFC in the regiment, smiling that twisted smile of his.

"That way, Sar'nt Thor... when it bite, it don't bite so hard."

Embrace the fantasy.

Sergeant Thor wondered if they, these Spartans who called themselves "Devils" to one another, believed in the priest's religion as much as the young man did, or were they simply resolved to the combat that must come if they were to see the dawn.

But the head vampire...

Hudu.

She'd die.

Now... with the dead vampire mercenary disintegrating into drifting dust behind the Ranger, the press of Hudu's damned faithful circled around her, protecting her, beseeching her like players in some bad community theater musical, losing their shattered minds while others prayed to the Vampire Lady like she was some kind of minor rising deity who could hold back the coming sure damnation of the daylight, a thing they greatly feared...

The Ranger stalked forward with the shank in one fist and the tomahawk in the other.

As though it were nothing at all.

CHAPTER SIXTEEN

SERGEANT THOR HACKED AND SLASHED HIS way toward the vampire vanguard surrounding Madame Hudu like a tornado of sharp edges, swift kicks, slammed fists, and even a savage headbutt that cracked the skull of one fiend so loud it sounded like a bag of potato chips being crunched under a sledgehammer.

He didn't care if they were powerful or lesser vampires, they were in his way. He destroyed them and kept moving on his target.

The high dark lady raged and shrieked as she tried to control her fear-stricken flock. The village she'd promised them rest and respite in from the relentless glare and consuming of the sun soon to come, was simply burning down all around them.

And there was nothing any of them could do as the horror of what would happen next dawned in their dark-circled haunted eyes. Her ringing words and angry promises became lies with each flaming collapse and fiery engulfment of a structure within the cursed ville.

And yet... despite the imminent end of all things bloody and eternal, they continued their hissing and whining appeals as though surely the lady had some power over facts and reality yet unrevealed.

She did not. The sun would rise soon, and they'd all be damned by its relentless glare, curling into black ash and hungry flame.

She flashed out over them with contempt and disgust hurled like coppers at beggar children in all the mean streets of the Cities of Men. All pretty guise and charming guile gone now. There would be no more promises. She would command them, and they would obey.

Even if it was against a will they no longer possessed. She was their queen, their dark master, and they were her servants and even lesser than that.

She would make new blood-hungry sycophants another dark night in other alleys and along other lonely byways among the unsuspecting, and the living...

After she'd had her revenge in full on the Ranger.

After...

But she was doomed. Some small part of her that was still sane reasoned it was time to flee by mist or transformation, or even just running for some cave in the high rocks and bloody cliffs...

Even the terrible Lady Hudu knew this, and her features practically trembled with unrequited rage as the heat of the wind borne of the dancing flames whipped and tossed her multicolored skirts and glittered the magic protective charms she wore about her thin chest and in her long curly and kinky hair of both dark and blond.

She never knew where she really came from or who her parents truly were. She too had started as a street urchin. And then one cold night...

She gave a bloodcurdling cry of rage.

All... was lost.

One of the buildings collapsed, and she could hear her followers who'd thought to bury themselves in the cellar there screaming in horror as they were consumed.

All...

... was lost.

Never mess with a Ranger. Never ever, some coffee-addicted sage who knew such things might have told her. But he was not here and had many troubles of his own, even at that very hour.

But that is another tale.

Some of the minor vampires about her lost their minds completely then, keening and sobbing as finally a thin red strip of light began to grow in the east.

There was wailing.

There were prayers.

There was gnashing of fangs.

And there... was Thor.

CHAPTER SEVENTEEN

STILL, THERE WERE SOME WHO HEARD AND obeyed their dark mistress of eternal delights even as everything went to hell in a handbasket there in that little cursed and lost village in the high desert that would now... disappear forever because some angry little girl had decided to make an enemy of Sergeant Thor.

These last hard-bitten few were her hardened veterans of midnight assaults and sudden murders and even blood-drinking festivals out there on the high desert wastes and the lost highways where time and events grew, and grow, strange and stranger still.

Ask the lotus-addled sages of Kungaloor, for they know such things that should not be known.

A few of Lady Hudu's faithful ran into the flames, catching fire and batting out what they could as their rags were consumed, still hoping for the dark salvation of the shallow trenches they could find for her to rest, or dig for their mistress down there in the deep root cellars where they'd lain waiting for this much-promised ambush. This very hoped-for feeding.

All vengeful plans were smashed now. But they could still save her. Still save the Vampire Lady so devoted were they, or so they thought in their fevered minds, to her that they were willing to try even if it meant being consumed alive by the hungry flames that were everywhere now among the smoke and drifting burning ash.

Meanwhile…

Sergeant Thor heaved his tomahawk into the skull of another one, splitting the cranium and never minding to run the rest of the fiend through with the bloody gore-dripping shank as he made for the strange multi-garbed and wild-painted guard surrounding their queen of damnation.

He was close now to his intended target. But a final guard still lay between him and her.

"Not for long," grunted Thor as he pulled the shank savagely out from the side of the chest of one of them he'd just finished off. He wiped his mouth and pushed for the next one, knowing the chaos he was using to get close wouldn't last and soon they'd recognize the predator among them was more than just a wild animal.

Much, much more.

They were clowns. Mountebanks. And tumblers.

Performers. Caperers in city streets and the occasional palace.

To him. The Ranger on the stalk. Thor...

They seemed like comic medieval circus performers. They were strange and misshapen. Once-colorful silks and canvases adorned them along with tasseled boots and bell-flopped hats made filthy by the shallow graves they'd come to know since falling under the sway of the one who called herself Madame Hudu.

Promiser of dark dreams and bloody delights in the world she would make for them.

The world of the dead.

Lady Hudu.

And they were hers... forever.

Thor didn't care what, or who, stood between him and the one he would slay tonight. Clowns were clowns and these were gonna die, as was their leader.

He surged into the largest of them as Madame Hudu, carried aloft by two strange Grim-Reaper-like stilt-walkers, bellowed and shrieked that they should attend her and rush the "cursed holy place now!" That there they would be safe from the "Fiend of the Sun that will soon destroy them all!"

Her voice had become stern and deep, like some prophetess of old showing them the way...

Surely this was the way?

She hadn't seen how close he was. The smoke and the fire, the wailing and screaming, and yes the burning alive of her followers... had distracted her almost as much as her insatiable lust for revenge against the Ranger she'd thought she'd run to ground inside the church.

In that instant, even as her plan fell apart all around her in flames and screams, she'd been debating whether to order her followers to burn the church just so she could make sure Sergeant Thor was dead, or take it and slay everyone there so she could go into its catacombs and sleep...

She had no idea that neither was an option and the sands of the hourglass of her life were few indeed.

The Ranger made the inner guard and drove his shank deep into the muscle-swollen back of the troupe's strongman. The hulking brute who wore a cheap leopard skin like he was some kind of ancient caveman, now turned vampire by betrayal and hard times, tried to roar, but the blade had penetrated to the lungs. He was bald and mustachioed and when he turned to face his attacker his haunted dead eyes, ringed in black by death and undeath, by delayed thirst and sleep-torment, were suddenly wide and filled with fire and anger at the blow he'd received.

But the stake of the shank was already in past the lung and into the heart.

The strongman wrenched himself away from Thor and went to his knees, hauling his two great brawny arms up and behind him to the blade's hilt to pull it free even as gray wisps of snaky smoke crawled and writhed away from the vampire-killing wound the Ranger had created.

Thor backed away, heaving for breath. Feeling himself near some edge and end of endurance.

The wizard, as Rangers say, *approaches.*

Fatigue, exhaustion, defeat…

The wizard.

Vampires along the edge of the inner guard, minor mewling faithful, were bursting into flames at even the hint of coming dawn as that thin red stripe of first day began to groan and lengthen across the morning dark.

Thor told the wizard of fatigue, exhaustion, and defeat what he could do with himself and pushed the assault against Hudu's vanguard, swinging and hacking as he dove into the press of those who'd pledged themselves to protect the lady.

A sad troupe of comic performers fallen on hard times just weeks ago who'd been dealt the last cheat of hard luck in meeting a "gypsy girl" east of all the Cities of Men.

East is curst, so they say.

Strange wraith-like shadows ran off into the desert wastes that surrounded the lost and lonely town as though hoping to find some fox's den and crawl into its narrow crevice to somehow avoid the coming judgment of morning light soon to reveal itself in the new day.

Thor jumped forward, lead boot out, a Muy Thai defensive kick with the leading leg, and slammed the sole of the heavy new Forge-printed combat boot courtesy of the speedball down on the end of the shank in the undead heaving strongman's back, driving it deeper into the haunted blood drinker's corrupted heart even as the brute tried to save himself and pull it free.

The vampire had almost done it on raw strength alone...

Now...

Now it was deep in the giant and would never be yanked free by the strongman, and the costumed thug seemed to realize that with a slow horror and just pitched over into the sand to finally die.

Again.

Other nearby demonic wildly made-up clowns reacted to the Ranger's attack with python hisses, sensing imminent dangerous-danger itself in the person of the Ranger suddenly and somehow among them. As one, they rallied to surround and defend their new Queen of Undeath, reaching for the wild and raging untamed Thor as he slashed and hacked at them, the very picture of fury even though it was clear he was surrounded and they had the advantage of numbers. Painted claws and flesh-white pancake makeup reached for him and tried to drag him down with hopes of tearing him apart and perhaps drinking a little blood before the sun destroyed them all.

Thor hacked at their reaching limbs with the tomahawk, removing some, savaging others beyond use.

The clowns hissed and seethed, righteous in their indignation at what threatened them and what was being done to them even as they objected like feral cats being drowned, or caught garbage raccoons in the dead of night about their garbage raccoon business of feeding.

The clowns.

Mountebanks.

Tumblers.

The performers...

Once, long ago, they'd been a ceremonial troupe out of the witch city of Caspia who'd failed the wrong sorceress and had to flee east and into the desert, tumbling and miming in the haunted cities there along the hazy trade routes from the east.

Here was their story...

They were assassins by trade. Performers by need. Often the two at the same time to effect just the right acquisition of coin in stamped gold, and it was just such a ruse they'd been tasked with in Caspia that had led to their downfall and fleeing into the desert wastes south and east of Umnoth.

And the arms, and fangs, of the Vampire Lady. The "little gypsy girl" they'd thought might make a slick addition to their various acts.

Back in Caspia, performing for one of the grand trade lords, the deal had gone wrong with one of the chief crones of Caspia. They were to make sure the trade lord was either strangled with a scarf of dancing or run through with a thrown knife during one of the playlets that dared such feats.

The old crone wanted the fat trade master dead for reasons not disclosed.

They failed.

The witch's curses to aid them and blind the guards and create just the right amount of unease had been of little effect, for the merchant lord had charms of warding of his own, and a pretty little witch as a concubine who made deals with demons and the dark to keep her lover safe. Her silks were very fine indeed.

So the assassin clowns of Mumry Bill, leader and impresario of the troupe, had been summoned and given a fat sack of gold to make the merchant lord die for the witch of Caspia, and they'd failed.

Mumry Bill and the odd flotsam of humans that was the troupe were forced to flee off into the east with the night, and all the hard times that would follow them after that, and the worse ones that would find them there after they met the "little gypsy girl."

In the City of Palms they'd lost their jiggle-and-giggle girls. One of their best attractions. Lost all five to the Priests of Susumannanon the Lover. As fine and slender and as acrobatic as the girls were, of course that lecherous lot of priests who served their bloody and bloated love god had wanted them all for themselves.

But on a permanent retainer some called slavery.

So they were down the dancers after that fiasco and on the run from temple stranglers who wanted to make sure the city was cleansed of this low sort as the troupe had revealed themselves to be.

But Mumry Bill had been through worse. He knew their luck would turn, and so they made for other cities and rumors farther out near the edge of civilization.

"A total washout!" a tattler might have cried. "They bombed in the Palms!" another may have whispered after all their ill luck there.

But they still had the Three Clowns. Everyone loved the Three Clowns. Once a famous violent comedic trio loved by children and men, now forgotten and grown old and mean and certainly bitter in their middle years. Yet surely they could keep the troupe in coin until the next assassination came along.

"Then our luck will change, my poppits!" cried Bill. "I'm certain of it! These Three Clowns have yet to see their best days. With them we'll tour all the grand Cities of Men and become the toast of kings and ladies."

Then he chucked into his long mouth the moldy cheese and hard crust of bread they'd been reduced to that night for a meal, somewhere between nowhere-special and can't-remember-the-name-of.

Things would certainly change. They certainly would.

A few towns later, Moppy, Toppy, and Slow grumbled that their luck had changed anyway and said they might take themselves off along the ports of the Sorrab to the south and try their act there.

Alone and without Mumry Bill and the other losers.

These three did an insult and outrage act that convinced audiences that permanent harm had occurred. Bottles were smashed over lumpy heads, owlish eyes gouged out, and each clown, one short and angry, another tall with crazed hair, and the last slow, fat, and very stupid, or so it seemed, tried to trick and murder each other with fiendish intrigues and more outlandish harmful delights with each passing moment. Every watcher was sure, so sure in fact, that true injury and even death were shortly to be witnessed. That one of the violent and angry little clowns would surely kill another.

In a certain way it was impossible to take your eyes off them when they were doing their act.

But Mumry Bill would have none of their glowering murderous grumbles and instead promised them riches and fantastic whores the likes of which the three freaks had constantly dreamed of...

They were freaks indeed.

Very ugly, and not just by half.

Smelled like cabbage.

Small hands.

... if they would but stay and try to make it as far as the fabled pleasure dens and gossamer courts of Akazong, promised Mumry Bill, riches and beauties they would have and dandle. Or even perhaps distant and mythical Kungaloor itself was for them where the lotus-scented streets were said to be paved in gold brick and the delicate jasmined beauties said to be skilled in the arts of love so deft that men forgot the pain of ordinary life.

The Three Clowns yearned to forget who and what they were each time they looked in the mirror or at any woman.

So Moppy, Toppy, and Slow stayed and grumbled as the gigs got worse, and worse, and worse still, and the weather got colder, some nights spent positively miserable out in the howling wastes, stalked by wolves and raiders, eating moldy cheese and stale bread.

Orcs ate the troupe's Fat Bearded Lady when a town with a scheduled performance suffered a raid.

Gnolls carried off the Donkey Boy one night.

Things got worse and everyone complained, and one late and windy night when there was no food and definitely no coin or fantastic whores...

Not even moldy cheese and stale bread...

A fight broke out and the Three Clowns almost killed each other. The Fish Girl of the Red Sea was stabbed to death.

It took the two stilt-walkers and the strongman to stop the spreading despondency-driven violence. The stilt-walkers who did their "Death Twins" act and seemed like two Grim Reapers making a graceful if not haunted dance of scythe and height, reminding all who witnessed their performances that death would have its way in the end... and that everyone dances with death. In the end.

The Death Twins beat Toppy, Moppy, and Slow senseless with clubs. But they didn't die. Not yet. That was coming soon.

And there was the charmer too. Her snakes writhing about her body constantly. Her sumptuous curves writhing and promising too. She was old and ancient, probably a witch of some sort or the other along the way, but charms and spells made her seem a comely thirty-five and so, because she was Mumry Bill's lover, she too had followed their downward spiral out into the wastes, and complained in her own ways though she was not above a good poisoning of anyone who threatened her lover's troupe. And her grift.

Like the escape artist who'd tried to depart with a slave girl they'd stolen and were training to become a new giggle-and-jiggle girl. He died after eating an asp-venom-saturated roll the Donkey Boy had stolen off the street. This was before the Donkey Boy was carried off by dog-men.

The escape artist thought he deserved more than the rest. And the slave girl had fallen in love with him.

Then the Two-Headed Freak drank her nightly sleeping aid and was dead by dawn, one head purple, the other green with death. One head had complained about the latest payout after a poorly attended performance at a mean and desperate little caravanserai and tried to hold back some of her "private show" fees from the traders who had sought the twisted delights she offered.

After that the grumbling got a lot quieter.

But these were gone now. And the Three Clowns seemed to settle down and keep their uneasy mutterings to themselves.

Things got worse.

But they were a troupe, and along with a few others they made their way from town to town until they met the "little gypsy girl."

There was the knife-thrower, not to be forgotten. Agile and lean, adorned with knives of all sorts and shapes, he could put them anywhere in a blur and the audiences were always left in amazement at such displays.

And of course there was Mumry Bill himself.

He was a grand figure in a fine "actual and authenticated" Accadion wizard's coat he'd contrived and spent much of the troupe's coin on. He was tall, and his voice was rich and sonorous like that of a real tragedian. He would tell tales of great fables and myths of the Ruin's epic past as he waved his silver-skull-topped cane with the two fantastic rubies in its eyes over the enthralled audiences they had managed to lure into their tents.

The cane was spell-worked, and that was half the game of the troupe. Great flares and pyro came from its eyes, and the minor hedge magician Bill was, he could create menacing shadows and otherworldly lights, even staging and scenery straight from the most fantastic of painted palace walls, with but a mere wave and dancing of its magical and arcane length.

And here's a bit of lore...

The cane was, in actuality, a fantastic artifact Mumry Bill had inherited when he took over the troupe via murdering its former master, who likewise had done the same to get the position of impresario.

Bill was unaware of its true origin, or its more sinister and dark powers. He just used it to entertain and enthrall as a prop with some capabilities magical.

Where the fantastic artifact came from, no one really knew. But the secret a sage might have been able to tell one who was interested... was that the Cane of Horrors and Delights came from deep up in the dark reaches of the Crow's March to the north where once a fantastic vampire wizard of the court of the Black Prince himself had wielded it as a badge of office in service to his dark and diabolical liege.

Slain by paladins of Accadios when the vampire wizard, a chap known as the Duke of Darkness, had ventured into the city of Accadios to feed on some of its finest beauties, disguising himself as an ambassador of Mourne.

The artifact had fallen into many hands along the way since then, its curses and dark alliances dragging it further and further off into misery and poverty and destruction, and of course... always east, for as they say, *east is curst.*

And that's what the malevolent little thing sought.

Finally, the arcane artifact had met the troupe of performers down on their luck. There were ups and downs, but if anyone had been counting and tracking, undistracted by the debauchery and mayhem the troupe always found itself in... the spiral was always heading down. And east.

East is curst. As they say.

It was like that was where the Cane of Horrors and Delights had wanted to go all along.

But this was all lore and unknown to the Ranger who simply slaughtered his way straight through their twisted and demonic playacting freakish mass. Hacking at the hissing undead, severing the reaching dried-blood claws that their performers' hands had become since meeting the waif of a "little gypsy girl."

The pancake makeup was faded and long cracked. Hunger and yearning for blood had consumed them and distracted them from their prior vanities and professional getup maintenance.

Dried blood, fresh on the new fangs, had been wiped away with silky multicolored puffy sleeves.

The once-sparkling eyes were dead, except for the glitter of hunger and hate and malice.

The silks were dirty from grave-dust.

The costumes ruined by the murders done along the way since meeting the "little gypsy girl."

Why, one night a whole village had counted itself uncommonly fortunate when the troupe showed up just after dusk to perform their show.

The show would go on even as the sun rose and all things came to an end...

It was Moppy, Toppy, and Slow who reached out with their necrotic hands turned bloody and dirty claws, grasping for Thor as he smashed straight into the Vampire Madame's vanguard.

The terrible Ranger drew his Glock Long Slide smoothly and very fast, the one taken from a dream...

The one that said *Come and Take Them* in Spanish, stamped on the side.

Ven y Llévatelas.

Not that a sidearm would do him any good, as the priest was clear it was a stake of some kind, wooden or cold-forged steel, that had to be driven straight into the black vortex that was an undead bloodsucker's heart. So sayeth Major Baer, founder of the Karthian Spartans.

Thor dumped three rapid-fire shots, pulling the trigger fast and steady, more for the kinetic impact, on Toppy who'd had the reach enough and came snarling like a mad twisted feral and hungry thing right after Moppy, short and angry, not snarling but intent on murder and feeding all the same.

The look in their beady eyes was pure cold murder.

Three rounds struck center mass rapid-fire on the goony and looming Toppy, and the vampire clown clutched his chest and spun about, making some comedic lunatic sound even in death as though it were all a performance.

The division of the attack force caused by Sergeant Thor's savage gunfire gave the Ranger time to sweep his tomahawk straight across the bridge and brow of Moppy's bullet-shaped little head. His dirty clown's getup was black and white and adorned with spades as though sewn straight from the texture and tone of ancient very worn playing cards.

The blow wasn't intended to brain the dwarfish little angry clown that was the leader of the act.

But it was meant to blind.

The razor's edge of the 'hawk cut bone along the edge of the orbital socket, destroyed the vampire clown's eyes, and kept on moving because Sergeant Thor's strike was a straight-up reaper's caress. Bulging triceps and the extension of a powerful arm flinging forward and across the target with the 'hawk, anchored by a powerful core and jacked abs, instantly destroyed the wild and malevolent little clown's vision in a heartbeat.

Moppy shrieked in the languages of the states of Skeletos, which was much like ancient Greek, that he'd been blinded and would tear the numbskull's heart out and eat it raw who'd done this to him.

But he didn't finish that last part because all the breath went out of him as the tomahawk was deftly reversed and went right in, spike at the end of the shaft, straight into the evil trickster's heart, smashing through sternum bone and piecing into the ventral sac.

Which was good enough.

Moppy gasped, mouth working. "*Moúdiasma,*" he seemed to rattle.

His harsh growl just a whisper. Just the barest hush of spoken sound as the vampire harlequin caught fire and began to die, crumbling away from the Ranger holding the smoking long-slide Glock and the foul and corruption-drenched war axe called a tomahawk so favored by those of his kind.

Moúdiasma.

Numbskull.

A performer's word. Something from the act, spoken at the last of the little freak.

Toppy, undaunted by three nine-millimeter rounds in his undead goony and loony body, made even more ridiculously so by the purposefully bad tailoring of his clown's costume, grabbed a rock from off the ground and heaved up savagely within his chest a wild yell as he sought to smash it down on Thor's skull.

But the Ranger was faster, lunging forward and sticking the still-smoking *Come and Take Them* right under the dead man's pointy chin and firing another round right up through the skull.

Vampire or not... bone matter and then brain volcanoed away against the dawning bloody-red light of the new day as Madame Hudu, aware of the close and deadly attack against her person, shrieked in outrage and horror.

"Interloper! Ruiner of all my beautiful plans!"

Her eyes were wild and dangerous as Toppy backed away from Sergeant Thor, squeezing the sides of his head as though it were all just part of the act of humorous violence he and his fellows had once made play of for the clatter and toss of coins of all types in the streets.

His mouth worked and he made an idiot's sound now that his mental processes were run through by fast-moving lead at nine hundred feet per second.

But he was still a vampire...

His eyes flashed red...

... and then he began to burn as the rising sun roasted his skull, his wild sideways hair turning to curling flame in an instant of dawn.

The deranged Toppy flung himself at Thor, and the Ranger slammed his knee into the goony undead clown's body and pushed him off and away even as he continued to hack and slash through the press of other fiends guarding their shrieking queen.

Many were smoking now.

Some were on fire already.

Thor slammed his axe into Slow when the corpulent and disgusting bloody clown tried to turn into a murderous rolling ball of fat and jingling bells. The clownish whale reached out to grab Thor, but the Ranger moved like greased lightning as he struck out with his axe again and landed a blow in the knife-thrower who'd come into the fray flinging knives.

Thor was sure he'd been hit, but he felt nothing as he coldly swung with all his might and decapped, mostly, the expert blade master with his bright little knives.

Severed head, hanging by just bits of muscle and tendon, flopped to the side, and the knife thrower's body, still animated by undeath, just staggered away, reaching for yet more of its many bright and shining knives to hurl at a target he could no longer see.

"Defiler!" shrieked Madame Hudu indignantly above it all like she was a half-mad child driven insane by a tantrum that would never ever end.

Mumry Bill turned from his adoring fascination with his vampire queen. It had been he who had willingly sold himself to her charms and promises of dark eternal wealth unending, when things looked so bad after the debacle with the priests in the City of Palms...

She had delivered.

"Things will be different now," he'd told each of his troupe as they'd been led ever closer to her vampire's cursed kiss on the edges of the towns they were poorly received in, or off into the howling winds beyond the light of the fires they huddled near on the way to the next worse gig than the last.

All to have their fortunes read each night by the "little gypsy girl."

"Things will be different now..." she purred to Mumry Bill when she first took him.

And now his queen was in trouble. In direct jeopardy in fact. All... was lost.

He whipped the Cane of Delights and Horrors from under his long showman's cloak, the spangle and pomp of his badly sewn "actual and authenticated" Accadion wizard's getup revealed for a moment in the half-light of dawn.

Bill's black-dyed hair that pasted itself away from his widow's peak was beginning to smoke as the rays of dawn caressed him and he reacted to save his dark queen with whatever he had left. The diabolical cane up and flashing. Its ruby eyes glowing with bright burning hell.

But the Ranger drove on, hacking and smashing the tomahawk toward his target.

Madame Hudu.

Arrows, targeted and well-fired, found purchase in the throats and upper backs of those servile fiends who'd crawled along the dust near their vampiric mistress, wailing and screaming, and now suddenly attempting against their will, for strong is the will of a Vampire Lady such as Madame Hudu, an ancient and old thing she was, to save her.

It was Alluria who fired these well-placed shots into the press to maintain Thor's corridor across the body-laden dusty street at morning's first light to slay the tormentor of souls and collector of victims.

Some arrows merely struck and added to the pain of the dying catching-fire vampires. Others actually found the black fiend-heart and destroyed it much like a stake would, and in this the fiend was well and truly slain.

The Cane of Delights and Horrors, a powerful artifact the damned showman had only ever used to entertain by tricks of light and shadow, never discovering its deeper and more vast powers, suddenly threw the dawn's light back in an explosion of shadow and darkness that erupted from its silver-skulled tip.

Surrounded by enemies, Thor suddenly found himself in total pitch-black darkness with nothing but the bloody-red murder glares of the last vampires all about him like a savage kind of illumination in the suffocating nether that had enveloped him.

The Ranger roared and waited for them to come at him, intent on holding his ground and killing them all as best he could.

Until there was nothing left of them. Or of him.

CHAPTER EIGHTEEN

A CLAW TORE INTO THOR'S FLESH. A BITE SANK into his muscled forearm. And the sound of the sucking of his own blood thundered in his ears instantly like he was listening to some industrial pump and drain at the bottom of a titanic well.

The Ranger roared and swept the tomahawk into one of the unseen bloodsuckers near at hand in the consuming darkness, taking half its head clean off on raw kinetic power alone, tearing the hungry beast away from his punctured flesh.

Another vampire, one of the high desert village dwellers made rag-stick thin by a hard and thankless life in such a strange and remote land, came at him like a shadow in the night, the screaming red murder eyes suddenly growing wide among the others all around him, and Thor lashed out with his combat boot and drove it down where a knee, or the rest of the leg, should have been.

He was rewarded with a sickening *CRUNCH* that rang out in the desert morning turned blackest midnight under that umbrella of the *Cane of Horrors and Delights.*

The tomahawk came round fast once and cleaved undead flesh. He was almost to her, and he could hear her screaming promises of eternal suffering close enough in his ear that she could have whispered and the words would have been clear as a bell.

Madame Hudu's eyes bored into him through the dark, and it was then that Thor realized there was every chance he would die now as a mob of shadows cold as death reached for him.

Her lips parted, and even in that choking darkness he could see pearly-white fangs become like beacons in a storm-tossed sea at midnight.

But the shadows were everywhere...

Fine, thought Thor as claws dragged at him and teeth opened for a taste of his living blood. *Then I'll take her with me.*

At that moment...

Fearing for his lady and dark savior, Mumry Bill cried madly and struck out with the ancient artifact he'd used as little more than a prop and special effect maker.

A very bad thing happened.

Who knows the whys and the hows of the Ruin. The negatives and positives. The energies and the opposites of such powers...

The mysteries.

Or how... if you believed the half-mad sages who studied such relics and said... there was an ancient Spider Queen who'd made a powerful magic that destroyed the Before and made the Ruin what it was...

All for revenge.

All for setting things right.

Depended on which crazy sage you talked to who knew of such mad things.

Coded for revenge as Talker and Kennedy had gone on and on about while Vandahar had listened, nursing his long-stemmed pipe and adding quiet comments of gravitas here and there about why the angry Spider Queen had supposedly done what she'd done.

Sergeant Thor cared little for such talk and so he'd never listened much to such fanciful tales. War. Combat. Obstacles against which to test himself... these were what the Ranger cared for, and such were more powerful to him than the calls of sirens on the rocks to lost sailors in peril at sea.

But artifacts...

Very powerful. Very powerful indeed.

So powerful that when two connect, strange things happen.

The Cane of Delights and Horrors was an artifact. And by its very definition as such... very powerful. No mere little imbued magic item incanted by some devious wizard atop his midnight tower. Or found deep in a dungeon where dark entities might be bound to a sword, a bow, or even a ring so that the item might use those same powers and abilities and get more than either wizard or wielder ever bargained for.

But by the standards of artifacts, it was not *extremely* powerful.

It was no *Sword of Cas. Malroc's Ring of Planes. Amulet of Depthless Witchery.* Or even *The Book of the Other Worlds.*

It was none of those things.

Now, the Pearl of Fate on the other hand, which Thor had in his cargo pocket... inside a clamshell he'd repurposed from the speedball resupply, well the Pearl of Fate, known to some as the Pearl of Great Price, was far greater than all those ancient and fabled artifacts of myth and renown.

Put together.

So...

It happens to be that when artifacts get near enough to each other, strange things happen. And had already been going on unnoticed since the ambush and the battle inside the cursed high desert village had developed.

The howling of the wind and the gnashing of the vampires' teeth had mostly disguised the growing dull buzz that had built and grown more ominously as both artifacts began to get closer and closer to one another.

At one point the stars had shifted to a point in the sky that, had anyone noticed, would have indicated not just a different year, but a different age altogether as though the night had become a glassy window into other times and other places. This was a side effect of both artifacts coming together, and the inherent weirdness of the Great Rift within the Eastern Wastes in general.

Insects swarmed and died.

Ancient phantoms crossed the night unconcerned with the petty battle between the night feeders and the survivors within the ancient church.

A deep bell from another plane tolled from some vast and unknown reality not of this timeline as Thor closed with Hudu, blocked by the glamoured Mumry Bill, slamming and hammering his tomahawk to within five feet of the Cane of Delights and Horrors.

The showman's artifact sprayed starbursts like defensive fire off some naval vessel seeking to shoot down incoming missiles in the age of Before that Sergeant Thor and the Rangers had come from.

The Pearl was already glowing pink and white and warm, destroying the charms of magic the performers had acquired for luck and treachery.

A sacrificial dagger of some magic called a Soul Harvester, twisting intertwined snakes about the pommel, shattered and sent hot flying sparks into Madame Hudu's caramel hip exposed by her flying gypsy silks, as she turned and whirled in terror at the judgment the Ranger had become, finally come for her and all her wicked misdeeds.

Burnt ash, whipped by the devil winds, passed between them in the cane's contrived darknesses.

A pack of werewolves howled from afar and the sound was cold enough to chill the blood.

But it was when the wielded cane in the ragged gloved hands of Mumry Bill snapped out and caught the Ranger in the ribs—a solid blow, not enough to break, but at least torque the ribs—that the artifact called the Pearl of Fate asserted its mythic dominance and smashed the spell effects of the cane all at once with a finality that contained an audible *POP!*

A mischievous demon illusionist had been imprisoned within the cane during its manufacture in the Grand Age, as it was known, of the rise of the Dragon Elves who were long ago destroyed by their own vanity, and hubris, thinking to make themselves not just like the gods... but gods indeed.

The harnessing spell was one of Dark Enslavement, and even the wild and uncontainable Sergeant Thor would have bent the knee to its powerful capture had the spell been cast on him.

But wielders of such mighty magics had long passed from this world into other planes, and their spells, left hidden in deep dungeons and diabolical tombs, were said to madden the mind upon reading.

And the Pearl's power... was rooted in the truth. In what was long ago. What might be even now. And what the world was as viewed through its silky depths.

The powerful Dark Enslavement spell shattered as the Pearl struck back even as the blow from the cane savaged Thor's midsection.

And the dreaming demon was released to giggle maniacally and scamper off through the darkness and into the lonely and haunted places of the Eastern Wastes.

The Ranger turned, roared, and swung at the vampiric showman in the black nepenthe of the cane's spell-woven realm of darkness even as the spell-cast dark began to disintegrate.

The leering, laughing, ensorcelled showman ducked and barely missed getting brained by the scythe of the 'hawk's blade.

At last the Pearl simply dispelled the darkness created by the cane, and so powerful was its true vision that the cane and all its trickery collapsed, imploding in reality, and then the vortex that was created... *hauled* the vampiric showman down into a suddenly created Orb of Destruction that howled madly for the half second of its existence as the hungry void slaked itself on the cane and the showman who would not release his grip from the coveted artifact that had given him so much power, never realizing how much it had been taking from him all along.

Then Mumry Bill was gone and so was the darkness.

The sun blasted across the dusty little streets of the unknown village, rising just to the left of the little church that had become a last redoubt for the desperate Spartans.

Its light was a blinding glare, and instantly lesser vampires turned to smoke and ash as remnants of their corrupt bodies flittered away as though struck by nuclear horror.

The wind had stopped.

The air was still and silent save for the hollow dying shrieks of the undead.

Madame Hudu, smoking and still able to stand direct sunlight for just a little longer than those she had enslaved, sought to turn to mist and seep down into some nearby rodent hole to wait out the dawn and to start once again on her long quest for gained revenge against the Ranger who'd ruined her, and all her petty and diabolical plans for a more horrible tomorrow for the living.

But the snake charmer, the mistress of the showman... she'd loved him. Faults and all. She had loved Mumry Bill. And though she was on fire at the edges, she was not quite burned up.

There is revenge. And then there is the revenge of a lover. A woman.

The Vampire Lady had made the man the snake charmer had loved... into her slave. And her, the Vampire Lady's, lover too.

Mumry Bill, who was now gone off into the void of outer darknesses.

The wronged snake charmer flung her asps and other serpents coiled about her even as she burned a bloodsucker's death in the light of a new day. The hideous asps latched onto the Vampire Lady, Madame Hudu, shrieking her revenges and empty promises. The charmer's props, real snakes, connected Hudu to the positive plane of reality, negating her ability to enter the negative, become incorporeal, and then... become nothing more than a nightmare of mist biding its time for another full-moon fever to get her revenge.

The snakes held her to the here and now she needed to escape from as they coiled about her and sank their fangs into her chocolate skin.

The snake charmer burned an instant later, falling to her knees and reaching her painted nails out for the place in the sand where her lover Mumry Bill had gone from when the revealed Orb of Destruction at the heart of the Cane of Delights and Horrors had suddenly been created by the two artifacts colliding.

Then she was nothing but ash and smoke on the reawakened gentle breeze of morning. Carried off and away into the Eastern Wastes.

Thor rushed the vampire who'd set her trap for him. In seconds she would be consumed by the flames already running up from her hands and feet as she shrieked and screamed and tried to pull the charmer's asps from where they'd sunk their fangs into her spell-masked flesh.

She seemed a pretty and wild gypsy girl of the world. Caramel skin and wild long curling hair. Dangerous eyes and flashing white teeth. A pretty smile. Multicolored silks flashing like a wand of cinematic and scintillating wonders... even as she burned in that instant.

But her imminent death was not soon enough, or final enough, for the Ranger, and he solved the problem of her in his life by driving the tomahawk deep into her chest with a savage strike that was so final, it pushed the spike of the haft straight out her thin and shapely back.

Thor let her burn impaled upon his weapon and watched as her fanged mouth worked silently open and closed... open... and... closed.

Her hands clasped themselves around the tomahawk's hilt, in prayer it might have seemed to the priest, and her eyes fluttered. Then she was dead as the Ranger shook her from off his weapon and watched what remained of her burn like a clump of foul refuse in the sand around his boots.

Her body hissed once, and then there was only the sound of the greedy flames in the ville and the silent desert morning spreading across the ruined town and the vast waste that lay in all directions as far as the eye could see.

Thor turned and saw Alluria near the steps of the church, an arrow nocked against the string of her horse archer's bow.

She smiled brightly and waved.

The howl of a wolf turned their gaze toward the eastern edge of the town. Out there on the plain, in front of the rising sun, gathered a pack of wolves.

Huge hulking beasts.

The pack leader, the biggest, cast baleful eyes upon them for a long moment, and upon all the burning undead within the silent murdered town.

Then it turned and trotted back into the wastes, the rest of the pack following, or ranging out ahead, as they made their way off and away from the cursed place.

The battle... was over.

CHAPTER NINETEEN

By noon, the horses had been recovered from the vast wide-open spaces beyond the town where they'd run off to escape the battle and the chaos of the *X*. The burnt-ash remains of a few vampires from the village who'd committed the folly of chasing the mounts off into the desert, and then been maimed for this by the raging Stormbringer, lay in scattered places. These grim reminders gave testament to the bloodsuckers' folly of trying a warhorse for drink, and ultimately led to finding the frightened beasts. Litters were made for those who could not walk, and then the company of Spartans, their priest they called a jumpmaster, and Alluria, Sato, and finally the Ranger bringing up the rear and covering their tracks, left the village.

For three days they would head east...

East is curst.

... heading deeper and deeper into the mysterious Eastern Wastes to link up with the main body of the Spartans.

Those they traveled with would only hint that this was because they and their brothers had come to pay an ancient debt owed at some unnamed location within the Great Rift. As they went, time grew strange and stranger still, the days seeming longer and much, much hotter than the count of seasons indicated they should be.

But on that first day... before the strange passing of time and the miles that would wear wearily on beneath their boots... Sergeant Thor decided... to ask a few questions of those they traveled with now. On point and ranging forward, he began his interrogation. Alluria, Sato, the horses and the recalcitrant over-laden donkey, the rest of the wounded and the walking wounded, and the three Spartans comprised the main body and the rear, while Thor and one of the Spartans, or Sato occasionally, would scout the way through the strange and bizarre landscape that seemed to be at the very bottom of the Ruin.

A long time ago, when he was a kid, Sergeant Thor had gone to Death Valley. It felt like being at the bottom of some ancient primordial sea that had long ago disappeared. But there was that bottom-of-the-ocean feeling. The wastes they headed into now, with something called the Rift at their heart, felt deeper, quieter, and something far more other and unreal, surreal almost with their lost ruined cities and half-sunken statues of bygone kings and heroes, than that fabled landmark had ten thousand years ago.

For the most part Sato scouted the back trail, recrossing and crossing their track, keeping a wary eye out for those wolves they'd left on the outskirts of the village of the damned. Of them, there was no sign any longer. But on occasion, brief flitting shadows could be seen on the far hazy horizon, and high among the broken rocks and ridgeline where strange passes invited exploration, and also seemed to warn of the things beyond those barriers.

On one such occasion to come, near a pass they would not take, intending instead to skirt the ridgeline, they would hear a vast and titanic gargantuan roar coming from behind the pass. As though it were the call of some overlooked dinosaur, searching for more of its kind. The Spartans would stop to listen, adjusting their gear and weapons as though expecting with grim resignation that they might have to fight this thing, and then would hustle themselves and their own quickly past the cursed place, laboring under their immense packs.

But those days were not yet at hand.

First came questions. And hopefully... answers.

That first day's road march deeper into the wastes, leaving by noon, Thor took the priest forward with him, and for a while they stayed in sight of the main body, making sure their trail through the desert wastes, heading north, was easily followed as they entered low narrow arroyos and even quiet wadis, all the while tracing the falling elevations of the enigmatic land. A series of draws led down into a narrow twisting canyon, and it was here that they began to follow its length, the priest indicating his rough map pointed this way for them to reach their final destination.

In the silence of those twisting places, as the air grew hotter and stiller, the sound of the priest's strapped sandals and gear the only sound in such lifeless terrain, Thor asked his first question of the ethereal youth who, to a Ranger from long ago, had the air of an officer and at best a lieutenant doing his best to navigate on training and little experience.

There was nothing wrong with that. *"Experience is a great trainer,"* Sergeant Joe had liked to say. *"That is... if you can survive the lesson,"* the whiskey-barrel-chested Ranger would add with a laugh.

In time, the priest would make a solid leader.

"Why was your element... do you understand that word? *Element...*"

The priest nodded and continued scanning his sector as he hung back and just to the left of Thor, following their course through the graveyard-quiet canyon as the sun blazed and beat long after noon's zenith.

Then he answered softly in patrol *sotto voce*.

Quietly.

"Yes. We use it as part of a larger military group. For us, the main body of Spartans is a company as we are the last of the battalion that was once us and by which we were known in the Age of Heroes."

Thor grunted and they continued on downslope, scanning the blue shadows growing longer ahead, deeper down there toward the depths of the canyon, as the day lengthened and closed in on its finish.

The air was still hot and dry, and they were tearing through the water they'd brought from the village well after making sure it was still drinkable.

The day was not done, but the cracked wadis created their shadows, and it was here the Ranger guessed ambushers might stack for an attack if they were to find one.

So he was humping the SAW, which would be quite a surprise for them when it came. Sweat had replaced dried sweat, but the Ranger stayed vigilant, worked his dip, and calculated the danger areas they'd need to cross and how to get it done.

It got done. And so far... so good.

But as the smaj would often say, "But that's what the man who jumps off the top o' the building without a parachute says all the way to the bottom. Then... *not so good*, boys. Just 'cause it's goin' solid on the stalk don't mean it can't go pear-shaped in a New York second. Then you teach it a lesson for even messin' with you like that."

But it didn't go pear-shaped, and the thick silences continued, broken only by the occasional call of some unseen hawk hunting the dry hills for prey.

"And you are Spartans? You call yourselves by that name?"

"Yes," said the priest and seemed to want to say more, but then restrained himself.

Thor waited a while, worked a possible ambush problem in the direction they were heading, deviated to get overwatch on a likely ambush spot, sent the priest back to the main body with instructions on how to proceed, waited until they were through it, then rejoined the priest forward of the main body.

"From a place called Karthia? Which I have never heard of," he said to the priest and spat dip onto a dry rock, scanning the terrain forward with a watchful eye.

To the rear he could hear the horses get upset about something. But Sato, or someone, got them to play nice and they quieted almost as soon as they started up.

"Yes," whispered the priest. His sonorous baritone was ragged and dry from the heat and dust and fatigue. But if he was tired, he didn't show it. "Few these days have heard of us or where we come from. Some say... our glory has passed... and the days of shadow will see our end."

He coughed to clear the dust from his throat. Thor stopped and indicated the man should drink some water from his skin. The priest did, and in the space of the hydration break the Ranger asked his next question.

"Where, or what, is Karthia?"

The priest stood for a moment, panting, holding the skin and debating whether to hit it again. His eyes were clear, and his voice was too.

"It is a great city fortress we took from bandits when we first came to the Ruin long ago. So say the ancient scrolls of our first warlord, Major Baer."

Again Thor grunted. Things were lining up. Or at least, the hypothesis he was developing had a good possibility of being true. And... he didn't know how he felt about that.

If it was, it meant something. Something important. And... it might mean allies for the detachment in their march and war on Umnoth.

But he didn't know yet.

So he continued his slow questioning in the intervals of hump and rest, watch and scan, sectors and danger areas, keeping his cards close to his chest. Which is the way of Rangers when they are not among their brothers.

They are men of action, and words are important. So important in fact, that often they use very few of them, valuing them like precious gold with which to buy their survival.

And the death of those they hunt.

"And its location?" asked Sergeant Thor.

For a long moment the priest was silent. Thor knelt near a rock and drew out one of the canteens that had survived the City of Thieves. He drank and so did the priest, hitting his skin once more, then using a gourd strapped about his armor to get some more refreshment from another type of drink. The Ranger reached into his cargo pocket and took out one of the tins of dip some smart brother Ranger back in the detachment had insisted be included on the resupply speedball. His money was on Sergeant Chris for that bit of grace and mercy.

He tapped the can and opened the tin, noting the priest staring in amazement at what lay within. Then the youth closed his eyes and crossed himself as though some unholy sin or unexpected temptation had just materialized in the form of a tempting succubus offering fleshly pleasures unlimited that must be resisted.

Thor extended the tin of dip after he'd taken a pinch.

The priest looked confused, but not because of what was inside. He glanced about cautiously, as though enemies must be on the high rims of the small hills and broken cliffs they were descending into.

"Do you expect desperate combat?" whispered the priest.

The Ranger nodded and looked away. Then rumbled like some summer storm far out across the horizon, "Always."

The dip was still out and offered.

"This is…" said the priest cautiously and didn't continue. His features twisted as though he were having some inner argument with himself.

Then…

The priest reached out and expertly pinched some of the dip between his thumb and forefinger. He held the pinch before his eyes, looking at it, inspecting it, marveling.

And then…

"Dip?" said the priest. And for a moment he seemed to shudder as he held the stuff in front of his eyes.

"Yeah," grunted the Ranger. "Put it in your cheek like this." And then Thor demonstrated with a little more from the tin. He had several tins now thanks to the speedball and Sergeant Chris most likely.

The priest nodded as though he already understood its usage.

"But… but this is… sacred… to *us*. How do you know of it?"

Thor made a small, rare smile.

"Where I come from, soldiers, infantry in combat and patrol, generally use it because we can't smoke and give away our position by fire or smell. Or at least, that's how we get started and what we tell ourselves."

The priest opened his mouth as if to say something, thought better of it, and instead stuck the pinch of dip in his mouth expertly, closing his eyes and mumbling a small prayer that ended with a barely audible... *"No matter what happens."*

Thor smiled again and shook his head, getting to his boots and stowing the tin of dip with a swift practiced gesture as he scanned the hills and the shadows ahead. Then he started off with that fabled road-eating stride of his.

The day wasn't done, but it would soon be, and they needed to find a place to hole up for the night. He had to identify a place, get them into a halt, go scout the position, and then get everyone in and set up for the night with their sectors and watches.

The priest hustled after him, taking up his position in their small two-man wedge scouting forward.

Someone had trained him well, thought the Ranger. Someone had trained him to patrol.

Later, as the canyon opened up below, Thor stopped and scanned what he could see, looking for enemies within its twisting and prehistoric length. Finding none but feeling there were some in there... somewhere... they moved on slowly now as Thor scanned for a place for them to rest for the night.

Only silence and the stifling heat surrounded them, and it seemed even birds and small animals had rejected this place, or were biding their time until evening.

"If I were to say to you..." said Thor in the silence and fading heat as the shadows began to cool and lengthen even deeper and longer.

Thor searched his memory, remembering a day he'd taken a tour of a museum on a base where he'd been sent to do some training. A long, long time ago. The displays, the uniforms, the stories. The equipment through the ages. The iconic unit patch. The history of heroism despite the odds in battles thought lost even before they'd begun.

The most storied line combat unit in the American arsenal.

The priest remained silent and waited for Thor to finish his question.

Then the Ranger had it. Knew what he needed to ask after the long pause as he continued to scan and assess the terrain ahead.

The story he'd once heard at that museum had made an impression on him, and as a Ranger, he didn't just understand it, he lived it. As all Rangers expected themselves to when the time of Plan B came. Third-world hellhole knee-deep in a pile of expended brass. The tale was, for Rangers, a signal across the vastness of the military, from one unit to another. A message that these were brothers who would not relent, even if the odds weren't just bad, they weren't even odds at all by any bookie's make.

Rangers understood bad odds. Of course. That was just Tuesday for Rangers. By nature, they are trained to operate for at least three days behind enemy lines, surrounded and without supplies.

Bad odds... "That's just Tuesday here," Joe would indeed say.

The tale in the museum was the story of General James Gavin. The name suddenly appeared in Thor's mind like a message stamped in important letters. He recalled the displays and the plaques in the dusty yet lovingly kept museum. The artists' renderings of what had happened that fateful day when heroes were marked down, the dead and the living, in the book of been there, done that, and got shot to prove it.

There was, on a lonely wall near the main display, a beautiful pencil sketch of one of the youngest general officers to command any division, ever, in the US military. It depicted an officer who was nothing more than a young man in a big world at war when he was promoted to major so he could assume command of the newly created...

... 505th Parachute Infantry Regiment.

Amazing, thought the Ranger as it began to come together, and the young and handsome priest watched Thor thinking his deep thoughts, as though he were brooding on some decision that meant life, or death, for someone. To create the 82nd Airborne Gavin had begged, borrowed, and stolen whatever, and whoever, he could to get it created. He was the first commander to ever lead a regimental airborne attack. An attack on the island of Sicily right there at the bottom of the boot of Italy.

Accadios was now Italy, or what remained of it... but if the Ranger's recall of the maps was correct... Sicily was gone, or fractured into lesser islands when, as the withered old sages of the Ruin told... "the stars fell one day."

Leading that ragtag force cobbled together after the jump into Sicily to divert the Germans from the attack on Italy, vastly outnumbered already, Gavin, a new major who would soon be a general, told his men, fighting for a foothold and their lives against overwhelming odds...

Hey that's just Tuesday for Airborne and Rangers...

He told them...

"We're staying on this ridge... no matter what happens."

No matter what happens.

Like what the priest had whispered after partaking of Thor's dip. After asking... *Do you expect desperate combat?*

No matter what happens.

Thor said those words now, and the priest stared at him in horror and amazement, his mouth opening and making a small *O* of stunned disbelief.

Then...

"How do you know... these... our sacred words?"

Thor thought about that for a long time, and then finally just said, "My people were once brothers to yours. A long, long, very long time ago."

He watched the priest and wondered at what strange set of coincidences had happened that this moment should arrive.

The Ruin, the world, the universe was strange indeed, and for a brief moment he understood better why he wanted to find those edges.

Perhaps, somewhere within them, or beyond them more likely, was an answer. Or answers, to all that strange mystery.

Maybe that was why Thor was the way he was.

The priest swallowed hard, then asked, "In the Before? Before the Ruin became the way... it is? When myths and legends were real and then... she destroyed... it all... made the Ruin what it is now? You are... from those ages?"

The Ranger didn't know about all that. But basically... yeah.

"Let's go," he said, standing up. Hefting the SAW. "We'll discuss more tonight when we make camp."

The sun began its final descent and they passed into riven canyons of ancient red rock. There were ruins here, but the Spartans said they were haunted, and perhaps even gateways to other worlds from which there was no return.

Thor thought that strange but didn't talk further because the place seemed ripe for ambush or sudden mass attack.

And there were no easy defenses here. These ruins were great temple facades carved into the tall and scraping rock of the land with strange stone gods broken and lying sundered across the drifting white sands that stood silent testament along the canyon floor. The wind whispered and caressed them, coming through the smaller canyons, and from within these strange carved cities in the rock walls they heard haunted sounds, or even wild mad yells that suddenly came then were gone and would not be heard again no matter how long they stopped and waited for the attack to come that must have followed the signal.

"Perhaps some animal," muttered Corporal Maximus in the stillness that followed. "But our mandate says we must link with the main body ahead at the well. It is not our patrol to search out such places and never return. We must be on, Jumpmaster."

Then he spit in the direction of the temple and its blackness within beyond the tall fronting columns, turned himself into his cloak, and readied to lead the rest forward.

Thor extended the tin of dip to the corporal, and the look of amazement that crossed the man's battle-hardened features was abrupt and sudden all at once.

Then the Spartan warrior, older, a veteran, and more scarred than the pretty priest looked toward that one. Their... *jumpmaster.*

The priest merely nodded. Once. Silently.

The youth turned to Thor.

"It is our custom that we only take the dip when desperate combat is expected."

The two Spartans, and some of the wounded that could, depleted Thor's tin, and then he stuck it back in his cargo pocket and made no face betraying if he was displeased they'd just burnt one of his cans of dip in one go.

They were brothers. Of a kind.

And yes, there was probably some life-and-death combat ahead. That was an edge. And he'd come looking for it. So... they were ready.

They made camp as the winds moaned and unseen predators stalked the night.

CHAPTER TWENTY

ON THE SECOND DAY OF THE TREK THROUGH the Eastern Wastes they passed an ancient fallen temple carved into the rock of the red canyons. Its high and almost Greek-looking columns and front, to the Ranger who remembered such places from the Before, reminded him of the lost Atlantari Elven temples in the islands of the southern waters. The train of Spartans, the trio of adventurers, the horses and the thankless and constantly complaining Burūto, paused in the vast and empty silence to study the strange features of the forgotten place of worship, and then slowly, one voice at a time rising and holding a strange harmonious note, they heard the sound of a chorus coming from within the dark temple deeps high up on the massive cracked rock the temple had been carved into.

The Spartan priest said there were such places lost in the wastes and the great fracture at its heart, and that their commander and the wise warned that within such places waited death itself.

Tiredly they passed on, the beautiful song of "the sirens" waiting within, the haunting notes that seemed to promise cool deeps in the vaults and undiscovered fountains in secret sanctums down there in the dark of such long-untrodden places. The song lingered in their ears and seemed to go on even after it could no longer be heard.

The sun was hotter that day and the winds seemed relentless and scouring, turning their flesh dry and raw.

By the end of the third day, deep in a vast silent valley where there seemed to be nothing living and nothing but the remains of some vast great army long ago defeated to give no testament whatsoever to what had happened here, they found what the Spartans thought was a great cave to shelter the night in.

Out on the plain, among the bleached bones of the dead soldiers, their weapons broken and rusted, their armor rotting, lay the great bone structures of forgotten war leviathans. The scene was surreal and strange and without explanation, for no histories, or fragments, or lore told of such events.

Even Sato was at a rare loss to comment with some knowledge of the past.

"As a man's heart is deceitfully wicked and cannot ever truly be known, so is the Ruin and all the strangeness in it, Warrior. All I can think in seeing these withering dead... is that someone... somewhere... waited the rest of their lives for them to return home from this unknown battle, hoping they would, and knowing they would not. Ever. It makes me miss my mean and cruel wife. I have been gone longer from her home than I ever intended to be, Warrior."

The Ranger said nothing and stared in silent awe at the front end of the "cave" they would stay in for the night.

The cave.

It was a McDonnell Douglas/Boeing C-17 Globemaster III. And long ago it had smashed itself into the hill in the middle of the valley of the dead army and the bleaching bones of the war leviathans.

What had happened to the rear section, or those that had piloted and been transported in it, was a mystery. But it was clear the ancient aircraft must have crashed hundreds...

... if not thousands...

... of years ago, mused the Ranger as he walked its half-buried length in the pleasant evening twilight as night came on and the sky turned purple.

The sand was white and soft and there was a heavy scent of sage in the gloaming. The blistering winds had stopped with the coming of the night.

The Spartans had started their cookfire near the mouth of the "cave." Alluria played the role of serving girl and woman, nurturing them, dancing away from their playful and longing grabs, and making sure they were fed, and valued.

And perhaps... had a chance to be loved.

Markings on the ancient C-17 had long ago faded, or been scoured away by the cruel heat and blasting sand-filled winds. There was nothing, absolutely nothing, left inside of it. No equipment, no gear. No clue as to *who* had come here in it, or *why* in the first place. It was merely the inner hull of the fuselage, and the shattered cockpit that had smashed into the low hill in the center of the ancient and long-forgotten battlefield and then been half-buried as was much of the rest of the craft. The wings were missing, as was the empennage, or the rear of the aircraft. Tail, stabilizer, and rudder... all gone.

In the dark, Corporal Maximus walked out to Thor standing in the twilight and studying the enigmatic thing they'd found here in the center of this haunted and deserted wasteland so removed from the Cities of Men and the fortress they called home, it was as if they'd gone to another world in some sci-fi novel.

"I will take the watch for the first half of the night. Then Private Ajax will stay alert until dawn. You must sleep, one called Thor, and have done little since we met. Tomorrow bodes ill."

The battle-scarred Spartan stared off toward the horizon and the east where it was darkest now. "I can feel it. Rested, you will be better in battle alongside us."

Thor couldn't deny what the man said. He was down to chewing coffee packets and swallowing them with canteen water just like that craven caffeine addict Talker back in the detachment.

That way lay madness, the Ranger told himself.

Then he turned toward the weathered Spartan, certain the man had seen many fights and been one of the few to survive.

Sergeant Thor already knew he could trust this man with his life.

"Solid plan, Corporal. I'll rack out."

The Spartan corporal turned and stared out into the night, leaning on his spear.

"Why are you and your men out here?" asked Thor as the wind came up slowly and began to shift the long, tall grass that grew up and around the bleaching skulls out there.

"It is how we march toward our objectives when we do not jump. We are few in number since the glory days of Karthia. Now we break into smaller elements to avoid giving battle before we are ready to. We agree to meet at a location near our objective. Then mass for the jump, for the prayers of our jumpmasters do not have the range they once had of old."

Jump, thought Thor. *Now that's interesting.*

"Jump?" he asked. "As in... from the sky?"

The corporal turned and, in the moonlit-blue night, made a face that indicated what Thor had asked was true.

"Once we were sky soldiers. So say the ancient texts. There were many of us and many... battalions. Do you know this word?"

Thor did and said so with a slight smile.

Then the Spartan, his voice clipped and hard, and some bitterness there too, spoke again.

"Our days have been hard luck and trouble, and jumps are no longer assured. Often we must march into battle like common legs, for the faith of our priests, and their numbers, wanes. When I was young... we jumped on a city in the wars of Skeletos and filled the sky like winged black panthers, and the commanders and sergeants led us into battle shouting, "Aitch-Minus!" as we came at them from behind their lines, slaughtering and laying waste to all who dared oppose us. And it was good to be a Spartan then, one called Thor. There was nothing better. Things were different. The priests had not lost their faith, or their way.

"Now the battles are more desperate, the stakes higher, the margins thinner, and the belief that we will get it done... it must be carried in the hearts of we NCOs... for our leaders are few, the young have no expectations, and the priests... well...

"But all that doesn't matter. We will go. We will fight... and if I die... then that's someone else's problem, is it not?"

The veteran Spartan sighed and said nothing more.

To Thor, he sounded like every twenty-year line infantry NCO. Expecting the worst, and just angry enough to get it done and expect no thanks in return.

Same as it ever was.

Thor went back to the "cave," and within minutes he was passed out with his assault pack for a pillow. Later, when the night grew cold and the Spartans were gathered near their fire, the serving girl Alluria came and draped a saddle blanket over the Ranger, and then, kicking off her sandals, crawled under the heavy woven cloth and curled her slender arms around his hulking body.

He neither woke nor moved, and in the morning, she was already gone before he turned over, arm flung across face, reminding himself where he was now that the new day, and more challenges, had resumed once more.

For a moment in the dark before dawn, he lay there and listened to the Ruin.

Here in the wastes... there was some quiet unheard ominous buzz... like that disconcerting chorus at the beginning of the movie *2001*.

You couldn't hear it... but it felt like it was there somewhere.

Their company left with the morning, and it was a strange misty day as they followed the rude map the priest indicated would take them to a place called the Well of Zanis where they were due to rendezvous with the main body of their brothers before the final attempt to reach their destination and pay the mysterious debt the Spartans owed and would not speak of.

The Spartans grew quiet and kept their business tight as they moved with caution over the alien and bizarre landscape that seemed to be at the bottom of the world. By noon, the strange primordial mist had refused to clear, and they encountered a dangerous and weird monster near a mysterious rent in the rock walls of another impossible canyon they had descended into.

CHAPTER TWENTY-ONE

THE CAVE WAS NATURALLY SHAPED. IT WAS A mere dark slash, or rift, in the rock within the canyon wall as they left the valley of dead bones and the strange remains of an aircraft lost long ago.

Thor and some of the Spartans out front.

The rest and the horses and the thankless mule bringing up the rear.

In the morning mist, the lost and broken aircraft had been like a riddle with no answer in and of itself to the Ranger whose mind was constantly working.

But since there was no answer... how could there be... it was therefore uninteresting to the practical and steadfast constant survival-minded Sergeant Thor who seldom wasted time on anything that could not be solved, or challenged, in some real way.

Whatever the story of the remains of that long-ago aircraft was, it had been lost, long ago. There were "tomorrow problems" as the Delta Boys liked to say, and then there were "yesterday problems" that men like Sergeant Thor had not time or use for. The only thing that mattered to such hard and dangerous men was the knife fight in the dark alley of the right here and now that was every day for those who got called by others "the tip of the spear."

And then there was the enigma of these "Karthian" Spartans, now heading toward a link-up with more of their kind on some mission, some debt that needed to be paid, a "jump" as they called it among themselves in whispers one to another reminding each other that the clock was burning for them. Thor remembered enough of the map to know the Karthian rock fortress stronghold was far, far away, along the southeastern edge of the Land of Umnoth which was where the Black Sea had once been.

Far away from here deep in the mysterious Eastern Wastes.

And so there was that to consider.

The "stars fell one day," the sages of Sûstagul had crooned to Talker, and ever-watching, ever-quiet Kennedy. The face of the world they once knew, call it the Before, had changed, and thus become the Ruin it was now.

Places on the map erased, others re-formed in the ravaging of some colossal comet or meteor strike, apparently.

Or was it something else? The sages said that was when the dragons came to the Ruin. And the Nether Sorcerer. The entity the rest of the Rangers were probably now on their way to smoke like a cheap cigar.

And for a moment Thor had doubts... about that. For a moment it felt like... the hour was late. The streetlights were coming on. And there was someplace other than the place he was at, where he needed to be.

Tomorrow problems...

Right now had enough riddles, enough problems.

So...

If these Spartans were somehow descendants of some long-lost 82nd Airborne unit, and the verdict still wasn't clear on that, but it was looking more and more likely with each bit of revealed information, then Thor highly doubted the downed bird they'd just left was the remains of the aircraft they'd come through the QST on.

That bird had another story. Another unit. And the details weren't easily detectable. And... it was clear a lot of time had passed.

And of course, there was all that *Ruin revealing...*

As he walked through the dissipating mist, the hot morning heat rising, he considered that back at Area 51 there hadn't even been any elements of the 82nd involved in the QST operation to save the civilization of the world that had once been. Spoiler... it didn't get saved. Back at Area 51 it had been all SOCOM and other special operations units, even some from other countries.

There was that to consider too.

But, Thor reasoned to himself, that had been in the two-week runup to the pump to jump all the aircraft and special operations units through the gate in a short period of time. *One night* had been the chatter, in fact. After the special operations units had gone through... perhaps then other units had been sent through as the days, and reality itself, grew stranger and came apart at the seams, making monsters of men and magic real.

Area 51 could only handle so many troops... so...

Who knew?

Thor pushed those thoughts away. They were no longer important. He needed to get them to the rest of their kind. Then...

"Tomorrow problem," he grunted to no one.

The Ranger gave up on the riddle of the smashed bird and accepted what Sato had once tried to tell him of the region they were entering.

"Warrior... even as traveled as I am, I have seldom entered this diabolical land even though whispers and songs sing pretty tales of wealth and power beyond imagining contained within the vaults of the lost ruins and sunken empires here. Easy sirens' calls to one such as myself, a simple thief seeking only enough for his family and perhaps to perfect his trade. Nay, Warrior..." cautioned the older man, his normal smile gone across his tanned and lined face. Sato was serious here, and there was no mirth or hidden wisdom for the Ranger to detect and gain by.

"Nay, Warrior... I have avoided this region, for I wish to live long, and it is said by those who have come back from their treks here that time goes strange and the lands stranger still the deeper one goes toward the Rift itself. Few return from these wastes compared to those who have dared them for a stolen hoard. Whole armies have gone missing where we go into now. It is wise to consider this, Warrior. We could turn from this path and live another day."

Silence.

"Then why do you go, my friend?" asked Thor finally.

"Where you go, I must, Warrior. It is fate. It is a tapestry far bigger than one humble thief. And perhaps..."

Sato's sly smile finally appeared. He laughed a little but there was none of his usual good-natured mirth in it.

"... perhaps I am not too old to be wily enough to tease out a pretty gem from the clutch of some bony bygone warlord dead atop his hoard. A bauble that will buy me back into the good graces of my mean and vengeful wife."

Then he laughed. And he was Sato again.

"Remember, Warrior, there are some things that are impossible to know in this strange and cursed land where time has no meaning, and they say there are wells to other worlds unknown to the Cities of Men of these dark ages. Fantastic places more dream or nightmare than real. We must concentrate on what we *can* know, and if it cannot be known, then we must avoid it and put it far from our eyes and minds, for it may be a trap of the mind that will distract us from the danger at hand we must use our wit and steel to survive."

A trap of the mind. Thor thought of the mysterious Globemaster, or what remained of it all these years later, or centuries even, smashed into the hill. Anything of note long since hauled off by raiders, or worse.

It was a distraction. Nothing more.

The Spartans were determined to go deeper into the wastes to join their brethren on an errand the priest had not, and would not, reveal to Thor, Sato, or even the tempting Alluria who teased them all with her lilting laugh and shapely soft form, dancing just away from the wounded warriors when they tried to grab for her.

They would have told her, perhaps, but a price would have needed to be paid.

"Ah, you must be feeling better now," she'd laugh as she deftly avoided their grasping touches, for they were men, young, and warriors, and such was their way.

It was their defense against certain violent death. She was a reminder that for today, they were alive.

Later, when Thor and Sato ate the stew Alluria had made of the rations, and they were away from the others, the girl joked of the Spartan grasps and pinches. She would have them know she was in control the whole time, and that it was she who was truly their master.

"They'll fetch my water, and do whatever I tell them to do, faster than that young and handsome priest could make them do it. They may have their ranks and orders, but they'd kill one another faster than they think if I merely caressed one when no one else was looking."

Then she laughed at how simple they were. Not in a mean way. But as one who laughs at the naïveté of young and little children. Her look was knowing and sly, and for a moment she allowed her smoky gaze to fall on the Ranger.

Communicating some clear message.

He ignored her and worked at the stew, for he was hungry and his mind was weary from scanning the horizon all day looking for ambushes.

It was the old thief who told her the why of their actions.

"They are young, girl, even though some seem old by their scars and the desperate battles without honor or humility they have fought. But they are barely as old as the warrior here. They measure themselves as warriors, but they are not ready to meet death, though they are willing when it must come for them. And they sense certain death ahead. You are life, beautiful and silly girl. And they just want to hold life for as long as they can, even for just a mere caress, because they know they will soon die and will never have the chance to grow old with a girl. I may be old, and my eyes are not as sharp as they once were when I raided the treasure vaults of the Al-Khazir... but it is plain for me to see... It is not death itself they fear, but what it will take from them. Such is the way of all soldiers I have known."

Alluria laughed delicately and ate her stew hungrily.

"I know this, old man," she snorted. "But it is a game they cannot win, for I am young and fast." Then she laid her hand on the dagger she kept on her slender and shapely waist, rising to her taut belly.

"And if needs be... far deadlier than any foe they think to face."

Thor raised one eyebrow and finished his stew.

"There are mysteries in this land. And then," he said to himself and no one else, for such is the way of Rangers in that they keep their own counsel and make their own plans when others merely talk and talk and do nothing else but talk of the heroes and killers they might be, or the deeds they could do. Such talk is not for Rangers for they are killers, and they measure themselves only by the deeds they have done.

"... and then there are mysteries," he muttered and stalked off.

The girl, a mere serving wench and a messenger for a thieves' guild, supposedly, was a mystery.

And yes, he'd awoken some nights and found her clinging to him, and not always just for warmth. But it was clear she didn't want anyone to know.

She was soft and pleasant in the way women are. And he didn't mind that. She had a game she was running, but he wondered what her true intentions were and guessed they probably were designed around him. She sensed he was going toward where gold and loot might abound, and that was something she wanted for herself. If she was near the acquiring, then perhaps...

She had no idea that acquiring had nothing to do with why he went where he went and fought whom he fought.

But her passionate embrace and desperate secret clutch were pleasant. So...

Then they came upon that rift, that fracture in the canyon wall... and out came the twelve-legged blue lizard. Hissing and spitting lightning bolts. Its otherworldly serpent's eyes aflame with silver fire. It was a giant the size of at least five massive bulls lined up end to end. It hissed metallically and stormed like a stampede of many creatures from the entrance of the natural cave at the entrance to the last canyon they were to thread to reach the Well of Azzim where they'd rendezvous with the rest of the Spartans.

Its long, scaly, armored body undulated hypnotically as it roared and reared up, glaring pure hatred and hungry malice right at them all, there on the canyon trail in the heat of the fading afternoon.

CHAPTER TWENTY-TWO

LATER, AFTER THE SUDDEN AND INTENSE battle in which they'd been forced to fight for their lives, Sato would tell them the desert nomads sometimes called the strange twelve-legged predator a *lightning lizard*.

The air was still alive with burnt ozone and smoke. The beast's rattling hiss and deafening roar-crack still seemed to echo off all the far canyon walls and through the lands and ravines of the area.

"In their speech... they say it is *akhtinaq albarq*... the *lightning choke*. But most travelers I have heard tell of it simply call it... a *behir*."

When the battle was given, the terrible lightning lizard was longer than it was large, but its body was the width of a large crocodile not even prehistoric in nature. When it roared, it crooned madly in a metallic hiss and charged forward from the large rent in the canyon wall, right at the Ranger leading in the point position.

In that first terrible moment the hideous thing attacked, it seemed impossible that such a beast of that size could have moved so fast.

But it had many legs, and it was a serpent too. If the opening moments were strange, what happened next defied logic and reason as the battle began.

Its swiftness wasn't even due to the twelve legs, six per side of its long undulating and scale-armored cobalt-blue body that seemed to go on and on.

As the fight began, the legs tucked under massive shining scales as soon as the thing had finished its rattling battle-challenge roar, then suddenly it slithered forward like a swift-moving python that was more zigzag lighting strike than a thunderbolt of poison and claws.

The beast was hypnotic to watch, and the Ranger had to tell himself to do something right now even as the ground began to shake and rumble as the thing suddenly charged for the nearest horse, its fangs open and dripping hungrily.

The horse was ridden by the beautiful and silky Alluria.

She shrieked indignantly as her terrified mount reacted in utter terror, rearing high as though that might save it from the serpentine behemoth's sudden assault.

The slithering behir moved fast as though aware the Ranger just ahead of the main body and carrying the SAW was the danger to be avoided. Thor had reacted immediately, rising to his full height, standing his ground, and getting ready to drag the SAW around and engage.

But within seconds, the lightning lizard had impossibly altered course and shifted to a new attack angle to strike and take the terrified horse while avoiding opposition from Sergeant Thor. The Ranger had already jerked the SAW up with a swift, much-practiced motion, eye to scope, ready to engage and cut loose with a sudden hot savage burst of feral fast-moving death to give the monster something to think about.

Alluria deftly slid free of the horse, her survival instincts honed and ready, scrambling free with her archer's bow as the terrible behir reared high above her with its narrow undulating armored torso, its silvery malevolent eyes alight with hunger and horror. Then it struck oddly and all at once, its serpentine body coiling around the screaming terror-struck horse all in the blink of an eye.

It was both unbelievable and grotesque.

Thor couldn't fire without hitting the strangled horse, and weighed his options as the Spartans reacted quickly and hurled their spears, making ready to defend their wounded to the death.

The three killers still on their sandals formed a wedge between their brothers and the raging horrible beast that was the behir, thrusting out their large round shields to protect as best they could.

Sato controlled the angry mule, who seemed to want to surge and run off into the desert with all their stuff. Two Spartans atop the other mounts kept them under control even though Stormbringer, Thor's dark warhorse, angrily stamped the ground and made clear his intentions to give battle even though the odds were clearly bad.

Stormbringer lived to fight. And a battle was at hand. The dark warhorse neighed not in terror, but like some barking challenge of what he was going to do to the creature that had just slain the mare he'd favored as he stamped his thick hooves in the dirt and fought to ignore his rider's sharp commands.

The savage *snap* and *crack* of Alluria's horse's neck and body within the sickeningly embracing curling coils of the behir made up Thor's mind, and with a decisive yank he snapped the SAW up once more and began to fire.

The first burst ravaged the swiftly moving coils of the giant cobalt-skinned lizard, and instantly it reacted, retreating toward the dark fissure from which it had just issued forth.

Black blood splattered out, and the beast screamed horribly at the impact of fast-moving seven-six-two, then...

The earth between Thor and his target erupted all at once like the ground strike of a bomb run from off a B-52. In the chaos and confusion, a wall of lightning spat forth from the needle-fanged maw of the terrible blue beast screaming in pain. The blast shattered rock and exploded dirt between the Ranger and his target.

Thor swore and threw himself off to one side at the last second as the canyon rock fissured and exploded in every direction beneath his boots. He barely escaped the streak of chained-lightning blasts that had erupted from the great wounded lizard's drooling greedy maw.

When he got to his feet once more the thing was gone from the field, having retreated back within the dark fissure in the canyon wall that was its home. The dead mount had disappeared with it.

The priest rushed to Thor's aid, fearing the Ranger had been struck down and killed instantly by the lizard's lightning bolt attack.

Assured the Ranger was not dead, the priest swiftly said, his voice almost breathless, "We must move on from this cursed place now or surely more of its kind might come up from the deeps to feed upon the rest of us. Hurry now..."

He pulled at Thor's sand-covered and bruised shoulder.

"No," muttered the Ranger grimly and stared at the black void of the fissure from where the thing had come and gone back into.

John of Towle's mouth opened wordlessly as though he were asking some question with an answer he surely could never comprehend. It was clear they didn't have the numbers to confront the thing. It was time to flee.

Then...

"It has our gear," grunted Thor, wiping blood from his mouth. "We'll need it to survive."

The priest closed his mouth as the other two Spartans and Sato came forward to make sure Thor still lived.

"Plus..." Thor said, straightening the links of the ammo feeding his smoking gun from the Bag of Holding. "Never killed one before. And now it's going to die."

He retrieved *Mjölnir* and the strange northern battle axe he'd carried since the weapons bazaar of the City of Thieves.

Then he went down into the fissure the behir had disappeared deep down into.

Sato and Corporal Max went with him.

CHAPTER TWENTY-THREE

"It is said such a beast is an eater of fine gems... Warrior," whispered Sato in the darkness of the deep cavern as they followed its winding rocky path down into the depths of the lair of the behir.

They passed bits of gear that had come loose from the dead horse and the blood that had spilled from the beast where Thor had shot it several times.

From below they heard a titanic wail, and for a moment they stopped, listening to the immense bellow that seemed to come from a far way off and then lose itself, echoing off into other depths of the vast and unknown place.

"There may be more to this place than just the den of a hungry beast who has taken one of our mounts," said the gravelly-voiced Corporal Max, who held one of the spears of the wounded he'd repurposed for this descent into the darkness beyond the fissure in the canyon wall.

"It may have gone deep…" ventured Sato, bringing up the rear of the expedition.

"No," rumbled Thor. "It's hit bad. Whatever made that sound… that's not the same sound as the lizard. That's farther down. Probably something else."

Sergeant Thor didn't want to say *monster*. He'd never liked using that word since they'd come to the Ruin. The Rangers. *Monster. Monsters.* It sounded too… PFC Kennedy. He wasn't ready to embrace that level of the fantasy.

"It sounds a lot bigger and a lot more dangerous than the thing that attacked us. My guess is the lizard-thing attacked us because it was hungry. Because it can't hunt farther down because whatever it was we just heard is a lot bigger than it. So we'll go a little further, and if it's not to be found too far ahead, then we'll turn back and accept the cards we've been dealt on this one. But if there's a chance to get our gear back, we need to make an effort."

He didn't tell them that the margin for survival in this area, in this terrain, surrounded by enemies, unknown by either type or amount, meant every piece of gear was absolutely vital. The margin for survival was thin.

Too thin.

He would do everything he could to improve, or at least maintain, their odds.

Silence. Neither Sato nor the Spartan corporal added comment to the Ranger's plan.

Then Thor added, "There was good gear on her horse. And her... possessions. She'll want them back. Girls are like that."

Corporal Max grunted his assent. Perhaps the serving girl was right: they would do anything for her. Anything like go down in a dark cave where there were clearly dangerous monsters... and perhaps worse...

It wasn't too much further down into the dark passage before they found the lair of the wounded behir. They heard the bone-cracking and the slurping long before they got there. The sickening sounds resounded off the walls of the passage ahead. The sounds of tearing flesh and feeding were clear and apparent long before they caught sight of the hungry yet wounded beast.

Injured or not, the beast was busy at the meal of the horse it had taken in prize for its surprise ambush.

Its lizard-breathing hissed and rasped raggedly as it crunched bone and flesh for its meal.

Perhaps its last meal.

It was clearly not doing well, and there was every chance it was mortally wounded and dying slowly.

Thor held up one hand in the near darkness, for there were strange mushrooms along the wall that cast eerie purple lights, allowing them just enough illumination to see the shadowy twists and turns and other features of the rock-hewn passage they followed to the behir's lair.

It was close. Just ahead...

Moving silently, Thor crept out of the darkness, draping the IR-resistant thermal shemagh he'd kept wrapped around his neck over his head to prevent the light from the powerful thermal scope from escaping the aperture.

He threaded the passage, hugging wall and pie-ing the corners, and then... the mighty behir appeared in all its thermal radiance, hot and beating red though its serpentine skin and scaly armor had been cobalt blue under the blaze of the afternoon sun.

It was entwined about what remained of the shredded and torn-apart horse, and Thor could see no others of its kind.

He flicked the safety off on the M105 anti-materiel rifle he'd scratched *Mjölnir* in. Thor steadied the powerful rifle in his gloved hand, falling into a sniper's crouch that allowed him to stabilize the rifle on his bent knee. Not optimal with the powerful anti-materiel rifle... but he didn't want to chance disturbing some unseen rock and making an unwanted sound in the moment before fatally employing *Mjölnir* with deadly surprise.

The Ranger didn't want to fight that thing down here. It probably had other unseen secret passages it could scramble into and cut them off by.

Or... worse.

He motioned to Sato to cover his ears. A gesture the thief had grown accustomed to over his travels with the strange warrior he'd come to bet his life with. The suppressor was attached, but *Mjölnir's* titanic blast was still going to be loud.

Sato had balls of wax ready and handed two to the Spartan, motioning for the corporal to insert them in his ears just as Sato was doing.

Thor was already canned with his ear pro and he could hear everything, as the Peltors amplified all sound below thirty decibels.

Handy on the stalk. Like having super-hearing powers.

Horrific when listening to something the size of five bulls and as wide as a crocodile consuming its lunch... raw.

Sinew and bone crunched and broke as powerful jaws tore and champed, ripping free what it wanted most of in the next hungry bite.

Thumbs up from Sato... a gesture that amused Thor since it seemed so modern and from his time but was in fact something the thieves of the guild had used extensively in their arcane silent cant to mean a variety of things especially when it was accompanied by other smaller, almost insignificant gestures.

It was almost a whole unspoken, or barely spoken, language. Each guild had its own and apparently there was a universal one used by all thieves. That was how thieves communicated and it would do for here on the stalk now, hunting and killing the beast that had dared attack them. Thor had learned the language well over his long stay inside that dangerous and intriguing city called the City of Thieves.

They'd also taught him many new skills and... even improved on ones he thought he'd mastered.

Stalking. Both in a city, or in the bush. What spies would have once called "tailing." A skill employed deftly through warehouses and wizards' vaults. Along busy streets, where targets that needed to be robbed were handled without a trace.

Locks and lockpicking. Rangers had that down due to airfield seizure operations, or so Thor had thought. But the thieves had shown him not just more ways to pick a lock, but how to do it faster and in the dark and almost by second nature while maintaining watch as though the tips of the fingers had minds and eyes and ears all their own in which to get the business of releasing done while security and alertness was handled with the other senses.

Traps and poisons too were taught. Disarming and setting. Thor had shown them a thing or two about setting traps. A common skill used by Rangers on the fade. They'd shown him some nuances there too.

Then there was the climbing of walls thought to be impossible to be climbed. Or listening over vast and great distances and being able to distinguish what was a long way off and what sound or noise was closer at hand, and how sound could play, and deceive, and be used in certain situations.

Now, in the cave deeps of the behir and whatever else was down here...

All quiet and thumbs up, Thor re-draped the shemagh about his head, activated thermal, landed the target reticle, adjusting for extremely close range, and waited until the triangular head of the hideous thing tore some more flesh away from the half-eaten horse. The malevolent behir raised its head as was its way to gulp down the great hunk of horse flesh it had torn free, and in that instant provided a perfect sight picture in thermal heats to put a fifty-caliber round straight through the roof of its crocodilian jaw and right into where its tiny brain should be.

Thor pulled the trigger and released the thunder.

The shot was a bolt of lightning in the dark of the cavern.

In the blink of a thermal eye, bright hot brain matter raced off into the dark void behind the behir and the massive and mighty coils of its length went rigid, tightening about what remained of the horse as the thing simply got switched off at twenty-four hundred fifty-caliber feet per second.

Nothing moved after that for a long while, and the sound of *Mjölnir's* sudden thunder raced off into other districts as did the brief flash of the lightning it had made on firing despite the suppressor.

Ahead lay the small ledge that was the lair of the beast they'd stalked down into the depths after.

They sat there for a long second. Waiting.

Nothing.

Thor lowered the shemagh and put the weapon's safety on, slinging it back over his shoulder with a minimum of noise.

They listened again.

Still nothing. No mate coming to the behir's aid. No other... *entities* coming to see what free meal had just been provided for the scavenging.

Thor cracked a green ChemLight and went forward, unsheathing the strange northern battle axe. It was good he'd brought it. The beast had turned to iron bands in death rictus about the horse and would not release its prey, or the gear it had borne as its burden.

They would have to cut it free.

Beyond the fatality-frozen coils of the behir was a great black void of some other large cavern which the ledge looked out upon.

At first all was black, then...

Details in the shadows and the gloom out there were revealed.

It was some vast and titanic well worked into the rough stone of the great cavern, and the more the trio of Spartan corporal, thief, and Ranger looked, the more new details came to be revealed out there in the dark.

It was a deep pit, at least a football field long. And all along its sides had been carved dwellings of... giant-sized proportions.

Towers and stairs. Small walled towns and other strange places and fortresses carved into the dark stone along the distant walls. From the ledge, colossal stairs ran down along the sides of the well, weaving in and out of these structures like some gray brick road of doom leading to some unknown silent and forgotten hell farther below.

"I have heard tales, Warrior..." said Sato softly. "Tales of a strange race of underground giants who once plagued the Ruin and the wastes after the stars fell. Perhaps... this is one of their lost cities. They were giants of fire, and it was said they found the doors to the hells and were never seen again having gone that way for all time. They were feasters of men."

Thor said nothing, staring for a long moment at the dead city lying down there along the cyclopean well it had been carved along. It was dark and there was no movement. No fire. No life. And it seemed to go on and on deep down there into other darknesses and places they would not know.

It was a city of giants. A dead city.

But... there had been that roar, thought the Ranger. That titanic... roar like some... thing... of *the Eld*.

It reminded the sniper of the strange giant that had chased the Rangers just after they'd come to the Ruin.

Cloodmoor.

That had been the name of the massive boulder-hurling giant that could step over hills.

"Let's get our gear and get back on mission," said the Ranger tersely. "What's down there..."

He watched the darkness far below for one moment longer, saying nothing and trailing off... feeling that call... of edges...

A new edge, perhaps?

"... doesn't concern us."

But I can come back, he heard himself think. *Some other time when I am alone and have no one to lose.*

See... what made that roar.

Then he raised the axe against the coils of the behir and reclaimed what gear they could from the rent and strangled horse.

In some cuts and hewing of the behir's scales and armor, behind the protection and the leathery armored scales, great and minor gems of good craftsmanship spilled out into the jade-shine of the cracked ChemLight. Sato collected these, murmuring, "I had thought these tales of such gem-swallowers, told to lure other simple thieves and luckless warriors to seek them, and their certain death, were mere fanciful tales, Warrior. I attend and know wisdom once more. A good old thief I am once gain."

Soon they were humping back all the salvaged and bloody gear for the surface.

Leaving all that tantalizing unknown down there along the walls for another time not this one.

CHAPTER TWENTY-FOUR

By the time they reached the well of Azzim, three days deeper beyond the village done to death by vampires for nothing more than petty revenge... revenge gone unsatisfied... most of the main body of Spartans had gathered and formed a small forward operating base. Bronze Age style, thought Thor as he surveyed their defenses and guard.

It was a fortress of raised dirt mounds, jutting spears, cleverly canalized avenues of destruction, complete with murder pits and slits in rock walls to fire from, and height enough to withstand an enemy that might come sweeping out of the desert windy wastes to foolishly raid them for gear.

Or slaves.

Or food.

Thor had studied enough Roman history, a favorite subject for most Rangers, to recognize a temporary Roman-style fort erected at the end of a day's march as the legionnaires were wont to do.

As has been said, the most important weapon the Romans carried was... the shovel.

And the lesson had not been lost on these Spartans out of time as far as the Ranger could tell.

Rangers hated digging.

And they had their own version of a base deep in enemy territory, being little more than a patrol circle. For defenses the Rangers merely went where no one would follow them. Usually a snake-infested completely inhospitable swamp laced with deadly traps all along their back trail.

If an enemy followed them into something like that they'd pay dearly for the stalk, then probably get murdered in a sudden ambush and dumped where no one would ever find their bodies.

Attend and know wisdom.

The Spartans on the other hand considered their shovels just as valuable as their short swords and long spears and impressive bronze-stamped shields.

"There!" shouted the priest triumphantly as they spotted the standards, spears, and helmeted Karthian Spartans in the distance on the approach to the Well of Azzim. The helmeted warriors could be seen high atop the dirt mound walls they'd flung up since gathering near the rendezvous.

The Spartan commander had chosen a large dune that bordered the well that wasn't a well at all, and was actually more of an oasis, to place his defenses. But among the walls and jutting spears there were the foundations of some long-lost desert oasis outpost, a played-out caravanserai perhaps, or even a more permanent settlement once. All that remained now along the hardscrabble desert floor and the thin weaving palms in the afternoon breeze that made their space among the high hard dune off the place, were enigmatic walls and old portals open to the skies.

Thor counted at least a company of the ancient, armored warriors who seemed cut straight out of some textbook treatise on Bronze Age warriors of the Classical Age. What was stamped on their large bronze shields, and sewn into their tattered pennants, plus a dozen other little signs, gave tell to the Ranger that once, long ago, they'd been soldiers in the US Army. Tip-of-the-spear warriors just like him and the other Rangers of the detachment that had come to the Ruin.

But it was also clear that whatever had happened had taken place long ago and these were the descendants of those long-lost sky soldiers.

On the armor, arcane and hard to detect, and more visible in the flapping pennants and tribal standards, were the signs of a lost unit from the age of modern warfare in what the denizens of the Ruin now called... the Before.

Once, they had been airborne infantry. Men from the legendary 82nd Airborne. Heartbreakers and lifetakers.

For a moment, Thor was intrigued to know... just exactly how that had happened. And what their story had been.

Whatever it was... it must've been a real knife-and-gun show when they got to the Ruin. Back in the Before, the 82nd was specifically used to go and break the enemies' stuff. And they were very good at it. They were the old-school savage Viking warrior cavemen of Special Operations command, and when they came falling out of the sky in a combat operations area, it was clear someone was going to have a very bad day.

Now, in the red light of late afternoon, cool wind shaking the palms of the oasis, the Spartans held their spears out and ready even though Corporal Max and the other Spartans insisted Thor, Sato, and Alluria were no threat to their brothers in arms.

More and more Spartans were appearing along the walls, staring in rapt fascination at Alluria.

She made a show of ignoring them all.

"These are dangerous times, Maximus," said the NCO guarding the entrance to the base as they'd approached the watch there. This was merely an open space in the wall that gave way to a channel leading within the defenses that zigzagged deeper into the dunes. It was atop these dunes that the archers of the Spartans stood ready with small yet powerful curved bows ready to pincushion anyone foolish enough to try for the entrance uninvited.

"Witches and phantoms mark this land," said the gruff NCO, whose look, and scars, were all business and indicators he knew his craft of killing and combat well. "Skinwalkers and demons we have fought as we closed on the objective and the jump against the tower. The commander has ordered full alert and no breaches in protocol, Sergeant..." Then the NCO paused, corrected himself. "Corporal Max."

This was not said with contempt. It was merely a correction, and some look between the two passed in the lightning flash of a brief second.

"They are friends," said Max simply, and the other man accepted this, indicating without a movement that it was good enough for him. But...

There were others who might have more questions.

The spears of the Karthians were used to encircle the three, and even then Corporal Max remained in front of Thor and his companions, hands up and protecting them though he was beat, bloody, and dirty from the long hump through the wasteland, carrying more gear than even Thor thought possible so that the wounded might make the well as best they could.

There was a sudden commotion and the line of spear-wielders parted as a small, bandy-legged, older man pushed through shouting and muttering curses at any Spartan he noticed.

He had a patch over one eye.

The Spartan first sergeant stormed past the sentries guarding the main entrance into the dug-by-hand fort, pushing armored men twice his size out of the way and striding like some giant of an elder age straight for the young priest they called a jumpmaster, his Spartans, and these three very strange new strangers who had come into his defenses with his men.

He ignored Alluria and made straight for the NCO of the watch, barking murder and promising eternal damnation.

Two straight-up heartbreakers followed the first sergeant, and the Ranger could easily recognize the operator version of these Karthians. Each was jacked beyond belief, older, with a variety of weapons well beyond the standard gladius, spear, and shield of the rest of the troops.

Each was a killer.

One carried a battle axe, the other a bow with two arrows nocked.

Immediately Thor assessed who these were and what their real job was. These were the senior NCO's bodyguard and dirty-work goons who got done what the first shirt needed done with a minimum of fuss and notice. Thor clocked each's murder-panther assessment of him as they followed behind their leader, their gear making no sound, their tread sure and quiet, and their confidence and ease too casual even though it was clear they did murder on demand and were readily apparent to do just that at the merest of nods from their leader.

Sato caught their wind instantly.

"Beware, Warrior... these men are true killers," whispered the thief in sub-aural hand signals of the cant.

Thor signaled his barely noticed acknowledgment of the danger they faced.

Then the first sergeant was barking at the young priest. "What have you done to my men, you worthless eunuch of a holy man?" He added a "sir" that was clearly devoid of any official respect for proper rank, and almost as insult, the first sergeant saluted the priest in the same fashion ancient men of arms used to salute, raising one arm and one fist against their chest and then snapping it outward.

To show they were not armed.

To show respect.

The first sergeant's salute was anything but respectful in its quick half-hearted throwaway delivery.

The priest nodded, accepting the pro forma courtesy though it wasn't even a charade of that.

Some NCO has taught him well, thought the Ranger and raised his opinion of the jumpmaster.

The priest visibly shuddered under the withering barrage of words from the raging red-faced one-eyed first sergeant, but he stood his ground. And the Ranger admired him more for that.

CHAPTER TWENTY-FIVE

The priest and the other Spartans had still not given up what the mission, or "the jump," as they referred to their objective in coming to this forsaken and haunted edge of the Ruin, was.

This had been what the raging first sergeant was after with the latest and last of his men to arrive and he ran his interrogations just short of full Spanish Inquisition.

It was clear the two heartbreakers who trailed him knew their way around how to make someone talk. So there was that implied threat.

Thor hadn't cared. The only thing that had concerned him was surviving the three days "behind enemy lines" with wounded and on the move. What happened next would be a "tomorrow problem." For whatever that was worth.

Sato and Alluria were, on the other hand, more interested in the reasons the Spartans had come this way.

But to their credit, the troopers, even the wounded, hadn't talked. There was always the corporal and the priest watching them. Reminding them what was expected of the Spartans even in dire situations that made bleak look like a Sunday picnic.

They'd hadn't talked on the topic of *why* they were going to where they were now at.

Satisfied, barely, the white-hot senior storm-cloud NCO allowed that everyone be brought into the Karthians' fort finally. The priest had explained that all that was told to the three new strangers who had come inside "the walls" was that the Spartans were operating deep in the wastes, well beyond the lands they called theirs. And all that was explained regarding this, insisted the priest and backed up by Corporal Max, was that they must link up with their brothers at the Well of Azzim. Then there would be further "operations." The trio of strangers who'd relieved them in the village of vampires had agreed to hump with them and hadn't pressed too hard.

When the corporal confirmed the OPSEC to the first sergeant, the senior NCO merely glared at him, then nodded as though Corporal Max's word was enough to satisfy him. Barely.

Again, some unspoken moment passed between First Sergeant and Corporal.

Thor noted this as... *strange*. Unfinished business or bad business, perhaps.

Again, not his circus, not his monkeys. He was just as ready to cut them loose and continue deeper into the waste for reasons he hadn't fully explained yet.

Even to himself.

But the smell of action was thick among the Spartans, and as an undead Ranger used to like to say whenever he got tasked with a pump in spite of his latest Article 15, "Action is the juice, Sar'nt."

Then Tanner would smile his half-undead smile and inhale the smoke that drove all the hard-chargin' Ranger NCOs nuts, letting the smoke spill out the ragged remains of his throat and the bony side of his face.

Thor could detect OPSEC when he smelled it. And something was going down here and that pointed to action and edges. The Spartans were good at keeping it secure, and no loose chatter was given away even though Alluria, who could not seem to abide a mystery unsolved or a riddle unanswered, no matter how small it was, had taunted them with food and teased them with suggestions of her curvy favors and longing glances would they but tell a poor little simple serving girl what their very brave mission was all about.

They would not.

They had not.

The younger Spartans, the ones who'd been badly wounded by the vampires in the running battle to reach the safety of the lonely church, swallowed hard at her simpering pout, clocked Corporal Max who gave them a patient yet knowing look, and then... *said nothing*. Looking like they were already dead.

She didn't make it easy on them. If she detected the slightest bit of weakness, she jacked her temptations up to eleven. A lot of things got dropped on the ground she needed to bend over and pick up.

Thor laughed. She was crueler than a drill sergeant.

And still... they said nothing about "the jump."

That was the way it had been for the brutal three-day hump through the strange desert wastes heading for the linkup at the Well of Azzim.

Alluria pouted harder and became more softly cruel to them. They may have been hardcore killers, but given time the Ranger was sure she would have broken them.

Thor, even though he'd respected their silences, would have liked all the same to know what he'd gotten himself involved in here. There was that. But if they weren't saying, he respected that and asked no questions.

During one of the night watches he and Sato had taken during a hard day's march to link up with the rest of the

Karthians at the well, the thief offered his theory of what was going down, for consideration, to the Ranger.

Thor watched the dangerous darkness out there beyond their perimeter, listening to the thief's speculations. They'd heard some desert jaguar calling out, hunting in the night, and it was larger than anything the Ranger had ever heard, by the sound of it.

And it was smart too.

"A phase cat stalks us," muttered Sato, and fingered his sharpest blade. "Very dangerous beast. The tentacles can paralyze even one as strong as you, Warrior."

Even on thermal with *Mjölnir*, Thor had failed to catch sight of the clever cat moving through the scrub and hard hills out there in the darkness and through the terrain they'd been passing that day. In the night, they'd sought safety in the lee of a dune. The moon was fat and full, and that was strange because Thor swore it had been merely gibbous the night before.

The Eastern Wastes were indeed strange, thought the Ranger. Time... felt *funny*.

"Warrior... more of the story of the Karthians occurs to me as we have crossed this dreaded land that you lead us into..."

Thor ignored the jab.

"There are told certain tales... songs and stories that tell of these legendary and noble warriors, and how they once followed a blood oath to their deaths. Unfortunately. I thought it was some ancient and inconsequential story, typical of such warrior cultures, but now in light of their unwillingness to share their... quest... with us, perhaps it is relevant now and we must consider the puzzle it presents if we are to unlock the chest of wonders that is another day of survival. I remember having heard the tale, long ago, as a cautionary one about never making blood oaths. I considered the warning well, for I was young and without wisdom then, Warrior, and so I have never made one, thinking it better to just steal and reach the nearest inn to live life as it should be lived."

Sato sighed longingly as though remembering the pleasures of a certain inn.

Then...

"This tale I once heard sung, tells of how the Spartans owed some service that was called to be rendered when least they were capable of the rendering they owed. And since they were men of their word... it was well known they lived by their deeds... they went to their death in some distant realm where the odds were thin. Because of what they owed. None ever returned. In the song. Fantasy and epic, the tools of every wretched bard.

"The tale of what truly happened to them... was never known. But I do remember this... having once heard a drunken bard who possessed a respectable collection of ancient lays. This drunkard sang in a haunting voice of the Karthians. Warrior, the performance was so unreal to hear, the lore of long ago presented in such a way... it was as though the images wove around me in the smoke of the den. This one sang of ghosts, wrongs, and revenge. Unfortunate tragedies that had befallen the fabled Karthians who had been greatly betrayed on that cursed quest in which they disappeared from history... forever."

Out there in the dark, the deadly phase cat yowled, and for a moment thief and Ranger were quiet, waiting for the attack that must surely come.

When it did not, Sato continued in a low voice.

"That they had failed in their quest was not due to their strength or deeds, Warrior, or even their honor. In the images of the tale, they were undone by some specific treachery this old thief cannot recall as having been part of the tale, but a very important theme within the song of that miserable and yet memorable bard. I apologize, Warrior. It may be of no use to us now. It is perhaps little more than a pretty lie, or a tumbler in the lock for another chest than the one we are presented with this night. And as we thieves say, *Work the lock that is before you. Not the one you want.* But as we have made this crossing, I have probed their speech and tried to ascertain what they are truly all about. Perhaps there is a great treasure we may steal. I am a thief after all, Warrior. A little more subtle than the girl, to be fair, but I am old and possess not her... *obvious* charms. As you well know. So I must be crafty and quiet in the business of unlocking prizes. And still, they are a tight-lipped lot about what their business is at the end of the known world where only haunting poems sung by drunken bards lying long dead in lotus dens are what passes for a decent map of where a trio of thieves such as we find ourselves in, Warrior."

Sato swore and spit.

"This much I remember. They were betrayed, Warrior. I am certain of that part of the drunken bard's remembrances. All songs sung that they were slain to the last man on the debt's errand. And so, Warrior, no great sage or philosopher am I... but the question does occur to this humble thief at this late hour of the night when a phase cat stalks our flanks... How is it that those who are dead so long ago, slain by some undisclosed treachery so near the Rift we approach... How is it then that they march these long hot days with us, and keep watch in the hunting nights with us and by our side? Are we, Warrior, in the company of long-dead ghosts ever about their cursed task? Unrevenged haunts who lead us to that same betrayal that took them? May we be exchanged like bad apples in the market for the souls they wish to set free from the debt they did not render? These are the things Sato considers, Warrior, late in the night of this strange and haunted land, hunted by deadly predators like fate and the cat in the darknesses out there. And... Warrior, as you lead us deeper and deeper into this cursed land for reasons... I must confess... I do not understand... yet."

Again, Thor ignored his friend's jab.

Sato fell silent, and it was clear the thief hoped Thor would illuminate him further on what, exactly, they were doing out here deep in the Eastern Wastes, so close to the Great Rift itself.

A place from which few ever returned.

The Rift of Madness, some called it.

But that was in other dens and cities far from the lonely howling wilderness devoid of life they now traveled through. Fear naming a place few knew. The safety of distant inns in which such wild speculations might be indulged over candlelight and meat and good brew with good and kind beauties in silks who smile and laugh and know nothing of... death in the night.

And... being right about it even in their ignorance.

Sato suspected he might find his end in this desperate wildness. And... perhaps there was even worse than death here. Sato did not know, but he had a very uneasy feeling about this whole expedition, and the Ranger could read his caution like the calculations for a shot in his playbook.

The thief had said as much in his own cautious way, though he kept many of his other, darker thoughts to himself.

The thief had long been at Thor to know why, exactly, the Ranger had wanted to fade into this cursed and haunted region from which few ever returned and of which strange and wild tales abounded.

Why had they come this way after the events in the City of Thieves?

What was the strange warrior's goal?

That they'd had to fade to complete the ruse of the misdirection of the stolen treasure they'd arranged and plundered in the City of Thieves was a given, but the why of going into one of the most dangerous lands the Ruin had to offer had escaped Sato, who'd suggested a dozen other fantastic cities the best of the maps of the Ruin had failed to name among the Cities of Men, where they might fade and wait out the storm of treasure hunters and worse who would try to find them over the next few months until some other greater treasure was rumored to be easier and readier to steal.

Strange and fantastic hidden settlements little known to most.

The pirate states beyond the Red Desert.

The Pleasure Palaces of Uran.

The Lost City of Ceylos where the cinnamon-skinned gnomes of that fabled jungle city created dishes of exotic spices and fires unknown to the palates of the northern reaches. The delights were said to be legendary.

Cazimoria the Snow Kingdom. Deep in the great Jagged Mountains of the east, far beyond the subterranean lands of the Dog Kings.

Perhaps even Kungaloor itself. Perhaps. And perhaps all the other fabled lands of the Golden Sun and the Azure Sea that were said to lie beyond that fantastic paradise of lotus-dreaming Kungaloor where the jade-green jungles and the deep blue seas met, the crossroads of trade and luxury on that side of the world.

Thor had shrugged at these tantalizing suggestions, and offered only this...

"Rangers go where others cannot follow, Sato. The treasure we stole was so fantastic, many would follow us now. Anywhere we went that they thought they could find us, they would hunt us. So we have to go where the men of this world fear to go... where no one ever returns from. Where things, and people, are said to be lost forever even according to your own tales. If they think we're dead, that's the best outcome for a fade. They will think the treasure we stole was lost out here and they will count themselves wise as not having followed, and found out, instead choosing to live. That's what Rangers do after we hit targets. Choose a place where no one else will go out of fear of death... and make it our home for a while. Of all the places I have heard of in the Ruin... the Eastern Wastes and this... Rift... seem to fit the bill."

Sato thought about this for a long moment.

Then he smiled knowingly. "You are clever, Warrior. But the death that awaits here under the mysterious sands of this land and along the strange Rift we head into, which even I have not seen, is very real. Many never do return from these haunted sands. They die here. And there is no denying that."

Silence. The great hunting cat seemed to have gone off for other, easier prey this night. Even its fetid smell was gone from the cooling hot air.

"Then," rumbled Thor, rubbing his jaw as he considered his friend's cautions, "we'll just have to be meaner than whatever it is that lives here and kills so many. We'll kill it. And we will come out the other side of this place, Sato. If we are thought dead by those who would follow and rob us, then we are free of their pursuit. And... maybe we'll find what everyone is so afraid of out here. See it for ourselves, Sato. See what treasure it guards, and take it for ourselves. For we are thieves, after all."

The Ranger smiled.

The thief had no reply to this and instead kept his counsel to himself, understanding the warrior less than he thought he had.

But to the Ranger, there was... another reason. Another reason why they had come this way in the first place. Or rather, why the Ranger had come this way. One the Ranger had not shared with his companion, or even Alluria when she'd whispered to him in the night, asking what would become of them if they continued into the face of certain death in the Eastern Wastes, perhaps being lost for all time.

Never returning to the Cities of Men.

In her own way, she was hinting that she was asking something deeper of him than just being lost to the Rift, and the wastes, and death, that certainly lay ahead of them.

She was asking about them, and what they meant to each other. In a very sly and circuitous way.

The Ranger ignored her deeper inquiries.

But such were her coquettish and manipulative ways, playful though they were. Thor had long been immune to such contrivings, having been off-post back in the Army in too many bars where comely young girls sought a way to make their living on the efforts of a poor soldier.

Despite the weekend safety briefs and off-limits warnings from the post commanders. Soldiers went and commanders wondered why.

But sergeants knew, for they had once been such.

The reason... why he had wanted to go this way... into the Rift itself perhaps...

... was the Pearl he'd kept from the Fates after their war between themselves.

The last remaining Fate had asked him that Thor leave the Pearl of Fate in the temple at the top of the volcanic island deep in the Sea of Riddles, indicating that it would call three more new Fates to itself to watch over the Pearl and all it would show to those who guarded it.

The Ranger had thought long and hard about this and decided the pretty thing had caused enough cursed misery for those it ensnared to serve it, and the temple, and that for a while... he would carry it with him in his travels.

Ar-Nahkt, the hawk-priest, had come to him on the last day on that island, circling down on the drafts and thermals in a noonday tropical blaze, landing on the burning white sands of the beach as the wind hustled and hushed the palms at its behest in the afternoon.

"*Kree-eee-ar!*" cried the priest bird as he stood before the Ranger. "What happens now... is unseen. And perhaps... perhaps that is the way it should be, for what mortal can handle the knowing of futures."

And that had been Thor's thinking exactly. It seemed the Pearl had seduced the powerful to play their games of power and politics and spend the lives of others on wars if the Pearl said it should be so, showed them the power they could have, tempted them, and that success was assured, or wasn't.

Thor hated absolute certainty in anyone, including himself.

He'd seen generals and politicians and Deep State scumbags back in the world burn hundreds of thousands of lives of young men who never should have been soldiers, because they were absolutely certain some war had to be done and won for no other reason than someone else made some money in the slaughter and bloodshed.

They'd never seen a dead barefoot kid holding an AK in the tall grass.

It was never about freedom or democracy or smiting evil like they said it would be and was for. No, it was always about the bottom line for them and the dark forces they served.

The money.

Thor had always hated seeing the dead body of some young kid lying in the grass with an empty AK he barely knew how to work and should have never been out there with in the first place with the real killers like himself and the Rangers.

Battle was for all the marbles.

He played to win.

He hated what had happened to those ignorant enough... who'd been forced out there against him by lies and games and whispers that they'd beat him.

He was a warrior enough to hate such sights of amateurs paying the price for someone else who'd never have to and was only interested in the profit and bottom line at someone else's expense.

What had been told to him about the Pearl convinced Sergeant Thor that those same versions of the Deep State the Ruin possessed, would come for the Pearl and use it to be "absolutely certain" about some next war or "battle that must be fought."

Sending off all those young, and ignorant, and inexperienced into a meat grinder where professionals stalked the nights like that predator out there.

The boys who never would have been out there had there not been temptations and inducements with ephemeral terms like "glory" and "fame," or even the press gang of a sword and a spear and "here's an ill-fitting uniform and bad gear" and war is horrible and there's dysentery and everyone dies badly in a knives-out trench fight.

Every day and twice on Tuesdays, as Joe would say.

Those boys all seemed to get sucked into wars of "absolute certainty." Wars the Pearl might promise petty tyrants they'd profit by without ever having to double-tap or swing a blade.

Thor had hated killing those boys who never should have been there. Even when they were called "the enemy." The ones who would have been something else had not some eunuch or simpering Deep State functionary come along to be "absolutely certain" the world, or the Ruin, would be much safer if they marched themselves off to their death so the dark forces could get paid.

And of course... there was that money those types always seemed to make, either way it fell out. Win or lose. Half the time both sides were in on it together just to get all that gold headed in their direction.

Or money, back in the Before. Foreign aid for the dictator's next Ferrari and mansion on some beach.

It was always that way. He'd soldiered long enough to see that.

Thor had seen that back in the world the Rangers had come from, and he'd gotten a whiff of it here again in the Ruin from the stories of the Pearl, and the City of Thieves, and all the Cities of Men which had smacked too much to him of the world they'd come from as all being the same.

As they say, some things never change.

Sergeant Thor had not liked that. Not at all. Maybe... that was why he'd gone off to find his edges.

The time of the detachment in the Ruin had been almost pure survival, and combat had been... *refreshing* to him.

Strange word. *Refreshing*. Perhaps only another soldier would understand that.

A break from all those sandboxes back in the world they'd come from ten thousand years ago. Monsters and demi-human enemies battling to see who won and who lost. Who lived, and who died. In its own way... an honest fight for all involved.

Survival and supremacy.

No trickery or Deep State games of eunuchs and cheap greed and cheaper power and losing is winning and here's some bogus Rules of Engagement because we need these scumbags on our side, sorry Sergeant So-and-So got shot in the head.

And yeah, to the Ranger, there was something simply noble in that time the detachment had merely fought for its survival in crossing the Ruin. No ROE. No Deep State games. Just kill, or be killed. He could live with that outcome. Either way.

But he was, as all Rangers are... *in it to win it.*

Now they, the detachment, Captain Knife Hand and the smaj, Talker and the rest... they were getting involved in the big struggle. And that would come with politics because things never change.

Out here, on the edge... kill or be killed. Winner take all.

In the Cities of Men, of course the inevitable eunuchs and functionaries who get paid... win, lose, or dead boys in the grass thinking of some girl they'd never make love to again... those scumbags were always clustered around such places.

The Cities of Men.

Thor spat, and he wasn't even working dip.

Always.

Somehow that particular horrible trait of humanity had survived ten thousand years of monsters and magic, and mayhem, when to every soldier, it never should have existed in the first place.

If the Pearl was gone from the sweaty grasp of petty would-be tyrants and their simpering Deep State eunuchs... then perhaps they'd be a little less "absolutely certain" to march young boys who hadn't had a chance to live, and no chance to survive, off to wars the inevitable eunuchs were hoping to collect on. Regardless of who got left dead in the grass at the end of the day.

There was some flaw in that argument. Thor knew it. The Ranger could see that. But that didn't matter to him. He had... an idea to flip the script on all the Cities of Men and the scum of tyrants and eunuchs.

An idea that if the Pearl got good and lost, or even destroyed, or perhaps... maybe just gone for a little while...

Then perhaps...

Two kids, some boy who thought he might be brave, and a pretty girl, could grow old together. Instead of one marching off in ill-fitting armor for glory... and never coming back again.

That thought had grown within him as he'd carried the Pearl of Fate away from its temple.

He felt the Pearl fighting it. Somehow. So he'd kept the lustrous pink thing in the clamshell and continued his journey into the wastes, certain...

There's that word.

Certain there'd be some place to lose it for a good long while out here beyond the known. Beyond the Cities of Men.

Beyond the scumbags.

Maybe not forever.

Maybe... just long enough for some boy to grow old with a young pretty girl.

Finding the Spartans out here, thought lost and dead, felt like a sign to him.

He was certain. But not... *absolutely certain.*

Thor didn't know.

Such things were above his pay grade, he'd told himself along the way, keeping his own war counsel against the whole world.

The whole Ruin.

He was a Ranger.

But soon there would be fighting. And for that... Rangers lived to excel.

What had undead Tanner said...

And that too... was a sign to Sergeant Thor.

CHAPTER TWENTY-SIX

THE "DIRTY LEGS," AS THE SQUAT BARKING first Sergeant of the Karthians announced them to the commander, were ushered into the presence of the leader of the mysterious thought to be long-dead Spartans.

Thor raised an eyebrow at this and said nothing. He'd correct that error soon enough.

It was a typical war leader's tent but not a warlord's tent. Not some savage chieftain's trophy- and booty-laden tent rife with languishing slave girls and steely-eyed killers in barbarian's armor and skins, eyeing who would die next so they might possess the title of khan, or chieftain, or whatever made them greater than the other wolves they traveled with, raided next to, and pillaged alongside.

That is until the other wolves came for them.

"But such is the way of such uncouth and savage peoples, Warrior," Sato might have said of such warlord's digs.

This was different.

Instead, the commander's tent of the Karthian Spartans was... spartan. Spare, clean, orderly.

But clearly a war leader's tent.

The soldiers who attended the captain were clearly hardened veterans, NCOs of some sort. Leaders of smaller units. Each hard-bitten and scarred with that *seen that been there done too many things and barely survived* look. Each was of the same pipe-hitter vein as the two killers who shadowed the perpetually angry first sergeant.

This tent was filled with studs who knew how to kill and didn't think too much about it.

The danger and lethality was clear to Thor as they were brought before a great campaign table spread with maps and styluses, scrolls and even a few actual leather-bound books. One large map was still being made as the Spartans went deeper and deeper into the Eastern Wastes. Large sections of it were unfinished and there were small, scrawled notes on it. Some of the symbols even vaguely resembled symbols once used on military maps of the Before.

The commander himself was... unimpressive. He was smaller than his men, but it was clear he was a warrior. He was older if only by middle age, and of course... like any good leader, he possessed that permanent look of indigestion.

And... there was one other figure in the room, and it was to her eyes Thor was instantly drawn, for she was strangely beautiful, and her hair was so red it was like living fire.

Her eyes were blue sapphire gems of otherworldly beauty.

He could see that she was a sorceress of some sort. Magical charms and amulets clung in great profusion deep in the canyon of her breasts. Her hooded robe was a luxuriant green, and she wore gold strapped sandals that seemed of little use in the rough terrain the Spartans had needed to cross to reach this deep into the wastes.

Her eyes were a brilliant blue and almost... ethereal, and when the Ranger entered the tent, those otherworldly orbs seemed to flash all at once as she took him in, her full-lipped pink mouth against her alabaster skin parting in stunned admiration at his considerable physique. For a moment she drank in his muscles and handsome features, then seemed to come to herself and once more regained her otherworldly bearing, more befitting a sorceress of some note and power and not some easily impressed tavern girl.

Alluria caught the interaction and made a small unhappy noise.

Thor ignored all this and stared at the commander, ready to kill everyone in the room, or make sure they never walked straight again, if everything went sideways and suddenly spears got pointed at them from every direction with the intention of being used.

Behind the captain, behind the redheaded beauty of a sorceress, were typical Bronze Age unit standards, adorned with trophies of silver chalices, teeth necklaces, captured ivory horns, and even a couple of fine weapons that were filigreed or rune-carved and seemed to be of remarkable if not magical make. But these trinkets and trophies were not what drew the Ranger's eye and convinced him all his suspicions were most likely very close if not right on target for the DZ.

There were three standards.

One with a painted devil, another with a panther, and the last one a falcon.

Thor gave a grim half-smile at this and wondered if they even knew what a DZ was. How much of their "Airborne" was just half or badly remembered lore passed down from generation to generation.

Then the smirk was gone, and he wondered if he was going to go in like a "meat missile" or a "dirt dart," again both terms that had once meant something to the ancestors of these men, if he had some detail wrong and played his hand wrong.

He had three weapons he could easily start killing them with. Besides his fists and boots.

But what did they know? What still made them what they once were...

Did they know what "How did you make yourself more lethal today?" had once meant? Or...

"Hold what you got, Airborne!"

Or...

"Keep your feet and knees together!" and "Knees in the breeze!"

And of course, "Strike hold" and "All the way!" and "And then some" and "Until dawn" and "Nothing to stop us!" and of course, always, "Airborne."

The killers all around him in Spartan armor watched him and waited for the signal to do what they did. The sorceress too watched Thor, practically purring, those huge gems that were eyes greedily drinking him in.

Thor watched only the commander but felt the hard-eyed presence of everyone in the room, ready and more than willing to do casual murder at the slightest gesture from the man they called their commander. Or the angry first shirt.

Thor spoke.

Betting all his hand right now. If it went sideways... *then we'll see who's meaner than it*, he thought to himself, cleared his throat, and spoke in that solid rumble of his.

"American parachutists..."

He did not turn and play it for the whole command tent, instead keeping his steely-eyed Nordic blue murderer's glare on the commander. But he sensed everyone in the room, every killer and even the sorceress who was a killer in her own right to be sure, that was more than clear, shift uncomfortably at his first spoken words in the crowded tent. What followed next left them all stunned and open-mouthed. How did this northern barbarian know their holy words? Their sacred histories?

"Devils in baggy pants," continued Thor, watching the commander, "are less than one hundred meters from my outpost line. I can't sleep at night; they pop up from nowhere and we never know when or how they will strike next. Seems like the black-hearted devils are... everywhere..."

Thor had spoken all this clearly and slowly. Emphasizing the words they surely had no understanding of because they were words from long ago, another time not this one. Betting these words, this letter from long ago... had survived as some form of holy text. He'd collected enough information to bet with intel. And now... he'd see.

Long ago, on other days lost across these new and strange ages none from the Before could have ever dreamed would become of the world turned and called the Ruin.

Silence within the tent so thick it could have been cut with a Spartan gladius.

The priest knelt swiftly a moment later, closed his eyes, and began to mutter some prayer.

Words familiar and out of order spilled from his swiftly moving mouth.

As one, every other Spartan but not the sorceress nor the commander, knelt following the example of their holy man speaking their "holy words" from the Before.

In the silence that followed, the low and quickly spoken words of the priest were clear in Thor's mind, and he knew them well, for all Rangers are Airborne Rangers.

The cadence of the priest was old and clear to any sky soldier. "Stand-up, hook-up, shuffle to the door..." The words were sometimes repetitive, but the basic gist was there, as was every hand and arm signal, every word a jumpmaster says, every movement highly scripted and identical every single time...

The sense of ritual had endured.

The JMPI was spoken like words from the holy books of all religions.

The smaj from back with the detachment snorted in Thor's mind and returned to the Kindle ebook he was perpetually at when not enforcing standards or quietly solving some problem before it got to the commander.

The words of a German officer written long ago to mark down in the permanent record his fears, his torment, his anguish that the ancestors of these men had caused him and his troops long ago... had been the key for Sergeant Thor to unlock these killers all around him, ten thousand years in the future...

American parachutists... devils in baggy pants... are less than 100 meters from my outpost line. I can't sleep at night; they pop up from nowhere and we never know when or how they will strike next. Seems like the black-hearted devils are everywhere...

Devils in baggy pants, the enemy commander had called them.

The Germans hadn't liked the fact that the 504th would go out at night hunting Germans in their foxholes. He'd written down all his terrors describing the devils that stalked him.

Thor had been sliced out for training with the 82nd a time or two. Jumped with them. Pushballed with them. And yes, even drank with them, for which they were, then, considered legendary in their own way.

His bet placed, his cards played... the Ranger saluted, slamming his assault-gloved paw into his chest rig and thrusting his hand out, just as the Spartans now did.

"All the way, sir!" he thundered in the tent.

And then, quietly, mouth agape, Devil Six returned the salute and replied in a clear crisp voice, "Airborne."

CHAPTER TWENTY-SEVEN

"How..." began the commander in a quiet yet firm and calm manner. His eyes went somewhere else, then to the map, a haunted look crossing that look of perpetual permanent indigestion. The face of leaders going back to Sparta and Thermopylae itself. The face of real leaders who lead real men.

Then...

"How do you know our... sacred words?"

Sergeant Thor had thought long and hard about this move over the hump through the desert as he'd put his final conclusions together.

The Spartan fort and what he saw there... the falcon, the panther, and the devil... just confirmed his hunches.

He'd considered what was known of the Before by the various peoples of the Ruin, that there was some fantastic civilization before the Ruin became what it became...

"The Before," they called it.

Obviously, this commander, or his counselors, would have some knowledge of that civilization they'd carried through the Dark Ages of the becoming of the Ruin. The Ranger detachment had encountered others who'd heard of "strangers" from the past, suddenly appearing in the Ruin with weapons and gear before they got "revealed."

The SEALs were an example. The rumors of an actual special missions unit called in Ruin history "the Delta Kings." There was that too.

D-Boys.

Tomorrow problems.

Thor cleared his throat and proceeded, certain he was halfway to where he needed to go, but not... all the way.

Just yet.

"Stand by, Devil Six," barked the first sergeant, suddenly thrusting himself right into the confrontation, putting himself between the strangeness of the Ranger to these Spartans, and his commander.

But the commander waved a hand, and as swift and righteous and angry as the senior NCO had been in his insertion, like a trained professional on the line of battle watching the commander's hand to see if they should push or give ground, the NCO halted.

With a mere turn of his head Devil Six nodded that Sergeant Thor should continue.

"You... are the descendants of men I fought with in the wars that marked what your people call... the Before. I come from that time. I know of your ways, and your unit... because of direct experience with them. In that time. We trained, and we fought together... and swore the same oaths to defend what we would defend with our lives. We were brothers. And time matters not to us."

Thor stopped and let that settle in for a moment.

The sorceress stepped forward and purred softly as she once more hungrily devoured the Ranger with her almost translucent rapacious large eyes.

If there had been a Hollywood in the Ruin, she would have been a B-movie actress who couldn't act her way out of a paper bag, as they say.

Here in the Ruin... it was her schtick.

She held sway over many in the tent, but there were some who seemed to regard her coldly, and in those faces Thor could see hatred and murder simmering.

Corporal Max's face gave nothing away and he merely stared forward, grim visage set come hell or high water.

Her eyes roved over the assembly, and she whispered a small spell, casting those large eyes about indeed. Eyes as large and as charming as other features she possessed in abundance. Hips and curves. She was tall, almost as tall as Thor himself but not quite. Her bearing was statuesque and almost brazen though she had the air more of a priestess than a worker of magics and charmer of souls.

Or an actress, thought the Ranger somewhere in the back of his skull.

"Oh please," muttered Alluria and gripped her bow tightly. Sato reached out and stayed the hand she might have been foolish enough to draw an arrow from her quiver with.

"Steady, girl. You are surrounded by real live wolves," he hissed softly.

"True this barbarian speaks, Achilos," the sorceress said almost breathlessly, her more than ample chest heaving, turning to the commander to make sure she had his attention.

She waved one pale alabaster hand across the space between her and the Ranger, and silvery starlight shimmered into sudden existence and disappeared a second later. Then she purred approvingly at the arcane results of her supposed "detections" known but to her.

"He is a man out of time, from times not known to the men of your tribe," she pronounced coyly, eyes roving over them all. Playing it cheap and theatrically. "But it is true and he says rightly, he is kin to your kind, Spartan, and..."

Her eyes went wide as though some horrible vision had just possessed her for a terrible instant. Then she shrieked suddenly, and her beautiful body shuddered seductively as she closed her eyes. They fluttered slightly, her long lashes dancing.

Finally, she spoke in a husky, deep voice with almost no emotion.

"Death and destruction follow this one, Spartans. Some even say he is... Death itself. The hawks... they believe he has destiny... *all wrapped up in him*... There is a lone sorcerer of great power who has made it known that this one is... *caught up in all of it*. That Fate has entwined itself about him and the Ruin must change as he treads the earth."

Then she lowered her head, clasped her hands within the long, draped folds of the wide sleeves, her rich wizardly robes forming about her shapely figure, and stepped back solemnly like some terrible actor overplaying their small part in the park for all the rubes come to watch. Done with all the gravitas she could muster in order to get some meaningless applause and perhaps a coin or compliment or two thrown at them.

The gathered Spartans, lifetakers and heartbreakers, killers every one, moved not nor reacted to her charade.

But they did not protest or scorn either...

The commander came around the side of the campaign table, his hand caressing his map for a moment as he stood in front of the Ranger, taking in Thor's full measure.

Then he turned back to the sorceress.

"Thank you, Skylla. For your magic and aid."

He turned to Thor.

"I do not know... who you are. But it is clear you have rescued and aided my men. And once, it would seem, Major Baer and the men of the five-oh-fourth... knew you, and your kind. Counted you as an ally. I shall not make that demand of you now. We go to our deaths. No ally should be forced by past loyalties to meet our fate. I offer you food and rest and shelter inside our fortifications. We march in three days from this night, heading for the great bowl of the Sands of Burning Glass in the deepest reaches of the Rift."

The Spartan commander studied his men, connecting with many, knowing all their stories. Then he continued.

"You find us much diminished, for the best of us was slain six nights ago in a battle against an ancient chimera that guarded a strange and lonely tower. Ajack and his element thought to pit themselves against the beast on the way here. Now Ajack of Petraeus has failed in his strength, and we are championless going into the battle we must fight. In three days, we must make war against the winged folk of the Tower of Flame and Air... there we must penetrate the gate to the Plane of Fire... and march to relieve the City of Brass and her efreeti queen who has called our debt in her hour of need."

The commander paused, swallowed hard, and for a brief moment turned back to his maps to stare longingly at them once more as if there were some other answer in them than the one he knew for certain. Then he faced once more Thor and his companions.

"I ask only this. If in your travels, if a stranger asks what has become of us... asks you if our courage failed in the hour it was most required... if we abandoned our oath..."

The commander's gaze took in his men once more as though it was the last time he would ever see them. Thor knew that look, having been on enough pumps and watched the wives of Rangers come out to say goodbye from a distance in the dark before dawn.

He knew that look.

And was glad he was never leaving someone behind to miss him.

Not everyone comes home.

"Please tell them... we did not. We went to die as men die. On our feet, swinging a sword. And that we paid our enemies, and our debt, tenfold for each death of our own."

Every Spartan nodded or gave a brief thump of their battered yet shining chest armor.

Silence in the tent.

The first sergeant cleared his throat.

Then Thor spoke in a low rumble.

"Sounds like a good fight is coming. I'd hate to miss that, sir. I'll go with you, and I'll lead the way. If you'll have me and my friends on the line with you... Devil Six."

There had been some heaviness and despair in the tent, and later, thinking back about it, the thief would observe to the Ranger that perhaps it was due to the recent death of their Champion Ajack of Petraeus. Whatever the reason, just for a moment, that pall of grief and despair and... *absolute certainty*... lifted... when the powerful new stranger who'd saved some of their own in a desperate last stand, said he would go where Spartans would go. Fight who they would fight.

For just a moment.

"What do they call you?" asked the commander.

"Thor," said the Ranger.

And a brief trumpet tattoo of hope seemed to run through the hardy and deadly Spartans lost deep in the wastes and headed to face their soon and certain deaths.

CHAPTER TWENTY-EIGHT

THAT NIGHT THEY WERE FED WITHIN THE dirt ramparts of the Spartans, and Sato, Alluria, and Thor gathered near their small cookfire and listened to the music of an army in temporary garrison, deep behind enemy lines. Readying themselves to march toward their destiny in just a few short days.

There was the sound of equipment being repaired, NCOs barking terse orders that were quickly obeyed. Spartans deploying to the walls just before dark, their gear jingling, their shields rattling against their armor, their long spears bouncing up and down as they went to replace those who'd maintained vigilant watch during the day.

The smell of other strange foods in the night as the relief of evening dark and cooler temperatures came on.

The priest came and brought them stew even though they had rations. He told them he would watch over their fire for the night even though they were as safe as it was possible to be behind the dirt walls and jutting spears of the silent Spartans out there, peering into the purple night as a soft low wind moaned across the strange and silent canyons near the Rift into which they were soon to march.

"The scouts say those canyons are filled with strange and dangerous mythical monsters," said the priest softly as he ladled out their stew. "We will have to face them to make it down into the Rift and to the tower we will jump on."

The wind passing through the distant canyons almost held a note, as though it were singing some forgotten song from long ago, and then, just when one thought they could hear it... it was gone. The strange note would come and go throughout the night, twisting and rising until around midnight the wind stopped and a deathly suffocating silence lay over the little valley of crescent dunes where the Spartans had encamped about the ancient well.

But the three adventurers were dead to the world and did not decline the offer of the priest who they knew was as tired as they were from the three days' running battle of a march across the southern edge of the Eastern Wastes to reach the linkup with the other Spartans.

Alluria was the first to fade, simply devouring her stew with a dead-eyed glaze, burping softly, then falling over wrapped in her riding cloak onto her pack.

And for a time, it was just the old thief and the Ranger he called Warrior. Neither making a sound as the camp got quiet and quieter.

Then Sato spoke.

"Warrior... it is time to tell me what you know of these strange warriors, for it is clear you know much more than the half rumors and barely remembered song-tales I have badly related."

Thor grunted and stared into the fire. He was so tired that even he was having trouble thinking, and for a brief moment he wondered if somehow the Spartans had drugged their meal.

Or that witch...

That's how tired he was. How tired they all were.

Poisoned?

Grim killers the Spartans might have been, scarred and tattooed by a hundred desperate battles with shield and spear and knives out, but they weren't tricksters in the backstabbing sense...

Thor guessed their little unit was probably quite good at a battlefield trick or two to make the odds more palatable.

But no, they were warriors. Not poisoners. They had honor, that was clear, and they lived by a code and a creed and the Ranger understood that, for Rangers had their own creed and all hell would break before a Ranger would betray that creed.

Or the smaj, or Joe, or any of the other lifer Ranger NCOs would... *roughly retire* that oathbreaker.

Back in the day they would have just drummed them out of the batts.

Now...

Well, now there were rumors, and everyone had a pretty good idea that the linguist had done some dirty work early on for the smaj in getting rid of a problem that had followed the Rangers into the Ruin.

The hard-eyed and scarred NCOs of the Spartans, ruck-humped and weathered, all seemed cut from that same Sergeant Joe and a dozen others Thor could name, cloth.

And that was the funny thing about Sergeant Thor. They'd made him a sergeant. In the Ranger battalion. A sniper team leader and for the detachment... a section leader.

But he knew he would never be like them. Joe and the rest. He wasn't as interested in making more Rangers like they were. Deciding who would make it, who wouldn't.

And this was the strange part...

They knew that about him. Knew he was just there for the fight. The edge. The practical application of technical perfection as a sniper, and... *a Ranger*.

So they let him stay.

They probably guessed it wouldn't be too long before the "Super Friends," or Green Berets as they were sometimes officially called, would want him to come try out for selection. That is if the Ruin hadn't ended any and all hopes of that.

And then Delta would have been the next step.

Would that, Thor had wondered, have been the reason they let him stay a sergeant in the Ranger battalion even though he was, in the words of the smaj himself, "a little too hippy-dippy for me"?

He wasn't that. But that was how the senior NCO had expressed it.

Yeah, the smaj didn't like Thor's extreme sporting side, and the times it got applied to a mission. Smaj called that "Hollywood stuff." Then added, "Ain't no place for Hollywood here in the Rangers."

But the other NCOs didn't wash him out, and along the way from Ranger private all the way to Ranger sergeant and then the job of, or calling some might say... a sniper. They let him hang.

They just accepted he was the way he was... a finder and jumper off of edges... and that it was probably good to have a dude like him on the team what with the way he could shoot, PT, and yeah... let's be blunt... *kill*.

He'd had that instinct ingrained in him like he was just some kid who'd been a hunter all his life. It was the scout section who refined his ability to fade afterwards, tripling his cred as a solid hitter.

Special Forces and then Delta had seemed written in his cards all along. But then the Ruin happened, and, well, as he thought to himself watching the broken glass wheel of the universe turn in his dazed fatigue, smelling the smoke of the fires on the desert, surrounded by like-minded killers used to the hack-and-slash, surrounded by enemies both of might and magic, and sometimes even stranger and more mythical than that... well, the Ruin had happened.

Plans change.

And Thor, not Sergeant Thor, or the Ranger, wouldn't have it any other way. He'd doubted in past moments just like this that he'd ever go back to the Rangers and their quest to smite the big bads plaguing what passed for civilization ten thousand years after the world ate itself and became something new.

Revealed...

And then again, there was that big battle in Umnoth shaping up to be something straight out of Tolkien or *Beowulf* or Henry the Fifth's Saint Crispin's Day speech.

Shame to miss that.

Thor yawned.

"Warrior..." prompted Sato as the Ranger stared into the fire dull-eyed from the stew and considered all these things once more, knowing he'd arrive at no conclusion this time just as he had not the many other times he'd done the same.

"It's what I don't know, Sato," rumbled Sergeant Thor finally, "that bugs me. But here's what I guess... happened... to them."

Thor recrossed his legs, picked up a stick from the fire, and poked it.

Alluria snored delicately, draped across her pack.

"They are the descendants of some... unit... that's what we called groupings of warriors back in the Before where I come from... but somehow they either got here the way I did, through a QST gate, or they held on through the becoming of the Ruin, what your... lore... says the Spider Queen... if that's the right way to say it... did to the world with her... magic, as you'd call it."

Sato made a long slow monastic *hummmmmm* and closed his slanted eyes effecting an almost beatific pose of rest and tranquility.

Then he snored once suddenly and woke himself up.

He coughed and sputtered.

"Q... S... T. I know not this word... Warrior. But I understand it to be the magic by which you and your brethren came forward to this time of need when the Ruin should have necessity of such expert warriors as your kind."

Then the thief yawned once again and leaned back against a pack, closing his eyes, once more effecting that dreaming gaze of restful sleep.

"I am a simple thief, Warrior," he said from behind closed eyes. "There are great forces at work as we near the Rift. Mighty players in the games of power and struggle... they seem to be... watching... how this plays out, as though..."

Then the thief was softly snoring to himself.

For a long time, even with the need of sleep overwhelming him like some prison sentence that must be served out regardless, the Ranger stared into the fire and considered all these things, feeling that yes, somehow his friend had hit the nail on the head.

The Rangers were well on their way to the north and the war there with the Nether Sorcerer. These Spartans had some kind of air about them...

As though fate and destiny were all wrapped up in them in just the same way the hedge wizard of the *Cyclops' Whore* had indicated it was wrapped up in Thor himself.

And then there was...

Thor's head flopped down on his great chest, and he snored once, loudly, waking himself.

Feeling the Pearl glowing warm within his cargo pocket.

That was somehow important.

But he was not awake... he was sleeping now...

He lay down, stared at the stars, and watched as two great sinister eyes peered down at him through the starlight, barely there. And there...

And watching...

Like stardust arranged to be just so.

"There you are..." whispered Tuth Evol from across the void of sleep. The Dreaming Sorcerer. "There you are, Ranger."

CHAPTER TWENTY-NINE

Thor found himself in another land not like anything he'd ever known before...

He'd known a fellow Ranger once, a guy who was really into online digital art. And the guy, a gunner on one of the batt gun teams with a background in anti-armor having first started as an Eleven Series with that identifier, was really into this strange, surreal art he called... Vaporwave. Thor had been a two-oh-three gunner that first year in the batts and had yet to try out for the scouts, or even get anywhere near the snipers.

That would be later...

... and his adventures with the Rangers, even before the Rangers went to the Ruin through time, were enough to fill a larger book, or a longer scroll, than the one you now read, oh wise and adventurous seeker of fantastic tales in strange lands.

But that gunner, he'd had an affinity for this style of online digital art called Vaporwave art. He was crazy about it. Constantly seeking it across all the major search engines and indie artist catalogs.

Thor thought it was a little mindless and sugary in that it consisted merely of images that were reminiscent of... something Thor had never experienced... but someone's idealized version of the eighties.

"Malls, *Miami Vice*, ethereal pink palaces, and misty pools and vibrant green marble columns, man," said the dreamy gunner almost in a trance when they hunkered for a long night in some smelly ditch in the jungle near a ville the Rangers had eyes on in South Am for an ongoing anti-insurgency mission. "All before my time, bruh," said the gunner. "But... there's something about it that brings me... peace. Un-jams my *chi*, know what I mean. Makes me think of... better worlds. Heaven, or even just some paradise I ain't considered yet because I'm young, jacked, payin' the rent on the scroll and I'll never die. Know what I mean? Other worlds than these..."

Thor had sighed, considered the luminescent and hazy pictures of strange palaces and neon signs and beaches at sunset, stately palms or slick sports cars... and he couldn't understand the fascination.

But everyone had their thing.

Talker, languages.

Kennedy, his game.

Each Ranger had a thing they dug and made their own.

Thor wondered what his was.

Sometimes he had no answer. Then he realized... it was his whole life. That was... his thing. The next adventure.

He'd seen that very same gunner lay patient murder-hate on some very bad guys out in the jungle who'd made the mistake of wandering into an L-shaped ambush the Rangers had planned. That particular X was so brutal, the team leader had designated the gun and the gunner to be the only ones engaging. Everyone else would watch the jungle, pick up the strays with targeted fire, and generally try to keep it hard and fast so they could get it done in one.

Then fade.

Like Rangers do.

That day was a message for the cartels. The Rangers were in the jungle now. It was theirs going forward. The cartel could have the roads for now.

Until the Rangers got around to those too.

The ambush was exactly what it was planned to be... quick and dirty and very deadly. The dead warm bodies were left on the X and the jungle was so quiet twenty minutes later it was like the Rangers had never been there.

You had to find the dead to know that they had been.

Thor had been positioned up on some rocks near a waterfall ready to drop some thumpers on any reaction force that might come in fast at the sound of gunfire in the jungle. Instead, all he heard was the sudden *dakka dakka* of the two-forty, six to eight and maybe a few more in each burst, tearing a patrol of hardboy tattooed cartel killers who thought they'd push the Rangers around, to shreds in seconds.

Some say life comes at ya fast. Death sometimes faster.

They found out.

Thor didn't flinch when he heard the medium machine gun suddenly open up out across the jungle down along the stream, knowing exactly what it meant. The targets were on the *X*. Now they were dead. Less than a minute. Much, much less than a minute. Seconds really. The usual jungle birds cried out indignantly at the sudden violence and sprang from the high trees into the hazy yellow heavy air to flap and call.

The deed was done, and the Rangers faded.

The gunner had lain the hate indeed and they were dead. All by himself.

The Vaporwave world of pink fogs and serene malls empty of life, marble columns and tall waving palm trees at the beach... was his center. Was the opposite of a massacre in the jungle for legitimate reasons. As the young Ranger Thor had once been closed his eyes and blocked out the smell of the fetid jungle night and the stinking ditch the team had chosen because surely no one in their right mind would make a patrol base in such a bug-and-snake-filled hellhole, the gunner stared into his phone beneath his poncho, the light barely visible, but a pink light, soft-hued... a paradise for a moment somewhere other than the jungles of reality and death that first pump was becoming.

Thor didn't mind action in South Am.

The jungle was the edge he'd been looking for. He'd win. He'd beat the jungle and pay the rent on the scroll. Then... he'd go find other edges. Other jungles. Other rents to be paid...

That was then.

Vaporwave images un-jamming the chi of the gunner who'd lain the hate.

This place he found himself now in, in nothing but his CryePrecision pants and boots, his bare hulking tattoo-and-scar-covered chest turned soft by the pink mists that seemed ghostly and ethereal and blocking off any kind of distant horizon, or edge to jump off of, was exactly like those images of that other paradise the gunner had once shown him in the stinking jungles of the night.

"There you are..." whispered the voice of the Dreaming Sorcerer in his mind as though he'd just woken from some sleep in which someone, someone he was supposed to have known, trusted, but now he couldn't remember who, had been saying something to him just as the dream ended.

As though he'd been asleep, thinking he wasn't at all.

"No," whispered the Ranger to himself as he stared around at all the soft neon and misty cotton candy. "*This* is the dream."

There U R appeared in neon script.

The Ranger was standing along a marble... walkway?

To either side was the most translucent beautiful pool he'd ever seen, not like a natural pool in the jungle or some outdoors place, but like the swimming pools of some incredibly rich sultan, pools of misty water and pink fog.

The light coming from within these places.

The water moved and steamed as though someone had just recently been in it, intimating that it was warm, and inviting, perhaps like a bath.

For a moment he was supremely aware of how dirty his skin was from the long march through the wastes, and how sore his muscles and body were from the combat and the humping of excessive gear and wounded Spartans to reach the Well of Azzim.

A swim would be nice, he didn't think. But the thought was there in his head. Inviting, and almost seductive. An offer of sorts...

On the other side of each pool guarding the marble walkway deeper into the... mall, palace... whatever this place was, were arches, and through these Thor could see nothing but pink mist. At first.

But he could hear the sound of distant surf, soft and gentle. Sloughing and hissing as it had on the Isle of the Fates. Rushing onto the unseen beach. Retreating just as it had come.

Sergeant Thor turned toward the marble walkway and saw it ended in a series of wide marble steps and more columns, pink marble, green filigree caps with hints of warm firelit bronze at the top.

There were two dark archways at the top of the steps and between the ornate columns. And each column was a star spray eye staring at him.

There and not there.

Watching the Ranger intently.

The Dreaming Sorcerer appeared in red neon script within the mist between the arches and columns.

"The Pearl, one called Thor..." intoned some deep and dreamy voice inside the Ranger's head. Both a whisper, and clear as a bell rung from the other side of a city wrapped in midnight dark.

Forever.

It sent a cold shudder through the Ranger even as he heard it. Yes, even Thor. Shuddered at the voice of the Dreaming Sorcerer.

He felt the Pearl, hot like a stone on fire, inside the cargo pockets of his CryePrecisions.

"Bring it..." whispered that voice of the eyes at the end of the pink marble columned walkway, "*to... me.*"

These words appeared across the misty waters of the pool in aqua-green neon script.

Within the pools, strange women, made of water and only now coming into reality, began to swim and laugh lightly like the sound of soft glass breaking. They weren't just beautiful, they were stunning beauties, and as they became real, the sun shone through the pink mist in the arches beyond the columns at the end of the marble walkway...

Sergeant Thor could see a beach out there. And palms waving in the sun and the wind.

The golden beauties, each a stunner and dripping wet, clothed in nothing but delicate golden chains here and there, or strings of the finest white luminescent pearls, left the pools slowly. Their curves and long legs undulating as the pink mist clung to their tight bodies.

They laughed and beckoned to the Ranger as they disappeared through the arches, singing a song that buzzed in his head like a lazy hazy afternoon.

"Come play with us, mighty one..."

The beach they walked toward was brilliant white sand. The sky cornflower blue. And so was the ocean, but with distant whitecaps. The palms shook and hustled in an offshore breeze.

Beyond all this... was the sea, and other lands few had ever known.

The girls ran across the sand and into the soft white waves of the sea, their voices still in his head.

"Come, swim with us in forests of azure..." they chanted in almost a round of a chorus, the lines fading and rising as each new one began.

"Bring me..." whispered the voice of the Dreaming Sorcerer as the pink mist became a fog, swallowing the palace of marble and pink and pool Thor found himself in. It felt like he was suffocating, or being drowned, in cotton candy.

The rushing of the palms in that offshore wind grew and grew until there was nothing but pink fog and he was falling through it, certain he would find its bottom, and that beyond that was some dark pit with no bottom he would ever find... forever be cast into...

"Bring the Pearl..."

Thor roared and woke himself from the dream, sitting up near the fire he had made with Sato and the serving girl, deep in the camp of the doomed Spartans.

"To Tuth Evol," whispered that voice from the other side of the terrible dream.

Neon letters appeared within the fire.

To Tuth Evol.

CHAPTER THIRTY

THE DREAM PLAGUED THOR THROUGH THE rest of the night, and in the morning he awoke and wanted free of it. He splashed cold well water on his face, chewed angrily at the rations, PT'd himself hard with bodyweight exercises, spent time on his gear... then got involved in a brutal game of pushball with the Spartans.

Thor had heard rumors of the game when he'd been at Bragg on occasion. Usually from the older NCOs who talked fondly of the competitive game between battalions the 82nd Airborne had once been "allowed" to play.

Officially.

It was beautiful and brutally violent. And the Spartans didn't hold back on each other, or the new giant who'd come into their midst to fight alongside them.

Thor was able to identify the team that made him their own. They were smaller, hearty, definitely more scarred, and ready to do as much harm and as much violence as they could to get the giant ball where it needed to go.

They were Panthers, one of the divisions of Spartans among the main body.

They quickly formed a small cohort around the hulking Ranger once they realized he was all but unstoppable due to his sheer size and mass. Then they found their rhythm as a team and began to beat, kick, trip, punch, and wrestle their way to repeated goals on the impromptu "battlefield."

Two hours of that and everyone was bloody and limping.

And smiling and laughing and taunting.

The one-eyed first sergeant came out and shouted at them, and the teams quickly broke up and returned to their smaller camps and their duties regarding the impending march to the objective. Thor, standing there alone on the pitch, caught the angry glare of the seniormost NCO, who seemed in his eyes to hold nothing more than naked, murderous contempt.

Thor turned and walked off, not interested in contests he didn't know the rules to.

And that was when he met "the blind Spartan."

Socrat.

"Ah..." crooned the ruined old spindly man who leaned on a long walking stick near the field where the violent game of pushball had been seen to its battered and bloody conclusion. The old man's eyes were missing and the badly healed flesh was ravaged and scarred by some hideous past injury. His voice was ragged like one who drinks too much, but he didn't seem drunk right now. "So, you're in this one... this time. Maybe we'll get a little farther along this time than we did the last. But either way... we always die, Ranger, don't we?"

Just like in that cold dream of fog and mist and piercing eyes made of starlight, Sergeant Thor felt a cold shudder run through him.

Then the blind Spartan began to speak, and what followed, was... *inconceivable*.

Even for Thor, who'd once seen the movie *Groundhog Day* on a Sunday in the barracks. He thought the movie was funny enough, but kind of stupid, and definitely a hell he'd never want to experience. Personally.

In that it seemed boring to have to live and repeat the same day over and over, again and again.

Though he did appreciate the aspects of trying to get things perfect. He strived for that in everything he did. Doing everything as though his life depended on it.

He could get behind that part of the movie.

The weirdness of the great Rift inside the heart of the waste... that was going to be another story.

And so the Blind Old Spartan made things... much, much worse.

CHAPTER THIRTY-ONE

"So far," began the blind old Spartan who hobbled along next to Thor as best he could. Thor was also hobbling in his own way after one of the Spartans had turned himself into a flying log to stop the Ranger and his team from scoring in pushball.

A for effort.

He'd walk it off. The kinetic force of the blow delivered by the sturdy Spartan had left a nasty bruise already turning from purple and red to a sickly yellow and even a deathly blue. Thor slammed his fist into the damage, grunted at the pain, and tried to trigger-release the angry knot forming at the center. The Spartan had gotten up, smiled, and shrugged good-naturedly at the failed crippling attack. By then Thor was already heading toward the goal and merely eyeballed the man for some deserved payback when the time came.

Such were the ways of pushball and airborne infantry, even ten thousand years later after the end of everything once known.

The Blind Old Spartan's voice was like a rusty screen door. His cane tapped, searching out in front of him for the way forward.

"So far... we've already lost half our number, and most will be killed in the assault on the Tower of Air and Flame that lies further down along the abyssal plain of the cursed Rift. Rarely do we make it much farther than that hell... but when we do it's the fire giants and their hounds that finish us. Every time. One time though," laughed the old Spartan. Not a pretty sound. "We did make it to the defense of the City of Brass... but the slaughter was so great... even I was put to the sword."

The old man coughed and hacked up a great wet loogie from within his spindly sunbaked chest. His voice was wretched. Unpleasant to listen to. As has been noted he was scrawny, thin to the point of being composed of little more than sinew and muscle, and he was bandy-legged, almost walking sideways like a crab going about the shore.

He was blind because he had no eyes where there should be eyes. Both sockets were ruined and scarred over by some horrid hideous injury making him seem like a truly craven thing with his wild wisps of hair and sun-cooked skin.

And his annoying voice.

And... the insane things he spoke of.

He wore a loincloth, no sandals, and leaned on a long, crooked staff. He had little else.

"What're you..." grunted Thor as he stalked toward the waterskins, never minding if the ruined old man and his annoying voice kept up the road-eating pace. Which he remarkably seemed to, despite his physical injuries and lack of sight.

The old man was covered in ancient scars and one tattoo.

A tribal Falcon.

"... the company wizard?" asked Thor. "And what do you go on about?" he spat, for the air was dry and he was parched and ready to slake his great thirst at the well and the skins.

He slammed his fist into the knot on his leg again and demanded it release.

The water was remarkably cold and refreshing at the Well of Azzim, and it was said to have magical healing properties. But the words the blind old Spartan spoke were colder, like the Ranger had been standing knee-deep in mountain ice water. And Sergeant Thor didn't like that.

The old man laughed raggedly.

"Nay, Barbarian... Would that I was... then I would cast some glimmer to get myself out of this hell before we die once again. Just like we die every time. I'd kill for a good pinch of dip and a spell that would do such. Nay... I was a warrior once like these young men. And you. Once. Battle at

Heart's Torn Crag cost me my eyes there on the rookery of the old watch fort. We was up against harpy witch-women who'd been raiding them grain fields of Athonia in Skeletos before that fine city was sacked and burned to nothing but embers. Nice whores that place had. Real friendly-like and skilled as they say. Painted and purty. I'd have to have a grain sack of gold for one of 'em to even consider me now. But back in the day, in kit and armor, cut a fine figure, Barbarian, did I. Standing tall and lookin' sharp every day the eagle flew I did. Was a sergeant of the rank."

Thor reached the skins near the well and had a long, deep, cool drink. Then he splashed some water on his face and a few of the cuts he'd received in the violent game.

The bleeding scratches didn't heal immediately and neither did he expect them to. Sergeant Thor had seen real magic in the Ruin. He'd seen a lot of bogus claims along the way, too.

Still, he splashed some on the rising ugly bruises of the pushball game and smiled, reminding himself he was embracing the suck, or the fantasy, because...

He heard the smaj's voice.

"Ya never know, Ranger. You just never know. Things are different here. Maybe PFC Kennedy ain't all wrong as a dog in a taco shop. Maybe."

Thor looked at the old wretch of a ruined Spartan and... actually felt pity... now that he knew the scarecrow of a ruined ruck-hump of a man had one been a warrior. A soldier. A descendant of that fabled unit he and many others had once known and had much, much respect for.

He reached over, took the dipper, and drew the old man some cold water.

Toothless, mostly, the man smiled and drank, making a chicken clucking sound as he did.

Every soldier can end up, and probably will, if they're lucky and they're the ones that survive... like this guy, thought the Ranger and hoped his end would be knee-deep in brass surrounded by enemies without mercy or kindness.

The Ranger had seen old guys with missing eyes and missing limbs going back as far as World War 2, and all the conflicts in between, making their way into the whatever base's PX to get what their service... at the cost of their limbs, and health, and youth... had bought them long ago.

And he'd seen men who weren't much older than he was now, hobbling into the Class Six on a Friday night, broken from the line, needing Rip-Its and vodka to get it all back together for Monday morning PT standing tall and ready to soldier.

Such is the fate of all soldiers if they live long enough, Joe had often said. *Dealer's choice how yours shakes out, Ranger. Just don't whine about it.*

"There's something different though..." mumbled the Old Spartan to himself, "... 'bout you. 'Bout this one. Never been a time through this when you had them other two... with you, y'know? Don't know if that means anything... but... hey... never know. I'm sure we'll all get kilt somehow. We always do. Still, I don't know what she looks like..." He laughed. "'Cause I got no eyes. Bitch harpy tore 'em out and cursed me even as I ran her through." He continued laughing like this was the funniest thing that had ever been said by anyone. Ever.

Then he stopped, his concave chest heaving. He wiped spit and sweat from his ruined old lined face. There were bad scars there besides the missing eyes and the ruin that remained. And what remained of the water he'd badly swallowed.

"I bet she is," he crooned to himself, rocking back and forth on his staff. "Shame to hear her die this time. But... things never change. Do they, Ranger?"

The words sent a chill down Thor's spine like no other. And he didn't like it. It was blazing noon, and he was cold with fear. A feeling he... hated.

He sat down on an old crumbling stump of some ancient bricked feature that had once surrounded the bygone well.

"What," he rumbled ominously, sure he was not going to like one bit where this was going, "do you... mean?"

The blind old Spartan turned his face toward the sun and smiled.

"Everyone always thinks I'm crazy when we're in it. At the last, when I tell 'em how they're gonna die, before they do... they get it when it happens. Gimme this look like... *You knew!* I gave up tellin' 'em several times ago of going through this same stupid game... of trying to warn 'em. '*Sir... we attack that tower, they're gonna shoot us up with their bows from the rocks up there. I can hear 'em. Heard 'em last time we made it this far. Sergeant Herc gets it first. Then the rest of the boys in the Devils. It's bad, sir. Watch them rocks. Best we go in at night when they can't see us... and the winged folk don't like the night, sir.*' Or... '*Kasseaus... mind the trap at the gate... it's magical and it'll fry you like an egg...*' '*How do you know that, ol' man?*' *Can you see the future?*' says Fried Egg Kasseaus before he's Fried Egg Kasseaus.* I always try to borrow some coin off o' him before the tower because he always dies early and at least I don't have to pay back later when we reach the city."

Again, the old man made a hideous sight laughing himself to death.

"But he never mind my... *prophetic*, as it were, words. He jes' goes and gets himself fried up. And so do the rest. Jase at the stairs to the high tower. All of Second on the slopes of the hot-coal sands where the air smells like sulfurous hell itself and the thunder of the fire giants is something that would scare normal men who ain't Spartans. One time we fought a good battle against them and the captain led us straight into them and our game was good and we speared the whole cohort of them and brought them down, keeping their fire hounds back with our teams, and we was able to go on a little farther toward the City of Brass and git ourselves kilt there. But... we always die, Ranger. Always."

Thor stared at the man, trying to... not think he was insane. This was the Ruin. What was insane, magical, or whatever, as he'd learned from Talker and Kennedy, was actionable intel.

And needed to be... considered.

Sergeant Thor cleared his throat and the ruined old Spartan fell silent. Dancing back and forth slightly on leathery old arch-fallen feet, leaning on his simple crooked long staff.

Then, "I only *hears* how they die, see. Ain't got no eyes. I gotta put the pieces together to see..." he laughed at this, "to see if I can save 'em. Some die in ways I don't know and can't never no figure out. That tears me up. On the march and hear 'em alive still. Again. Knowing we're heading right to where they gonna die and I can't tell 'em however even if they don't believe me anyway. I..." The old man sighed desperately, and it was almost like a steam-whistle's hiss. "I hate that," he said finally and stamped one dirty foot into the dust.

"You were an NCO?" asked Thor simply.

"Was," said the old Spartan brightly without his heart in it. "Till she took my eyes and cursed me with the knowledge of how we would all die. Over and over and... over. Again, and again, and again."

"Magic?" asked Thor, embracing the fantasy.

The wretched old Spartan nodded.

"Yeah. The curse she gave me was... good for a while. Like I could tell you how the dice were gonna come up or what the answer would be to the question. Sometimes I could use it in battle, change the outcome of a fight we was in. But over time... got worse. I started to see how my brothers would die and there was nothing I could do to save 'em anymore.

"Then we marched for our obligation... that's how we ended up here where we never shoulda been. And something about the Rift, because the Rift is strange and weird in ways men and elves have never known, it's like we have to live it, and die, all over. Again and again. So I been here before, Ranger. Every time. Just like you sometimes. You ain't always here. Those two with you, though... they's never here. She sounds nice, that girl o' yours. But... she got a secret. I can hear that. I hear the Spartans tell of that time one of the winged folk shot you straight through the heart on the assault up graveyard spine and the whole attack stalled and we died, them hunting us down in the days that followed. Heard the captain say he'd mount a rescue mission when you got taken by fire giants. They returned three days later, half of them dead, and had tell of you roasted over open flame by them giants, spitted and all. You've died a dozen other times when you've been here with us, Ranger. But, Barbarian, you ain't always been here with us. We do seem to get farther with you along most times. But like I said, we always die. Always. That's the play in the streets, and the words and what we do never really changes, and even if it do... the outcome's the same. Always. I gave up a long time ago tryin' to warn and change things. Now I just march along and try to have a good time as best I can, enjoying hearing my brothers alive again, for what time remains us, this time around. It ain't so bad when you look at it that way, know what I mean, Ranger? Know what I mean, Barbarian?"

Thor grunted.

"Why do you call me that?"

"Barbarian?"

"Yeah. I'm not one."

The old man laughed.

"Ha. That's funny. You've always sounded like one o' them from the Dire Frost to me. Met some who were serving a warlord in Skeletos. Wild and untamed in battle. Almost impossible to beat. Savage and not like us. No discipline. Only... bloodlust and like to get into the thick of it even all alone. I've heard you in battles against the fire giants, and the djinn, and even some of the other strange monsters we meet along the way, and sometimes don't. You sound like them.

The giants of the Dire Frost. To me. You sound like anger and battle are just... your way. Barbarian. Savage. Noble and terrible... in your own way, Ranger."

All right... embrace the fantasy, Thor told himself. He sighed. Took a deep breath and stood.

"Come with me."

"Where to, Barbarian?"

"The pretty girl has a stew on."

"I like the sound of her voice. And I am always hungry. Partial to stew, even if it's a pretty girl in the mix."

"Then you're going to tell me everything that's happened. Every time."

"You believe me?" asked the old blind man who was once something else. Something brave. Something noble.

Again, Thor grunted. "I do, Spartan. Let's see if we can change things around this time. Perhaps we can go all the way."

The blind old Spartan was silent for a long moment.

Finally, as if wanting to believe in something he wasn't ready to, he murmured, "Hold what you got, Airborne," trying for a moment to stand as tall as he once did.

CHAPTER THIRTY-TWO

IT WAS ANOTHER TWO DAYS BEFORE THEY HAD their first battle against the pyrohydra that guarded the narrow canyon pass leading to the tower where the gate to another plane waited for the fated Spartans to try their hand against the fire giants beyond its thin quivering glass-like barrier.

Marching now with First Platoon, the Panthers as they called themselves, Thor was able to observe and blend into their ways and ranks, working among them. Yes, the Panthers led by Sergeant Craius of Towle, or Cray the Crawler as he was called by the rest of the Spartans, were Spartans, but the Panthers were exceptional scouts and they ranged fast and far ahead of the main body winding its way through the canyons to reach the Plain of Burning Glass at the bottom of the Rift, and the passage they sought through the Tower of Fire and Air.

Here the air was hot, and still, and there was some gray lifeless death in it that could not be named or felt even as they closed for contact with the mythical multi-headed beast.

And there was...

... some strange lingering *hummmmm* of live and wild energy, electricity, barely there like some twisting ethereal note of madness from some bad sci-fi episode of some terribly cheap show about lost places from which no one ever returned.

You could feel it, but you just couldn't put your finger on it.

The whole plain was unsettling, but Sergeant Cray and his men ranged forward through its stinking salt flats and sulfurous lakes, communicating by hand signals, even tapping the ground with sticks just as the Rangers would have ten thousand years ago.

The sounds were easily detected in the vast silences at the bottom of the plain.

Thor added nothing to their tutelage and instead focused on understanding their ways as he ranged forward with them, staying near Sergeant Cray and getting his chi straight with their method of communication, and their way in which they worked.

The first obstacle they came to that demonstrated their formidable abilities was a narrow field between great tumbled red rocks full of death vines. The forward scouts alerted Sergeant Cray, and the small yet barrel-chested Spartan whispered to Thor, "Come see this. We found more of the killer weeds. Very dangerous. But not for Panthers."

Then the man grunted and laughed and hustled forward without a sound, his massive pack and armor betraying nothing in the deathly silence beyond the stinking pools of yellow water. Neither did his sandals seem to make any sound, and so was the way for the rest of the Panthers who wore standard Spartan gear, but instead of the red-and-blue-dyed horsehair plume of the other units, the scouts had gathered dead hiss-grass, a waving feathery bush that grew in abundance deep down in the crushing heat of the basin, and had woven it into their gear and into the catch atop their classical helmets.

It was effective camouflage, and many was the time the Ranger had needed to scan an area twice, especially if the Spartan scouts were hunkered and not moving. The camo of their armor and their skills made them all but undetectable under visual scan.

Movement, fast movement, betrayed them. But the sniper could find them with some careful scrutiny, for those were some of his best skills.

Target identification.

Still, their scout game was tight. And they ran it well under the constant direction and silent vigilance of their tough and hearty NCO who'd immediately enjoyed letting the strange barbarian among them observe the prowess of his trained and highly skilled men.

His Panthers.

It was midday, and Sato and Alluria were back with the main body, ready to come forward and interface with Thor should Devil Six need him. Thor had asked to range with each platoon for a time so he could adapt to their ways.

There were three platoons.

Falcons. Devils. Panthers. Some additional specialty units.

The Headhunters and the Troll Cutters were flankers and specialized platoons. The Werewolves were sappers. And then... there were the All-Americans.

The Spartans just said "Allamericans."

Even at first glance Thor had recognized the heavy hitters that the Allamericans were. They were clearly the best of the best. Each was a brute and a killer, and they were loaded with weapons, larger shields, heavier packs, fearsome spears, each with a battle-axe strapped across their pack and a wicked gladius that was thicker, longer but not by much, than the standard.

It was clear they were the anchor of the Spartan line and to stand and face them was to court death itself. They neither smiled nor talked, and their armor was highly polished as though it was their intention to draw all enemies to them so those enemies might die against their impressive round shields and under their heavy blades.

The shields were stamped with images of the ancient 82nd patch, but also adorned with fearsome tigers with huge fangs and claws.

Thor could understand why, according to Socrat the blind Spartan, many enemies had simply turned and fled the field of battle to avoid going up against the premier killers of the legendary Karthian Spartans.

"Deathweed!" hissed Sergeant Cray and spit off into the dust as Thor studied the boulder-strewn field that descended lower and lower into the sulfurous miasma the Rift was becoming by the hour.

The rock here was a bloody red, climbing and stacked all up along the low canyon walls that now seemed to disappear into the hanging and fetid air.

Throughout the broken field of death, along the length of the vines, long desiccated into little more than husks and crawling across and around the tumbled rocks, were what at first appeared to be small dried-out gourds. As the Ranger studied these, trying to guess first why the Spartan scouts called these vines a "deathweed" and then why they considered them dangerous...

He realized the "gourds" were not gourds at all... but tiny heads.

Tiny shrunken heads with malevolent dead eyes and razor-sharp fangs in slit-lipped mouths.

Nightmare fuel.

"Deathweed," smiled the Spartan NCO and laughed a little once Thor understood the danger.

"Very bad, those," muttered Cray the Crawler. "But not the real danger here. There's a giant mouth in the center of the field... it casts an illusion of magic to cover itself. Once one of us goes in there, the hungry little bastards will drag you to the mouth while the heads tear you to shreds to get what they can of the meat they can make from your bones."

The Spartan nodded grimly.

"Fire?" asked the Ranger.

The Spartan shook his head.

"We tried fire when we came to these fields. The vines with heads will go deep in the dirt and the heads will scream and we think that is some kind of magic that makes the hearing go bad and the head mad. And the fire does nothing to the mouth, as it is buried deep and will surface only to feed."

"Go around?" asked Thor when the smiling NCO stopped his explanation and watched Thor work the process, he and his having already done the math for previous deathweed fields throughout the wastes.

"Best solution, Barbarian. But these creatures cluster and know the trails to lay their traps along. My Panthers have already scouted some goat trails along the high cliffs, but it is a surety that more of these monsters have made their nests there so that time and need of food and water would make one foolish enough to try combat by fire or hack and slash against them. Looksee... the bones strewn about the field. Not all are lost goats. See those broken weapons there in the dust. There is probably much treasure buried deep here, and were we adventurers there would probably be a prince's hoard here underneath the bloody sands. But we are not such weak men. We are Spartans, and we answer a call to a debt we must pay. Time is of the essence."

"So what do you do then?" asked the Ranger bluntly, for such is the way of Rangers.

Cray smiled.

"Poison."

CHAPTER THIRTY-THREE

THE BEST SPARTAN STRIPPED DOWN TO HIS sandals and leather kilt and carried the carcass of a bloody goat wrapped in dried hides and packed in hiss-grass. Around his waist the Spartans had tied a knotted rope that reminded Thor, amazingly, of some Bronze Age version of paracord.

The Spartans even braided it just as bored soldiers and skilled operators had done since its introduction into the military repertoire of tactical equipment, knotting it back over itself four times so the length was shortened and could be unraveled with ease and skill.

It wasn't five-fifty, but it was silky and good, and the Panthers were proud of it and treated it like gold.

One of the scouts, Macamo, noted to Thor as he formed the anchor team of his fellow scouts, "Our wives back at the

Karthian fortress make the holy cord for us, and they make it well, for they know our lives often depend on it greatly."

Timothy, who every one of the Panthers called "Wildcat," was satisfied and tied off securely to the anchor team. The scent of the bloody fresh-killed goat shot by another Spartan with a hunting bow was safe from detection. The young Spartan kicked loose of his marching sandals and squared off against the field of death.

The Ranger watched as the kid took three deep breaths rapidly and then at the last... slowed his breathing, letting the air go slowly until it was literally barely more than an audible sigh on the dry desert dead air.

And then... he took a soft step into the deathweed field.

For the next half an hour, slowly, the young Spartan made his way to the center of the field, which was not more than one hundred meters distant.

But the one the Panthers called Wildcat had to move slowly, very slowly in fact, to not disturb any of the vines or the sleeping tiny demonic gourd heads that seemed to open their horrible fanged mouths wide in noontime slumber, and then suddenly gnash their teeth in some brutally pleasant dream of bloodshed and rending of the kill.

Their soft growls could be heard across the field in the silence of the afternoon heat. Beyond this the sulfur pools hissed and burped.

"The deathweed slumbers during the day, and that is fortunate for us that we found it then. At night it creeps away from the head, and hunts, Barbarian... and it is especially active under a full moon."

Wildcat dropped the stuffed poison goat and once more made his way, just as slowly, out of the field.

Once he was out, one of the Spartans expertly fired an arrow into a goat bladder of blood left on the outside of the bound hide-covered goat. Instantly, as the blood soaked into the hungry dry sands, the vines all around began to writhe and growl fiercely, muttering like small, tiny, violent predators.

Soon the goat was dragged into the gaping hideous mouth at the center of the field, and within an hour the plant began to vomit grotesquely, convulsing and heaving up the slowly devoured rotting dead within its bloated and deep buried stomach.

Putrefying bodies and rotting body parts came shooting out like hurl-spray as the demonic plant writhed and rustled, hushing on some loud and wretched note as it met its end.

It died quickly, but it died and that was the important part.

Then the tiny heads began to curl and writhe, tendrilling themselves toward one another and... ripping each other to shreds in a hideous feeding frenzy that defied belief.

When all was finally quiet after the gruesome self-feeding-frenzy implosion of the hellish deathweed field, Sergeant Cray smiled at Sergeant Thor and said, "The way is clear, Barbarian. Now we approach the Lake of the Hydra."

CHAPTER THIRTY-FOUR

Before the devlish weed-thing in the desert on the way to the Tower of Flame and Air... back at the Well of Azzim.

"Tell me..." said Sergeant Thor, embracing the fantasy. Doing his best to extract every bit of intel he could from the scarred and old Spartan who followed the hunting pack, doing his best to make them believe they marched toward their fate, carrying their baggage, and their memories, even as they did so.

Hearing Kennedy's admonitions...

The smaj's warnings...

"Tell me," Sergeant Thor asked that blind old Spartan whose ruined voice was like a broken screen door on a hot windy day somewhere in the badlands of the Texas that was long ago. "Tell me how it usually goes with this... temple in the lake?"

Embrace, the voice in his Ranger mind whispered. *The fantasy.*

The old Spartan was squatting in the dirt, working at the rations Thor shared with him after their initial conversation at the well, after the game of violent brutality the sky soldiers of the 82nd had once called pushball.

"We generally do well there," began the old Spartan. "Remember... everything I'm telling you, Ranger, comes either by my hearing, or secondhand from the survivors who make it past that giant seven-headed beast."

The old man spit out some of the MRE and made a face at something he'd chewed, then thought better of what he'd experienced and ate some more because he was hungry, and more was needed for the long miles ahead. And whatever dangers came with that march.

Standard with MREs, thought Thor as he watched the man.

He'd enjoyed the cake.

The old man had asked if there was more of that.

There wasn't.

"Usually, I stay back with the gear near the old guard towers beside the stinking cesspool lake of burning glass. But I know the orders we're under and the call of the march and them sergeants a'barkin' the way we used to do when we're headed into contact on the line. In other words…"

The ruined old Spartan rubbed the grey growth on his scarred chin.

"It's a straight-up attack, Ranger. If we make it down the causeway to the old tumbling temple at the center of that smelly burning lake, then all we gotta do is survive the wicked beast. 'Cept that's where… almost every time… we lose half our number. Ain't no joke about that thing. Seven heads and each a mind of its own. Each one has powers of fire and flame winds."

The old man was silent for a long moment.

"They worship that thing. Whatever the hell it really is. The bugbears that live in their muddy little villages all along the edge and stretching out into that nothing waste that's the bottom of the Rift we've marched into to meet our deaths."

"What's a bugbear?" asked the Ranger.

The old man rubbed his jaw again and thought hard for a second.

"Kind of a… large goblin. Bullies really, on account of their size among most goblin kind. We ran into raiding parties of them coming into Skelos during the wars there. These… these are… *different*. You usually find them other kinds in forests or deep down in dark dungeons and the Underroad places. So it's not more than a little passin' strange you find these kind here in the desert, raiding from the putrid lake and... protecting that damned *Daímones the Mad*. That's the name of the pyrohydra. It's a powerful thing even among its own kind and is said to have come up from the Temple of Ancient Dark, lost somewhere deep in the Rift."

The blind old Spartan snorted at this.

"If you believe them old scare-tales..."

"How does the battle go... normally?" The Ranger didn't need myths and half-truths. He needed to figure out how to kill this thing, and actual experience was far better to get that done than whispers and rumors that couldn't be confirmed.

"Well, if we have our man Ajack... then we usually win. I won't lie to you, our commander's not... a tactical genius when it comes to planning. Straight in and start chopping even though he don't look like it. Man can swing a blade and he's good in running a battle line and taking his place anywhere on it. He's a good fighter too, and like I said he manages the battle well. It's Ajack who often takes the daring and initiative... makes a good plan or pull a trick. But now he's dead on this run... so..."

The old Spartan shrugged. He'd been here before. With Ajack. Without. It was just the way of things.

"And if he's with you?" prompted Thor. He needed to understand what had worked in times past even if they'd lost a lot of men or gotten killed farther down the trail of their quest.

"Well now, Ajack... he's tried some daring moves a time or two... and even survived sometimes. Those usually ended in more casualties, though there was this one time we got real lucky and we had less. Less than usual anyway. But generally, Ajack leads an attack straight up the main causeway for the temple, and as long as we can keep the bugbears from cutting us off with their rafts and dragon boats as they attack from the sides of the lake... then we make the temple and fight the beast, sword against claw and fire. Now, here's a thing you may not know yet... about us..."

The old Spartan smiled wickedly and leaned close to Thor.

"Spartan shields is resistant to fire. Prayers our women offer for us make 'em so. As long as we maintain formation... fireballs of Daímones can't touch us more than singe and a bad sunburn. Then we close and stab that huge thing to the death with our spears, and once a head goes down, the sergeants lead the way in with the gladius to get the head severed off good and proper, and that's one more thing we... uh... the boys don't have to deal with. Damn. Sometimes I'm there I wish it so hard.

"Like I said... on a good run we lose half there in the lake. Which... when you consider what comes next... our march against the folk at the high tower on the lonely hill farther down in the bowl, and then through to the Plane of Fire itself and the ambush of the fire giants, imps, and hounds of hell... ain't good odds when so many have already been cut down. Maybe if we had more, we could make it at the Gates of the City of Brass..."

The old man sighed in the desert heat and Thor gave him some water to drink. He smacked his lips and coughed. Then continued.

"And that's a funny thing... you'd think we get some kind of... *jump*... on the jump. But we don't. Soon as we come through that gate at the base of the tower to the Plane of Fire... Repham and his giants are all over us with their flaming swords and hell bows. Now listen, Ranger... a giant, on a good day, is a bastard of a thing to slay dead. These Repham's boys are straight-up hell on wheels, Ranger, to kill. And only half surviving the attack on the pyrohydra up the causeway and making it to the tower, much less the gate and the Plane of Fire, is... as we used to say... standards."

The Spartan sighed and seemed to squeeze the ruin where his eyes once were. As though wishing for something and unwilling and lacking the faith to name it. But still wanting it all the same.

"Real problem is the damn bugbears. That's what starts the whole downward spiral off on the wrong sandal. If you know what I mean."

"How so?" asked Sergeant Thor.

"Well, like I said... they have several camps around that stinking yellow lake. It's a big foul-smelling mess of a sour lake at the bottom of the world, and why anyone would build a great white marble causeway, and then some old temple in the middle of it... don't know. Musta been a lost civilization of giants from ancient times. It's creepy... when you hear it told to you by the other boys. But you'll see it, 'cause you still got eyes."

"The bugbears," prompted the Ranger, getting the old man back on track and developing the intel on actual tangos in the area of operation.

Or...

The bad guys that needed to die in order to push forward with all players operational.

"Oh, yeah..." said the old man. "See, best I can hear, the boys have trouble makin' it up that causeway because they're under some serious fire from the dragon boats the bugbears use. Poisoned barbed javelins. Once they've lobbed their attacks, the buggers 'board,' as it were, the causeway from both sides, and... their attacks are pretty well coordinated, and you have to be honest about that. That pyrohydra they call a god seems to control them like some field commander that can message their fevered little minds. They hit that causeway from both sides supported by indirect fire... then... and that's the problem I go on and on about but everyone thinks I'm crazy because I'm talking about events ain't happened yet like they've already happened."

The old Spartan stopped.

"You know... the young never listen to one who's been there... done that. I wish it weren't that way, Ranger. But it is. I could save 'em... but they just see me, each time, as old drunk Socrats, the NCO who lost his eyes to a harpy and now's gone cray. A ruined man they're never gonna end up like. Old. Like that's a thing that never happens to you when you're young and strong. I wish I could tell 'em it gets us all and that there's something to still being alive, and old, in the war game. But..."

He harrumphed to himself as though reaching some bitter conclusion. Again.

"The problem on the causeway for us is when them fronts of the buggers hit our flanks as we move to contact on the hydra, we pivot and hold the line with our shields. Shouldn't be a problem. 'Cept them bastards use morning stars. Spiked ball and chain on a stick. Hook those over our shields, get a bunch of 'em pulling, and the shield goes down and the line doesn't hold integrity. Then they come in swingin' and cuttin'.

"See... Ranger... problem ain't the pyrohydra... its fire attacks ain't much against our shields. Still... thing's deadly up close all fire heads and claws and teeth... hissing steam and breathing fire... it's like fighting hell itself. Or that's what the ones who survive say. See, the real problem is if we lose our shield wall going in... then the fireballs of that wretched beast cook us alive. And the bugbears are good at getting our shields away from us and once they do, we still gotta push up the causeway across a stinking lake that will practically boil you alive. That Daímones can get in the water, under the temple pool, and start to hit the causeway and the temple ruins from all sides with different heads. On a good day... it's an ambush you know you gotta walk into. On a bad day... and that's happened a few times... everyone dies, and the bugbears come for the baggage train. Which is where I get hacked to death. Ain't pretty and I still got nightmares even though it's a new time through. I tell 'em that's why I drink. They laugh 'cause it ain't happened yet. Truth is... I just like to drink. Gotta be honest about these things as NCOs say for all times since the Before, and probably will still if we ever find out what's on all those other worlds the wizards say are around them stars in the night."

Thor was silent for a long moment.

"You don't run off into the desert when that happens? When all is lost? When everyone's dead?"

The Spartan stared sightlessly at where Sergeant Thor was speaking from.

Then...

"Never. We're brothers. We live together. We die that way. You know that, Ranger. I've heard everyone dead and dying... and *you* still swinging and roaring."

He looked at the Ranger with sightless eyes.

"And then you're dead too."

CHAPTER THIRTY-FIVE

In the darkness before dawn the little bands of Spartans, just as their predecessors had done to the German Army so long ago, spread out among the villages along the hot steaming lake that smelled of rotten eggs and lurking death.

Working in killing teams, the bands of Spartans slit the throats of the few sentries the bugbear chieftains had thought to put out on the eve of the coming slaughter along the causeway and meaty sacrificial fire to Daímones the Mad.

The giant seven-headed behemoth had been whispering to the shamans in their trances. Battle was coming. *Defend your god. Bring me their flesh.*

In the dark before dawn the Spartans ranged out among the villages, making their mayhem. Causing their mischief.

This was the Ranger's plan, and it was the words of that long-lost fear-riddled German officer who'd put it into Thor's mind to suggest this plan of action to the commander of the Spartans.

Attack before the attack.

And as the old man had said, in the past various outcomes of *Groundhog Day* Ruin-style, past runs the Spartans had made against the pyrohydra in its lake-center ruined temple, high numbers of the bugbears and their coordinated attacks had started things off badly for the attacking Spartan force.

Two things were certain.

The causeway had to be crossed by the Spartans in all previous "run-throughs."

There was no getting around that.

The sides of the lake were swarming with bugbear tribes under an alliance led by some great chieftain named Gulgumag Bone-Cruncher.

According to the blind Spartan, any attempt by the Spartans to skirt the lake met in getting surrounded and destroyed even if they managed to get a fighting fort up. The bugbears could call more numbers from out in the deeper desert there at the bottom of the Ruin, and other and more hideous foes promised a good feeding.

The water in the lake was undrinkable and the enemy easily numbered in the thousands, so swimming the lake, or making rafts, or going around... was impossible.

It was either up the causeway and through the pyrohydra's temple... or turn around and go home.

The Spartans had given their word. They would march and die. They would never turn back.

If they did, according to the old man, "Then we would not be us."

So, in formation and fighting the bugbears, the large goblinoids hitting them from their dragon boats on the lake, and massing forward along the causeway as the spear-chucking buggers "boarded" the ruined roadway along the unit's flanks up the giant white marble causeway through the water that lay before the giant sculpted temple in the lake, was the only way to go.

As Socrats stated... the Spartans usually lost half their number in just getting to the raging pyrohydra that hid within the temple pool at the center of the stinking lake. Four platoons of Spartans and a witch with little more than prophecy and supposed battle charms stood little chance against the kinds of heavy numbers the bugbears could bring to bear, surrounded and defending a fixed position.

"And who knows, Ranger," sighed the old man. "Perhaps that's why we fare so badly against them diabolical winged folk farther down the plain, and them fire giants the other side of the gate to the Plane of Fire. I've heard fifty men make it to relieve the efreeti queen at the gates to the City of Brass.

Ain't much. They always die before they can make the entrance... which... they say is something really ... fantastic."

"Why is it... *fantastic*?" asked the Ranger.

"Don't know. Ain't never seen it. Got no eyes. But those that survive seem real amazed by it before the djinn berserkers led by Repham hit them and wipe them out every time we make it that far." He paused. Cocked his head. "If... we make it this time... can you describe it to me before you get killed, Ranger? Or better yet... the fancy girl who got it real bad for you... I can hear it in her voice, Ranger. You know that, right? She wants you for her man? Somethin' else in her voice, too... she got a problem that's bigger than her. But I bet she's real pretty. Get her to whisper in my ear all seductive-like how beautiful them gates are. That'd be like bein' with a woman one more time to this old sergeant."

The old man laughed riotously.

Thor ignored the blind Spartan's observations and pushed on for other details about what they would face along the way to the mission's objective.

Every item, every detail, nothing was too small... everything was critical to the mission. If they were going to make it.

If they were going to survive.

The blind Spartan recalled everything he could, and it took time to do so. But the man seemed to sense that maybe this time... maybe this time things could be different despite so many endless slaughters that had come before... and so the ruined Spartan pushed himself and for that Thor gave him credit.

"If I could, Ranger..." the old man said later. "I'd swing a sword even blind and ruined like I am to get them outta this. I would, Ranger, I would. But... I'm blind and they won't listen to me, like there's some magic that's been spelled on them to just ignore me and march off to die no matter what I say. Or do. Sometimes I think it's that witch that's done this to me. To us. The vixen that sounds real pretty like a good whore that's always near the Six. Curse that witch. She's nothin' but trouble."

The Spartan spit.

"Curse that witch," he whispered again.

Then...

"But if we make it to the City of Brass... tell me what it looks like, Ranger. It sounds... incredible. I wanna... *see* it. Even if it's just words."

Thor grunted, studying the sand beneath his boots, and seeing all the enemies that lay in his way and how he would kill them now.

"We'll make it, old man. And yeah... I'll tell you what it looks like. But don't be surprised if it's not just some city that looks like every other city I've ever seen."

The old man made a face at this. But it was hard to tell what he meant by it.

The second thing that stood in the Spartans' way was the beast of the pyrohydra itself. Seven heads all spitting fire. The Spartans, even decimated significantly in the crossing under fire of the causeway, tended to do well against the beast. Their shields were magicked against fire, or fire resistant to some magical degree, and their tactics and movement to combat were effective in dealing with the snarling, fire-breathing horror. Even though they suffered casualties, they often made it through and got to the other side of the strange lake.

Once they made it to the other side, it was a straight run down the descending plain with little opposition until they came to a large hill, or small mountain, on which someone had built a tower and a fortified courtyard.

Inside the yard was a pool.

Except it wasn't a pool... it was a gate to another plane of existence. Apparently.

Embrace the fantasy, Thor reminded himself. But...

... that was a tomorrow plan.

So, in the march toward the lake, as the bugbear harassers came out to skirmish against the marching Spartans, hurling their barbed javelins and then running off into the barren desert, cackling and calling their hooting war cries to one another, the Ranger had gone to the commander of the Spartans, Devil Six, with his plan for how to survive the lake.

The commander agreed with the proposed plan after a long silence of studying his maps, seeing the sense in the Ranger's logic, and then tasking him with initiating the plan.

The first sergeant was none too happy, at first. It was as though the first sergeant's angry rage-driven brain for all things *Dress Right Dress* and *Spartan* suddenly skidded to a halt on the highway of danger and discipline he operated along. But he warmed up to the mayhem Sergeant Thor had in mind after the plan to split skulls, slit throats, and burn bugbear villages to the ground, had been laid out on a rude, boot-scratched sand table of the area.

Mayhem and murder in simple boot-drag arrows. Simple, eloquent, and utterly lethal.

The first sergeant pointed a steady finger at Thor and hissed… "You son of a whore dog. I'm in."

The march toward the lake continued even as more mobs of bugbears came out to scout and harass.

On the hot boiling afternoon they arrived on the low hill overlooking the steaming miasma of the battleground that was the lake, and the hazy temple at its center, the Spartans immediately digging in like they were building a fort to stay for a while.

Socrats had indicated when the Spartans had done this on run-throughs before, it took about three days for Googlemag, or whatever his name was, to get the local tribal chieftains worked up enough to conduct a frontal attack on the Spartan defenses.

The results were always catastrophic initially, for the bugbears.

They were innate cowards.

But... they had the numbers, and once they figured out they could surround the Spartans and attack from all sides, time and casualties began to tell. Cracks appeared, and troopers were dragged back bloody from the line as the shield walls began to collapse, and then... in the end they simply got overrun by sheer numbers and slaughtered to the last man.

The bugbears's god had the cowards more afraid of failing it than dying on Spartan spears.

"It's bad, Ranger," muttered the ragged-voiced old Spartan when he told of the slaughters that had happened before when this course of action had been undertaken.

Then Thor asked a question he had not intended to ask.

He didn't factor... *magic*... into his plans, usually, and so it was odd the question should occur in his brooding mind as he pondered the tactical situation. But he asked it anyway.

One commander had said during an op order...

"There are no stupid questions, men. Just stupid outcomes. Questions eliminate the stupid. Hopefully. So, ask 'em."

Sergeant Thor asked.

"What about the sorceress... Scylla?"

The redhead who hovered near the Spartan commander at all times and who eyed Thor like a meal she was looking forward to.

At one point she and Alluria had gotten into a shoving match, and Alluria had pushed the witch into a stand of stacked spears. The Spartans who'd been enjoying the developing catfight had to rush in to prevent the murder that was imminent. Both women were dragged away from the other's sight uttering promises and oaths at one another.

The Spartans made cat noises and laughed. But the mood after that was definitely ominous when either woman was around.

"What about her?" said the Old Man. "She's a witch. That's all. Armies of Skeletos always have a witch with them."

"She ever die... when you get surrounded in that fort... or you're with the baggage? You hear everyone die. That right? What about her?"

The Spartan made a face, lowered his head, and rubbed the place where his eyes used to be.

"Yeah. I do. I hear all of them die... but..."

He was silent for a long moment.

Then...

"I guess... come to think of it... no. Ain't never heard her screaming when the rest of us are getting cut up and stabbed and them bastard goblins are gibbering and yipping like monkeys in a madhouse."

More silence. Heavier.

"Now… that's strange, Ranger. Real strange. Never thought about it. And that… that's strange too."

So, they had three days until Goolymuffin got his act together and attacked in force.

Or whatever his name was.

By darkness the day the Spartans had arrived, the fort was up, the walls of thrown dirt formed, the spears jutting, the pennants flapping, the watch set. They were dug in and there for the long stay.

Three days.

Or so it was supposed to appear as such.

Instead, in the black darkness before dawn the very next morning, little bands of Spartans, just as their predecessors had done to the German Army so long ago, *devils in baggy pants*, but this time in leather kilts and armor, spread out among the villages along the hot steaming lake that smelled of bad eggs and death even in the hours before dawn… and began their attack.

Working in killing teams, they slit throats and torched huts. They burned boats and poisoned wells.

By dawn they had formed up into platoons and were on the march down from the fort for the causeway.

Out there across the lake, black smoke from a dozen burning villages boiled hard and rolled across the putrid surface. It looked like some dark and hopeless vision of hell, and the descendants of the 82nd Airborne had done it.

They'd done what they do best.

They'd broken up into teams and ruined the enemy while he was sleeping, deceived that he was safe, breaking stuff where they could find it. Slitting throats where they could. Spreading terror and chaos and then suddenly vanishing back and forming up for the real attack.

In some villages, the dragon boats had survived. In others, everything had burned to the waterline. All was confusion along the charred shores. Bears lay slaughtered, or in chaos and disarray raced about the flames, screaming like mad monkeys and sounding horned alarms that echoed direly out across the apocalyptic lake.

And now... the shining and orderly Spartans in their battle lines sounded their own horns and marched down to the white ancient marble causeway to give battle against Daímones the Mad at the ruined temple at the center of the stinking lake.

A beast of ancient fables made its lair in that fallen cyclopean place.

The Spartans would go there... and kill it.

Out there within the strange fallen marble slabs of the temple, Daímones's seven heads roared weirdly and titanically as the dawn rose and black smoke built and boiled forth.

And the Spartans, like some glittering snake, entered the causeway even as dragon boats full of bugbears pushed away from the distant shore.

Sergeant Thor, in a captured dragon boat with Alluria and the blind Spartan, pulled hard at the two oars, rowing at an asymmetrical angle for the temple in the center of the lake. The blind Spartan coughed as they passed through a bank of drifting black smoke, then smiled, a pack with strapped Carl Gustaf rounds heavy on his back. Alluria was in the prow, crouched behind the carved dragon there with her bow and an arrow ready, eyeing the way through the waters ahead.

Thor studied their approach to the island of collapsed megalithic cut marble that was the temple at the center, sighting the distance and where he wanted to land the craft.

The old, ruined Spartan spoke against the draft of the oars.

"It is good to be going into battle again, Ranger." Then his voice went dry and hoarse as the smoke, or something else, caused him to choke suddenly.

He wiped at the scars where his eyes once were.

"If we die today, Ranger... then this is how I want to die. Fighting. Every sky soldier would have it that way. Airborne, Ranger. Thank you for this."

The thin old man hefted the pack, hiking it up his scrawny hunched back, shouldering it proudly as though it were the most important gear in the world.

"Airborne, old man. Airborne," grunted Sergeant Thor at the oars, pulling for the imminent *Ranger Smash!* he had in mind for the pyrohydra they had to get past.

CHAPTER THIRTY-SIX

The spartan line smashed through the first waves of boarding bugbears who'd come out ragtag in their dragon boats to give battle against the Spartans along the causeway.

In this, the Ranger had also had a hand in the planning, organization, and assault tactics. The command team of the Spartans, mainly Devil Six, the first sergeant, and a particular few especially hard-bitten sword swingers acting in chief NCO positions, had liked what they heard and contributed their nuances, expertise, and insight to the final plan of attack.

With the Allamericans protecting the flanks—these were the Spartan heavy hitters—the main body of the Spartan platoons, Falcons, Panthers, and the Devils in support of the two forward platoons, hacked and slaughtered their way forward up the badly defended white marble causeway.

The bugbears were in total disarray from the surprise attack before dawn and were having trouble massing their numbers and coordinating their attacks against the Spartans on the march.

Many of the past runs, according to Socrats the blind Spartan, had involved putting the Allamericans forward, as they were the most heavily armed and armored.

And the deadliest in the pure straight-up brawl that was Bronze Age combat.

It was said that one of them was worth ten Spartans, and they really were hulking huge brutes who had achieved the perfection of the male combat warrior. They swung their blades fast, hit hard, and in trade it had to be a pretty good blow to get past their huge shields, which they handled easily and effortlessly with their massive brawny arms, or the armor itself which was thicker and covered more of the stone-cold killers' bodies.

This, according to Socrats, had always, "seemed like a good plan."

"Ever try putting the big guys on the flanks?" asked Thor.

The old man scratched his head. "Yup. Coupla times. That's always Max's position. 'Cept when we do... the crafty goblin bastards come in with their morning stars by the boatload and hook the ball and chain over the shield and then ten of them little demons get on the chain and pull for all they're worth. Then the Allamerican goes right over and into the lake and never mind the practically boiling poison waters... that takes him right to the bottom and as we say on the line... *he dead*."

Thor was quiet, thinking about the problem this presented.

Then...

"Corporal Max... what's the deal there?" he asked.

The blind Spartan ran his scarred old hand down his face and shook his head gently, sighing.

"Ain't time for that now, Ranger. Another story, another time."

Sergeant Thor let it go and continued on with the planning.

In the end they decided to put the heavy hitters on the flanks. Broken into two groups they could handle the action now that the bugbear attack had been disrupted. Many of the villages along the shore were still burning well into mid-morning even as the Spartans continued fighting their way up the marble white causeway.

These "villages" were little more than mud huts and desert bush constructions, and so the flames had spread quickly and greedily, reaching down to where the prized dragon boats were brought ashore when not in use. In these the hardest-struck villages, the tribal warriors were stranded on shore, their boats burning and their villages on fire. They had failed to answer their war chieftain's horned calls when it came to sally forth and defend their god the pyrohydra.

But in other villages the boats had been salvaged, or the village not struck at all due to Spartan considerations of distance and speed and time, and in addition a sizeable number of bugbears had boarded the head chieftain's massive war raft, and that strange vessel was now making its best speed to reach the pell-mell and very one-sided combat now going on along the causeway.

Sergeant Thor's answer to protecting the heavy-hitting Allamericans as they kept the bugbears from boarding right into the Spartan flanks, was to use the scouts and their amazing "five-fifty cord" to keep hold of the bruisers on reinforced drag handles the Ranger had instructed the Spartans make. Now the teams of scouts worked, and the massing goblinoid bullies that were the fierce and yammering bugbears could no longer drag the heavily armored Spartans down into the rotten waters of the lake, leaving the Allamericans on their spiked war sandals and fighting.

In short order, the now reduced and massively uncoordinated attacks of the bugbears failed against the Spartan flanks, and the main body continued to slaughter their way toward the temple at the center of the lake as the roaring multi-headed leviathan that was the pyrohydra began to surface from within the monument's sacred pool.

The battle was just underway, and from Sato's position near the front with Corporal Max, things seemed to be going their way already.

Then a new challenge revealed itself through the drifting black smoke and falling ash along the lake's surface.

The humongous war raft of Glimmerglub, the bugbears' chieftain, or whatever his name was, was on direct approach to slam right into the causeway just past the front line of the advancing Spartans.

Spartans shouted as javelin fire filled the air. The forward line reacted as did the other platoons, and the sudden rain of heavy missiles rebounded with loud clangs off the huge and heavy round Spartan shields.

A roaring cheer of derision went up against the bugbears approaching to reinforce and support the mass blocking the causeway ahead, already considerable. But to Sato it was clear that given their numbers, the fiends coming in on the chieftain's war raft, if they successfully boarded the causeway, would threaten the forward advance of the Spartans... and victory.

The crafty thief turned to Corporal Max.

"Spartan... the weapon the warrior gave you. Employ it now against the goliath of a war raft coming at us... or all may be soon lost."

Bugbears along the causeway yipped and gibbered like mad monkeys in their moment, sensing an impending change in the tides of battle. More of their kind were about to be alongside them and pushing into the outnumbered Spartans who were slaughtering forward at three-to-one odds.

Trampling the dead as they went.

Corporal Max grunted and dragged the slung M203 Sergeant Thor had bestowed on him around from his back to his chest. A grim look of both fear and determination in his cold, hard eyes.

Fear that he would not use this weapon right as he had been trained.

Determination that he would make his way through the slaughter ahead to put rounds into the looming war raft as its rowers slammed the water as fast and as furiously as they could while battle horns cried out alarm and the call to attack as one, in the bloody moments ahead.

All around them the combat and slaughter continued as man versus beast went on in unabated fury.

For this was... to the death.

And no quarter would be given.

CHAPTER THIRTY-SEVEN

EVEN WITH ALL THE RANGERS PLANNING ON hitting and fading, and the real *Ranger Smash!* that was coming, it was still a battle. And there are always unforeseen events in any battle.

That is battle's nature, after all. Life. Death. The chaos and utter strangeness that seems so attracted to life-and-death struggles.

Thor had trained the veteran Spartan corporal on how to use the M203, a variant of the standard M16 battle rifle with an underslung attached grenade launcher. A formidable and valuable infantry weapon that had survived the Cold War and made it all the way into the GWOT in some places. It was a solid weapon, and indirect fire in an intense gun battle was often the game-changer.

Ask any grunt who'd been in it a time or three.

Many older Rangers preferred the weapon to the modern equivalent M320 GLM grenade launcher, with its advanced features and specialized rounds for placing a launched fragmentary device just so.

The Air Force Forge technicians the Rangers back at the detachment had convinced to gin up the two-oh-three for Sergeant Thor's speedball had found a DARPA R&D dev model in the database that had been tested successfully to replace the "ancient," by some standards, tried-and-true small unit infantry indirect support weapon. Tested, tried, and true. But of course, some politician's buddy got the contract to make something else, something newer and totally un-battle-tested.

Neither the politician nor his buddy would be out there on the line, or at Khe Sahn, their lives depending on equipment to work in the most adverse of conditions and direst of circumstances.

That was the grunt's job. Let them bear the cost of development and lowest-bidder "military-grade weaponry." Only hack screenwriters in fantasyland thought that phrase meant something more than it did.

Before the M203, fighting soldiers in Vietnam had used the legendary M79. Solid weapon even pipe hitters in the here and now tried to get their hands on.

It had been, in fact, the smaj who'd been involved in initiating the speedball, the talk, the development, and the planning to get Sergeant Thor a resupply downrange and well beyond the wire. The smaj had initially considered sending the rogue Ranger an M79. It was easier to carry. Battle-tested and less likely to break down in that it wasn't that complex. But then some younger Ranger NCO had suggested the need for a primary battle rifle for CQB instead of the super SAW and definitely not the big-hitter M105A anti-materiel rifle Sergeant Thor carried.

Though Sergeant Thor had done CQB with all three weapon systems, a shorter battle rifle like the two-oh-three would definitely be optimized for tighter quarters and even... "dungeon crawling."

"'Cause that's a thing here in the Ruin, Sar'nt Major. Kennedy says so," perpetual PFC Tanner had offered out of the side of his skeletal face even though no one had asked for a seconding of the Ranger NCO's vote for the two-oh-three.

The advanced DARPA version they'd sent the Ranger in the speedball had some of the features of the three-twenty in range finding and sighting, digitally, and munitions selection. But it was still, at the end of the day, a solid rifle and launcher that worked and fired on iron sights if need be.

Those other "more advanced" features were too advanced for the Spartan anyway, Sergeant Thor had determined.

After putting the scarred and quiet veteran Spartan corporal through a basic rifle course using the primary rifle ballistically to engage with five-five-six fire—he spent some of his forty-millimeter rounds, and he had a lot in the magical Bag of Holding—and getting the Spartan to understand first the loading and operation of the grenade launcher, he then finally instructed in the employment... or *blooping*... of dropping rounds indirectly on fortified positions, or masses of troops to either destabilize an enemy attack ready to push on friendlies, or, as it often got used for... bunker-busting.

Blooping just meant aiming the rifle higher, guessing by the sights just how far out the grenade round would get launched, and then taking your best shot.

It wasn't so much science as it was feel.

The thief had been right there during primary instruction just as Thor wanted him to be. When they were done, Sergeant Thor put both through a small stalk and a series of sand table simulations for *when* and *why* to use the indirect fire feature of the M203.

Corporal Max had been spot-on after a few blooped rounds to get the hang of it, putting the fragmentation rounds exactly where they needed to go. He was, to the Ranger, a quick study, and sober about the whole thing.

The battle-scarred corporal gave a rare smile and laugh when the rounds exploded out there in the dirt.

Now, as the war raft came in and lines of Spartan and bugbear clashed forward along the bloody marble causeway, that training and those talks would come into play in the next few desperate seconds.

They'd known about the war raft via the scouts ranging ahead of the main body during the planning phase before their attack kicked off that morning. It was a massive snarling bugbear-laden hot mess of ropes and stolen wood and the remains of ancient ships that seemed impossible to be here so deep in the desert.

As though perhaps there had once been some great cataclysmic event that had brought the flotsam of wreckage here to this lonely lake at the bottom of the Ruin for the bugbears to make their rattletrap pirate ship.

The war raft had no weapons systems other than the constant spray of launched javelins from the bugbears manning its upper "towers." These were four ramshackle patchwork skeletons of badly made pyrohydra heads, painted and gaudy, from which bunches of the large goblins hurled javelin fire if they got close enough to their intended targets.

The raft, for all its fearsome bluster and fury, had, in past runs according to Socrats, been of little use and almost no effect against the advancing shield walls of the Spartans. It was always the smaller dragon boats making fast-rowed sallies in against the Spartan line-of-march flanks to hurl javelin fire before the Spartan archers, the very few of them there were.

Always, according to Socrats, "No matter how bad we fare, how wrong it goes, there's always loads o' bugbear bodies punctured by arrow fire and gutted by the boys up there on the line, then chucked off into the water. The survivors of the battle tell me that when I help with the wounded... reminding me that no matter how hard we got hit, we gave 'em back ten more. I like that, Ranger. I do. I'm that kinda man. Or I was... when I could fight on the line instead of..."

He trailed off muttering to himself, holding leathery hands out he could no longer see as though there should be a gladius in them.

So the immense and wonky war raft of Goolygoogoo the Indomitable, whatever, came screaming in all alone across the rotten waters of the lake, emerging from a bank of black boiling smoke, and this time barely supported by dragon boat fire. Its bugbears were shrieking bone war horns and hurling javelin fire like it was meat-on-the-street-grade diarrhea, when Sato directed Corporal Max to use the two-oh-three against it and shut down the reinforcements that monstrosity of a troop transport would soon provide against the Spartan front rank just ahead.

There were probably more than a thousand shrieking mad bugbears armed with morning stars and three javelins each, stacked and ready on its wide water-overrun sinking deck even as the goliath of a raft plowed forward under badly run oars.

The bugbear warriors sang some horrible chanting battle song only understood in their mad monkey gibbering language, but that it was a song and that there were words was clear. They stamped their claws and readied themselves to reinforce their barely holding line as the Spartan Falcons and Panthers slaughtered forward, hacking and slashing in every direction, relieved in their advancing shield walls by replacements from the Devils bringing up the rear, stabbing and stomping those not totally dead yet that had fallen anyway. The Allamericans were slicing at the few dragon boats and their troops stupid enough to attempt to attack the flanks further back. They raised their massive, heavy shields and blocked almost all incoming javelin fire.

Just at that moment, as Corporal Max pushed forward, there was a loud roar from the leviathan within the temple.

The pyrohydra was coming out to join the battle.

A solid *Whump* and *Crack* followed this war cry of the beast, splitting the air and making it feel alive and heavy with sudden pressure in the suffocating heat and gassy miasma that was the swamp rottenness of the lake.

Shield-blocking Spartans, bloody marble, the wounded being dragged back from the line, javelin fire increasing by the second as the battle reached its fevered pitch, the barbed missiles slamming into everything, all this faced the corporal as he shouldered his way through the armed press to get close enough, and gain enough of a picture to drop rounds on the incoming war raft before it could wreck all their plans.

Sato pushed forward past the corporal, both small curved razor-sharp blades coming out from within the folds of his loose shirt as he made ready to work.

"Make way!" shouted the thief in a martial tone as he reached the foremost of the Spartan lines where bugbears were being hacked to death in mass quantities, though even more were surging in to take up the slack.

Off to Sato's right, Devil Six, the steadfast Spartan commander in his fine silver armor, red-and-blue cape torn and shredded, spattered with the blood of his men, and the enemies all about him, hewed and cut at the nasty creatures who dared get near enough him as they sought to drag him down and make a prize of him.

As though they knew that every time this battle happened was not the first time. And that they had always won. And that killing the Spartan war leader was somehow a goal...

They had the numbers.

The arms.

And their great multi-headed lizard god sending them messages, directing their attacks, bolstering their courage, and demanding they sacrifice their cowardice on the altar of Daímones the Mad this bloody stinking day.

The first sergeant and his two hatchet men were busy at the killing work as well. The hatchet men cutting down anything that got near the senior NCO. The barking raging first sergeant pushing more and more troops into the spots where Spartans had been downed and the line was thin.

Too thin.

Almost... non-existent.

Suddenly, the first sergeant would bark some fierce order for replacement, catch an incoming javelin with his shield, then deftly hand out a killing injury on some fast-moving bugbear that thought the ill-timed moment opportune to make a killing stroke. All as he shouted orders and encouraged his boys to earn their place in the memories of their fellow warriors this day no matter what happened.

It was pure chaos.

As all battles are.

And they would remember that day forever if somehow the loop of the harpy's curse and the weirdness of the Rift could be broken.

But the plan Thor had given them was still in effect. Sato needed to get as far forward as he could to direct the corporal's indirect fire in order to make sure that colossal hot mess that was the bugbear war raft failed to board the causeway in time to reinforce and support by fire.

Victory was near.

But it wasn't assured, even now...

Battles have a way of turning on a dime.

Ask the dead who didn't think they were gonna die the moment before they did.

The Spartans gave no quarter, expected none, and amid their ritualistic shouts of *All the Way... And Then Some*, hewing and hacking, cutting down and spearing, they laid waste in every direction along the marble highway through the hellish yellow lake, even as more and more of their enemies piled up, making it clear they would not abandon their chimera god this day.

Sato weaved and danced his fatal cuts... and bugbears began to die as arteries got slashed in the blink of an eye. The dying beasts suddenly turning away from the deadly thief, spraying their dark inky blood across foes and comrades and the yellow air. Guts splashed out onto the bloody white marble of the causeway as Sato got close to the edge where he needed to be, destroying all who dared oppose him, to get ready to direct fire on a Bronze Age war line of shield and sword and raging feral snarls of life and death.

The war raft was almost too close now, realized the thief grimly half a second later.

"Fire now!" he shouted raggedly above the clash and thunder of the battle, the dying and the angry screaming at one another. The mad battle raged and cared not, even as the fear of the innately cowardly bugbears caused them to ululate and moan in high battle cries that they would spend themselves here this day even though they did not like it.

The already dead said nothing.

Corporal Max dropped the first round, steadying the rifle, raising it high over the press of Spartans all around him and pulling the heavy trigger mounted at the rear of the underslung launcher.

Bloop.

The round sailed high and came down swiftly on the center of the raft, detonating and killing dozens of the hairy beasts in an instant.

The screaming pain and wild, animal fury was sudden.

And even so... the raft was still inbound.

A tower, damaged by the blast, collapsed across the water and blood-washed ruined-body deck, spilling bugbears down onto their brethren along the chaotic benches.

The next shot needed to be lower to hit the front of the raft and disable it, or sink it perhaps, thought Sato.

The thief observed the shot, turned, and made eye contact with the corporal who'd ceaselessly practiced the reloading operation, dropping the tube, dumping the spent shell, and inserting a new one taken from a bandolier they'd contrived and draped about his armor.

Sato made the agreed-upon gesture to drop the next shot closer, but not by much.

Wincing as he did.

He'd seen the weapon used during practice. This was, as Sergeant Thor had put it... *danger close.*

The corporal fired and the next round went long as the raft was still closing. It exploded in the water beyond the raft, sending up a plume of foul-smelling stinking spray, along with ruined bugbear bodies that had been dumped into the lake after the previous hit.

"Lower!" shouted Sato angrily, then, "Spartans... pull back and get behind your shields now!"

There was time for one more shot. One... last shot.

Expended round dumped.

New round in, sighted, the corporal fired at what he thought was a dangerously low angle...

The bugbears surged, swinging their heavy chains and spiked morning stars against the shields of the hunkering Spartans who'd gone into a defensive turtle in groups at the last second per Sato's shout. The round slammed into the bow of the shipwreck junkyard raft and ripped it to shreds with a dull explosion. Shattered wood and fast-moving shards shredded the bugbears on the main deck closest to the front as the blast directed out and away down the length of the rattletrap war barge.

A second later, fastening ropes that had joined the various shipwrecks together ripped through, and the raft broke in two right down the center, spilling the warriors and their incredulous warlord right into the hot poisonous depths of the simmering lake.

Bugbears screamed in terror and pain as some were scaled by underwater volcanic fissures that bubbled up from the bottoms while others tried to swim for the edge of the lake, or even the causeway.

Those that swam for the Spartan-held road through the stinking lake were cut down without mercy. Those who boarded forward of the Spartan position ran for the protection of their multi-headed lizard god.

The battle was over, here...

A moment later the pyrohydra's heads began to surface from the waters around the temple ahead of the main body of the Spartan line.

Devil Six raised his bloody gladius and pointed toward the emerging beast. "Form up and prepare to march into battle, Sky Soldiers! All the way!"

The massive leviathan and all its rearing heads roared deafeningly. The Spartan battle line, in an impossibly short amount of time, was formed and marching forward, spears out, the first sergeant shouting curses and insults to tighten the line and eliminate the gaps in the shield wall.

"Pull your heads outta yer fourth point of contact, boys! This is for all the marbles, Spartans! Ain't nothing to stop us!"

And then finally, as Sato made it behind the line, he heard the senior NCO mutter, "Courage now, boys! Show that thing why you're Spartans! Show the Ruin what it means!"

CHAPTER THIRTY-EIGHT

AS THE STURDY LEGIONNAIRES MARCHED into the teeth of the terrible seven heads of the pyrohydra, hardened though they were, it would have been impossible for them to be anything but purely awestruck at that very moment.

Some were injured. Most were bloody... with theirs or more likely someone else's... but almost all marched forward as one to give battle against the fabled hydra at the center of the lake.

The ancient temple was once a place of fearsome giants gone long ago from the realms of the Ruin.

Thousands of years.

The hydra had been their... *guard dog*, those terrible dark and fiery giants leaving it behind to guard a vast cache of ancient gold they'd hidden deep down in the watery vaults far beneath the temple at the bottom of the steamy lake where even other monsters lived.

The buried treasure vaults of these giants were long forgotten, but the sleeping gold, the curses and spells laid over it, and the traps and the tricks of the sunken vault, still waited for those who could pry its location from some dusty scroll long unconsidered.

And there also waited an ancient guardian of a giant Death Knight who slumbered in a hidden throne room, guarding the vault far below the waters of the lake.

Within the vault was a massive sword of great power.

But the Karthians, once the 82nd Airborne, were not here for that.

They'd come to honor their word, and that they would do now even if it meant certain death in the face of seven-headed breathing-fire death.

Lost treasures were not the Spartans' concern this day as they marched, spears out, shields locked, breaking off into various elements to orient themselves against the individual snaking malevolent heads of the ancient pyrohydra as it undulated and prepared to strike to defend what it had been placed to defend.

The triangular heads rose dripping from the waters of the lake, hissing steam and breathing fiery blasts that made the lake burn with flame.

It was true Daímones the Mad had come to think of itself as a god. All seven heads a pantheon of gods, each one made with some facet it thought it controlled in nature, and in the wills of others. It had grown mad with these delusions, mainly the chief head, a psionic-capable powerhouse that bent the tribes of the bugbear goblinoids to its petty whims, over time.

They hunted on behalf of the beast.

Brought treasures for it.

And, in times of leanness... were sacrificed to the hungry, slavering heads. Because Daímones must be fed.

All feared the pyrohydra.

It was such a towering and terrible thing that in that instance, as the Spartans prepared to meet it in battle, it should have stood some chance against them.

But the Spartans, firm and steady and still fighting the innate fear the thing radiated, failed to notice it had been badly wounded already in some recent assault.

Whump and *Crack*.

Just moments before.

As Socrats had assured the Ranger, in past run-throughs of the Spartan battle against the hydra heads... things had gone... "well" for the sturdy sky soldiers, mostly. They had fire-resistant shields. Teamwork. They were tough and capable. And they had a plan and solid NCOs to execute that plan.

But men still died.

If they had the heroic Ajack they generally fared better, losing less with him leading the assault from the front and wielding his gladius at point-blank range against the darting heads seeking to haul any Spartan off his sandals and into the steaming waters where he could be drowned, and feasted on later, down there in the depths near the sunken monuments of those lost terrible giants.

But there were still losses. Spartans died.

Daímones the Mad was a six-story, seven-headed, fire-breathing monster after all. It was very dangerous on any day that ended in y. And as it rose out of those steaming and stinking waters, dripping putrescent liquids, roaring like some mighty leviathan from an elder long-ago age, its fantastic bronze and crimson scales shining in the bright late-morning sun, its huge fangs practically dripping and bared for the meal after that battle, all the eyes seeming to greedily take in what it was about to devour...

It was a real gut check.

It took everything not to just be surprised and simply stunned by the sheer immense size of the terrible beast and to not halt, or even to fight the urge to run...

But on this time through Socrats' curse... the thing had already been badly devastated by a surprise attack from the rear, even as the battle between its servants and the intruders raged out on the causeway along the lake.

It was already wounded in hundreds of places from fast-moving shrapnel.

Many of its organs, mammoth things, were ruptured from overpressure.

It was bleeding internally.

Several of its heads already had concussions from the blast wave of a rucksack full of explosives, most of what had come in the speedball, that had been tossed down into the waters by Sergeant Thor.

The det ruck detonated fifteen seconds later, on the submerged beast down there in the yellow and shadowy depths of the lake. In the pool beneath the temple. Though the injury wasn't great in the form of savage wounds or ragged gashes and rents in its great scaly armors... the blast had been effective in that the beast, or rather all seven of its heads, had had their eardrums shattered, and some of their eyes were now dripping and pulped from the explosive released pressure of the submerged detonation.

In short, all seven insane heads had had their bells good and rung with the tremendous concussive effects of an underwater explosion.

Up close and personal.

In the darkness before dawn as Sergeant Thor, Alluria, and the blind old Spartan carrying the overloaded pack of explosives, and four strapped Carl Gustaf eighty-four-millimeter rounds, made their way, the serving girl guided the blind old man, gently leading him.

Two ADMs. Area denial munitions filled with eleven hundred fast-moving steel flechettes that explode over a wide area.

And...

Two direct-fire-impact HEDP rounds for hot and explosive penetration inside an enclosed area. He'd use these rounds if he had to, if the main body of the hideous beast surfaced and he could put one of the delayed impact rounds right into it, center mass.

The Ranger had told himself on the way to the hit that he would get it done in one, probably. The recoilless rifle launcher the Rangers called "the Carl" was a fearsome weapon, and to get hit with one was a real bad day.

Even if you were a six-story-tall seven-headed dino.

On the way in, rowing in the dark across the foul-smelling lake, and as they made their way onto the tumbled megalithic cut marble stones of the temple as the stinking lake water bubbled and lapped at the blocks in the darkness, Thor had debated between going for the main body of the thing with an HEDP, high-explosive round, or just trying to gut-shot it with one of the ADMs.

In the end, he figured the heads would come out to play first and he'd try to get a lot of them with the fragmentary shotgun effect of the ADM.

It was armored just by its sheer size and the dragon-like scales of its hide. True. But an HEDP round moving at high speed with a blast effect that was nothing to joke about... was something to be considered.

What if it was magical? Or rather, had magical armor or charms that protected it?

The Rangers had fought one dragon, and the hide of that thing was almost impenetrable.

How close was this hydra to that, wondered Sergeant Thor as he pulled quietly at the oars, forcing the stolen dragon boat forward through the pre-dawn dark.

Concerns for "armor" moved the Ranger's thinking toward the heads and just taking them out. There were seven of them. If he'd taken *Mjölnir* in, that would have been some tricky shooting trying to hit seven giant snaking heads at relatively close quarters. The temple was the size of a modern basketball arena, with no security to keep any guards off him while he worked the rifle.

Alluria and her bow weren't gonna give him enough time and space to dome all seven weaving, undulating, hissing, fire-breathing, fanged heads...

And getting this thing to a state that minimized Spartan losses, giving them a better chance going forward, was the goal of the *Ranger Smash!* he was about to execute.

Hit it before it had a chance to go out against the Spartans. Maybe kill it. Maybe make it weak enough to be killed.

And the fire-breathing was another consideration...

He didn't have a magic Spartan shield, and he couldn't use one while running modern weapons.

So he'd rigged his "det ruck" full of high-ex and made sure it would explode once it was at a certain depth based on timing alone.

Then he'd use the Carl on the beast if it survived the explosion, and try to take out the heads as they came out to respond to whatever it was that had just attacked them.

It was a plan.

As the three had made their way onto the marble blocks after getting out of the dragon boat, Alluria cleaned a few of the bugbear "holy guards" that patrolled the temple and guarded the monster in the arena-sized pool. Easy work in the blue dawn. Her shooting was expert, and Thor, carrying the launcher, crouched down next to the old man and admired her work as she shot the guards down in the darkness.

She'd put one arrow right into a bugbear's skull.

Another she shot through the throat. It gurgled, choking, but it didn't give an alarm and a few seconds later it fell over dead, or dying quickly. A third she hit in the back, and it screamed a little but none of the guards on the other side of the temple came running to see what the matter was.

Then they mounted a collapse of blocks near the rear of the temple, Thor going first, quietly and moving like a great hunting cat up the tumble-pile of fallen white marble as the first rays of dawn touched the skies in the east. Alluria led the blind Spartan with her cool hand, and it was clear the old soldier enjoyed that as he labored quietly, and cautiously, up through the giant stones to get to the top of the circular ring that was the roof of the open temple.

Later, when Thor complimented her at her skill leading a blind man through the near dark upward along uneven terrain, she merely sighed and said, "Serving wenches get a lot of that with good customers who drink too much and need to make it home through the streets at the end of the night so they can come back and drink themselves silly the next night."

For a moment, Thor doubted she'd ever done that at all. For a moment, to him in his mind, that was clearly just a story she told so no one really knew how she'd gotten so good at moving in the darkness like a cat, even in charge of someone who had difficulty.

She had skills and experience in this kind of stalking work. And it was to be admired.

But that... that lie... was a tomorrow problem. For another time. Not now with killing work close at hand and the Spartans already engaged out along the causeway.

Across the lake, villages burned like torches in the fading dark as dawn took the day and claimed it for itself. And for a moment, Thor stood and watched the Bronze Age destruction, thinking how few had ever experienced such a sight.

And this... was an edge.

Then he quickly turned and prepared the explosives as the day commenced. The battle along the causeway began, and at just the right moment, from the height of the stones that ringed the temple, Thor tossed the det ruck into the waters below.

It sank.

Seconds later it sent a plume of stinking corruption and water high into the air that rose well above the top of the fallen temple where they waited to make their next move.

In that instant, the Ranger was aware of something he had not taken into consideration during all his planning...

The stones did not shake in the slightest. They should have, because, as Thor thought to himself, he'd forgotten to consider that they might just collapse from the detonation even though they were so monolithic, and they didn't.

The heads of the terrible pyrohydra began to surface even as debris and water rained down from the detonation, and already Thor was dragging up the Carl, round in and ready to fire. Alluria and the old man were well out of the way, but he shouted "Back blast area clear!" anyway and fired an ADM round dialed for the range he needed.

It was short-range, and he'd have to cover from the flechettes himself.

He felt the overpressure not just from the launch of the powerful rocket inside the tube, but from the detonation just seconds later because the range wasn't far to go at all.

He'd had to contend with that too. But he calc'd that into his planning as he'd assessed his position and the battle he intended to give there.

He fired and instantly dropped behind the cover of a massive broken capstone jutting up from the top of the temple. Blast shrapnel scattered in every direction. Fast-moving steel flechettes savaged snaking lizard heads dripping water and blood and ichor as they rose from the pool at the center of the temple.

Whump and *Crack*.

The roaring heads, rising from whatever damage had been done beneath the waters, were screaming in pain and receding beneath the turbulent foam-chopped waters an instant later, reacting and fearful of the predator that had been waiting for them beyond the surface.

Beyond its underwater world where it was a god in its own minds.

Seconds later it was clear the thing was snaking its heads out through submerged portals in the stone, keeping its leviathan's dragon body bulk down deep to avoid more pain from whatever savage warrior was raining down death from above on it.

But the Ranger was already readying for crime scene number two.

Thor could see great billows of its inky blood blossoming in the putrescence of the waters it lay within. It was dying and probably wouldn't last much longer. But it was deadly and still dangerous, and it would kill anything that tried to stop it from escaping the *X* it found itself on.

But now he had no shot as it went deep for the submerged exits from the temple.

Thor loaded another ADM round and ran along the top of the temple, hefting the Carl as he dashed surefootedly forward.

Below, along the causeway, the Spartans were advancing against the titanic beast by the time he got another round loaded, still racing along the edge of the temple.

He had a gut feeling he wasn't going to need it at all by then. The thing sounded fearful instead of angry as already the first teams of Spartans were chasing down the snaking heads and spearing them as fast as they could like some prison assassin shivving a target at blinding and sudden speed.

Two heads had already been hacked off.

One head, larger than the rest, lolled drunkenly, dragging itself through the water. This was the powerful psionic-capable head. The overpressure of the det ruck had scrambled its fantastic brain and it was literally throwing up.

Not a pretty sight to behold.

But there was no need to even use another round on it, and so, as the killer Spartans finished the beast off, Thor collected Alluria and the old man and made his way back toward the Spartan line down on the causeway below.

The holy guard was seen fleeing from the island on an overloaded dragon boat as their god was hacked to death by dozens of armored warriors shouting, *"And then some!"*

Twenty minutes later the goliath was well done and dead and the Spartans had finished hacking it to pieces. Now they were either putting their bloody sandals on the severed heads or taking the opportunity to piss on some of the skulls, laughing breathlessly as they did so.

They too had been afraid, the Ranger could tell, but they'd gone right into the face of danger swinging hard and dealing death.

Now the fear was expelling itself in the form of laughter.

And the rush of being still alive when your enemy is dead.

Life-and-death fights are weird like that.

The first sergeant came in roaring, but a smile on his hard scarred face nonetheless. The Spartans were formed up and moments later marching for the other causeway on the far side of the temple leading to the far side of the lake.

And the Tower of Flame and Air.

Later, when the NCOs reported casualties, the first sergeant sat in stunned silence listening as there were no serious casualties reported among the platoons or special teams. No deaths at all. Merely bad cuts, a few broken bones, and the occasional Spartan who'd been knocked unconscious in close combat but was already back on his sandals, or soon would be. And getting gently harassed by his brothers who were glad he was alive when... they had most likely thought him killed in the thick of battle.

The Ranger fell in alongside them and so did Sato and Alluria, the two surviving mounts, and the thankless mule... and for a moment Sergeant Thor felt something different moving among these men.

Some mood that was different than they had been.

Some unseen change in the weather.

The priest came marching swiftly past. He was covered in blood.

He smiled at Thor and made the symbol for dip. Thor popped the tin and John of Towle reached in and took a hefty pinch, nodding his head in thanks as he hustled up the line of march for some job he had to perform.

"You wonder at their nature, Warrior?" asked Sato as he walked with Sergeant Thor.

The Ranger grunted and took some dip.

"They are men who thought they were dead, Warrior. Now, without even realizing it... they feel like they have a chance against a game that has been cheating them for some time. Call it life. Call it fate. We have all been there. A little victory is like that for the young, and soldiers. On a good day like this one you have a hope that perhaps... you might just win. Your plan was effective, Warrior. The wind is in their hair."

The young Spartan who'd poisoned the deathweed, Timothy, was with the other scouts as they hurried forward under overloaded packs to get forward of the main body and range out ahead. He paused next to Alluria, giving her a bashful smile as he pulled a hydra fang he'd taken as a trophy from the slaughter.

He handed it to her and mumbled, bashfully, almost stammering, "For you."

Then his platoon sergeant and the other scouts were laughing and telling him to keep up. He was hustled forward, still looking back at her. Moving ahead. Ranging.

A hope of his own in his heart.

"What am I supposed to do with this?" snorted Alluria, holding the large bloody fang.

Sato laughed.

And so did Thor.

"I think he's sweet on you," rumbled Thor and continued his long-legged, road-eating stride toward the front and the next battle that lay ahead.

She watched the Ranger go, then shook her head slightly.

Men had wanted her badly. Had killed each other for her.

Other men and wizards had offered her large fortunes for her favors if she would but...

A faithful priest had once sold his sacred idol just to buy drinks from her for another night more.

And then... some young soldier with dark eyes had given her a trophy from a battle where he'd almost died. And she was life to him. And worth it all.

There was something powerful in that. Something she'd never... considered before.

For a moment, a single moment in time amid the toss and turbulent pass of a universe... she saw another her that could exist. And be happy...

The other side of the lake was reached by the long column, the Spartans marched hard for most of the day, and by late afternoon they saw the rising hill. There lay the strange tower, dark and bloody red at the end of the long and victorious day. In the sky all around its tall heights, strange winged creatures flapped and soared, rising as high as they could in the last of the sun.

To Thor they looked... evil. Wicked.

For no reason he could name.
It was just a feeling.

CHAPTER THIRTY-NINE

IN THE EARLY EVENING DARK AS THOR STEPPED from the commander's tent, the sorceress Scylla motioned to him from the shadows nearby. Beckoning him with her wanton eyes and generous curves.

Her cloak parted just so to reveal the canyon between her ample breasts.

She smelled of perfumes and exotic scents and her voice was a delicate purr promising much, much more.

For a moment Sergeant Thor thought better of it. There was much to do this night if his plan was going to execute in the morning. After that, things would move hot and heavy until they found themselves attempting to relieve the City of Brass against a sizeable army he had yet to have a clear picture of.

Socrats had never seen the army.

He'd only heard the shouts and roars of the death of his own when they'd been overrun every time they'd made it that far.

Thor was having trouble visualizing how such combat would go. But in the end, he decided that if what they faced could be hurt in some way... then he'd hurt it until it didn't breathe anymore.

Or... this was all someone else's problems. But they'd never mess with another Ranger once he finished with them.

And that was a vow he'd kept to himself.

But now here, in the twilight outside the commander's tent... something bothered the Ranger about the witch. And had bothered him all along since first meeting her. She was of little value to the Spartans and seemed more of a tradition than anything else, but what the commander had told him inside the tent when Thor asked the man to share the nature of their mission with him... had tickled something in the back of his mind.

She was always looking at him.

Always devouring him.

Some knowing smile that wasn't just about sex... but some smug sense of satisfaction on some other issue the Ranger was guessing few knew about.

Clearly it was some eastern game. Some intrigue...

But she'd bothered him all along.

Inside the tent, the Ranger had asked the commander of the Spartans to tell him everything. At the time it had nothing to do with her. Scylla. The war witch of Caspia in the service of the Spartans to cast charms and make predictions about the battle and weather. She'd done little else.

Nothing easy to measure.

She bothered him. But more so after the honest conversation with the commander in which all... was finally revealed about why the Spartans had marched to their certain deaths that lay just ahead.

"No," had said Devil Six quietly once everyone was gone from his tent, from his precious maps, maps he'd made, save the Ranger who had done so much for them. The two men had been running through how things would go in the morning as they swiftly moved toward the final battle. The plan was not fully revealed to all because both Thor and Socrats had begun to wonder in the telling of what would happen soon, and on the Plane of Fire, if there was not... *some traitor*... in their midst.

"No. I cannot tell you why, Ranger. To do so... obligates you to die as we die... if we must die."

Some dark look crossed the man's concerned face as though for one moment... he was aware of all the times they had died before. Every time. Every failure. Always his.

As commanders of men... *must*.

As Socrats had said... none of the other Spartans had the same knowledge the blind old man possessed. But sometimes they had that feeling, just before their deaths on the current run-through... that all this *had happened before. And... would happen again.*

Their words.

"Gives you a creepy feeling, Ranger," Socrats had said. "Even if you do know it's true. Creepy all the same."

And then the old man shuddered.

"Doesn't matter, sir," said Sergeant Thor in the tent. "We're not going to die. And if you do, out there on the battlefield against the giants... then I'll die there with you. Sir."

The captain sighed and once more looked longingly at his maps. His passion.

"Tell me," rumbled Thor. "Why have you come all this way... just to pay a debt?"

The captain cleared his throat.

"We are men of honor. There is no length, no city too far and unmapped... that we will not go to if our honor is at stake. And in this..."

The man trailed off for a long moment.

Finally he straightened himself, moving to his armor where it lay polished and ready for the morning and the battles and the death that would come.

"A long, long time ago..."

Devil Six laughed slightly at this, but it was not a happy laugh, and there was some quiet bitterness in it.

"Isn't that how all these stories always begin?" he asked.

Thor said nothing.

"A long time ago... we Spartans were surrounded at the siege of Ankarrum. It is... was... a city that lay south of Caspia. This was five of my rank ago. As I said... a long, long time ago. The Devil then, Marcus of Ridgeway, he and his men, then we were battalions... Panthers, Devils, Falcons... four companies each... we were surrounded at that city by a vast horde of orcs as big as the sea, who came raiding out of Umnoth under the Bloody Khan himself..."

The commander looked at the Ranger.

"Do you know of the Bloody Khan?"

Thor shook his head.

Devil Six cleared his throat.

"He was greatest of the orc khans of old. Even still by these dark days. He conquered from the Crow's March, making war against the Black Prince himself, as far as the Redheaded Giants of the Jagged Mountains in the far and unknown east. It was said his emissaries even reached Kungaloor and were given princes' ransoms that the Grand Khan of the Orcs of Umnoth might not 'turn his wicked eyes' upon the east and think to plunder it."

Silence in the tent.

The captain rolled out a fine map and used it to illuminate his story as it progressed. It was one of the most beautiful maps of the Ruin Thor had ever seen. It was inked in gold, and the parchment was heavy and well-made. The names of many unknown places the Ranger had never seen on any other map lay along its surface, and for a moment Thor wondered if he was seeing a map of the Ruin... from long ago.

"So instead," continued the commander, "the Bloody Khan turns his eyes upon beguiling Caspia. The witches of the council were said to be counseling him in his conquests and providing him with the comeliest concubines and courtesans of that fabled and wicked city of liars, thieves, and witches. So... of course this was a betrayal to those hags in the Great Khan's turn toward the south, and their lands, roving his eyes where he would for plunder and spoil for his vast hordes."

The captain moved his scarred hand to where his beautiful map marked the Karthian fortress.

"We were mercenaries then. With orc hosts on the march out of Umnoth, massing for an attack on Caspia itself, the diplomats of the witches were dispatched to the Karthian rock to hire our might for their own. But we were already deployed forward to protect Ankarrum out of friendship, and not pay. The witches seethed at this, feeling they'd been betrayed once again, though they had not. Dark threats and promised curses were delivered by a two-headed crow to our Six telling him the price of his friendship with Ankarrum. *Murder, betrayal... revenge*, croaked the two-headed crow... it is said. And Caspia was almost burned.

"Instead, the orc army parted with much of the populace in chains and an entire treasury of the greedy hags given willingly if the Grand Khan would but gaze farther south and consider the port city of Ankarrum instead of Caspia."

The commander moved his finger toward the markings of Ankarrum on the rocky coasts south of Caspia below Umnoth.

"Fifty thousand orcs came sweeping out of the eastern mountains and fell on Ankarrum like death itself. We were just three battalions led by a brilliant commander I pray... every day... I were half the man..."

Devil Six lowered his head and removed his finger from the map.

"The long story short is... we fought until many were killed and things seemed... utterly... hopeless. The enemy dead were heaped high to the walls, and the orcs were using those dead to surmount the walls in the last hours of the battle. The end wasn't just near for the Spartans... it had arrived. The slaughter had gone on day and night, and by then only fifty Spartans remained on their sandals.

"And then..."

The captain paused. His eyes on the map. His thoughts elsewhere. Another time. A place he'd never been but whose ancient fate now charted his footsteps.

Honor.

"The commander made a deal with a wandering efreeti vizier, who offered a *wish* in exchange for a deed to be claimed later by the sovereign of the efreeti court at the City of Brass. On the Plane of Fire.

"Devil Six had no choice. The deal was struck. The *wish*... cast. And the Bloody Khan was consumed in a dark and tempest night by a greater storm elemental summoned by the vizier.

"Of the twenty thousand orcs ready to storm the inner city of Ankarrum, estimated by our generals in our ancient scrolls... not one of them, including the Great Bloody Khan himself... remained at break of day. By dawn they were gone and nothing remained of them, and the Bloody Khan disappeared from the pages of history, and the Ruin, forever."

The commander raised his head and stared at Thor.

"But the debt was owed now. And here, on this day, on the Plane of Fire, an army of djinns, the sworn enemies of all efreeti, have besieged the City of Brass and intend to take it for their own for a thousand years to come. They are led by the terrible Repham himself, augmented by many other enemies such as air elementals and hellhounds from the lower planes. And of course, the Goblins of Torment who make that plane their home. The City of Brass lies surrounded by an army greater than our own power to match at this hour. Soon it will fall. And still we must answer the call to pay the debt incurred so long ago. And so…"

He trailed off and said nothing for a long passing moment.

So the Ranger finished what the man was going to say.

"You go to your deaths."

The commander looked up and said nothing, only giving a face that seemed to ask the Ranger, *Do you know nothing of these powerful creatures of the Plane of Fire? Of hellhounds, chaotic and wild djinn berserkers, and a cohort of fire giants under the command of a named war general from the lower planes who has served the demon lords?*

Socrats had told Thor of these foes, but never of the debt the Spartans owed. Because, even blind and unconsidered…

"I am still one of them, Ranger. And we have agreed it is our debt, and not yours."

Now Sergeant Thor knew.

"I can't tell you if you're gonna die," rumbled Thor quietly after the long pause. "But the debt will be paid. Sir."

Then the Ranger turned and left the tent.

CHAPTER FORTY

Later, as the night wore on, after the meeting in the commander's tent and the ambush of Scylla, sitting around a small fire with Sato and Alluria, Thor finally spoke and told them all that had happened.

"The witch that travels with them has been betraying the Spartans. Tomorrow she'll probably signal this giant we're going up against, Repham, that we've crossed through the gate to the Plane of Fire, and that's when his quick reaction force will try to come out and hit the Spartans before they can reach the City of Brass. That's what I'd do if I had that intel."

Both serving girl and thief were silent for a long moment, still holding their rough wooden bowls of the night's stew.

Then.

"I knew it," hissed Alluria and made to get up for her bow.

Sato reached out a hand, stopping her, his face betraying nothing.

They knew of the Ranger's conversations with the blind Spartan who seemed to have some foreknowledge of what would happen.

They had taken his words as truth.

"And how do you know this, Warrior?" asked Sato impassively. "How do you know she intends to betray us?"

Thor cleared his throat and looked at Alluria, steadying himself for the storm that was sure to come soon.

"She cornered me after I finished the brief with the commander for operations tomorrow..."

Alluria hissed like a deadly snake warning of its strike, and Sato's firm grip moved to her arm, resting lightly on a control pressure point.

She squirmed but did not scream. Then she stilled herself.

"Scylla said I must meet her at midnight so we can..." continued Thor, keeping an eye on the deadly girl across the fire from him.

Alluria glared back at him.

"You know... for..." said Thor sheepishly. Uncommon for him. But then, Alluria's eyes burned with pure malice. So that was jamming him up a little.

"I'll murder her," whispered Alluria coldly. And that was a promise if Thor had ever heard one.

Sato nodded.

"You may still, girl. But let us hear a good reason why we should pierce her heart this night. First before knives."

Thor nodded as though Sato had just saved him from some terrible fate.

"The commander told me of the Spartan debt they must fulfill. It involves, indirectly, a perceived betrayal of the witches of Caspia a long, long time ago. Scylla is a witch of Caspia. Yes, witches are common with these eastern armies... in the Ruin..."

Sato nodded at this and that it was so.

"But, in listening to Socrats, it's clear these Spartans have suffered a serious run of bad luck, if his stories are to be believed. So much bad luck it's... probably not bad luck at all. I've wondered if there's someone here who's feeding information to their enemies, trying to make sure the Spartans never return from their mission. I've thought about that a lot in hearing how many times things have gone bad for them. And no matter what or which time through... things get real pear-shaped after they go through the gate to the Plane of Fire."

He stared at both of his friends.

"I've even suspected it was her. And yeah... I get she finds me... attractive."

Alluria hissed a vile word. Unprintable here on this scroll.

"But tonight, she practically confirmed... to me... it was her doing the betraying."

"I bet she did," hissed Alluria again. Her eyes were practically shoving knives into his eyes.

"I... Alluria... be cool. I had no intention... I was just buying some time to get rid of her..."

The girl snorted derisively.

"I have no idea what *Be cool* means, Warrior. But I will tell you... I am anything but... cool. Right now I am hot for her blood on my dagger. And I will—"

Sato shushed her.

She stopped.

The Ranger continued.

"It was when she told me we... I emphasize this word... *must*... that we *must* be together tonight. I asked her why. She said there would be no time tomorrow, or ever again for that matter, for she saw only my death and that she wanted to... lie with me. Before."

Alluria said nothing and remained totally still.

But her eyes.

Cold. Cold murder.

And that mind inside that pretty face was working.

"I asked her how she knew that," continued the Ranger. "She said, 'her powers.' Said she can see the future sometimes. That it was *now or never* and she feared... and this is the part that busted her out... *that you will all die*, she said. Not *we*. But *you*. As in *us and the Spartans* will die. But not her. If I had to bet right now, I'd bet she's sold out our location to this Repham, and once we cross over onto the Plane of Fire, we'll be hit by Repham hard before we can make it to the City. Hit right where we are and when we least expect to be."

"But your plan, Ranger..."

"She doesn't know the whole plan. But she will in the morning when we march. That's enough time for her to use... spells, I guess... to inform on us. To communicate with our enemies."

A long silence followed in which each of them thought their thoughts. Thoughts of *how*. Thoughts of *murder*. Thoughts of... *opportunity*.

"Warrior..." Sato said slyly. "I am disappointed in you."

Thor studied his friend, unsure where he was going but suddenly concerned he'd made some mistake in his calculations.

"Warrior... if our enemy is as close as you say she is with this little bird going to tell on us... then perhaps we have a chance to misinform this... Repham. And play a game of deception we thieves are best at. Even if we do find ourselves in battle among warriors... we are still thieves. Thieves of the Queen of Thieves, in fact."

Thor hadn't clocked that. And now...

A smile rose on the side of his face as he considered the possibilities even with the plan that was already in place.

If she thought the plan was something else, communicated, and then the plan went the way it was arranged...

Advantage.

"So..." Alluria whispered softly. "I can murder her then? After we lie to her. Right to her fat cow face? Then I can shoot her in the back and gut her?"

Sato nodded.

"But first... we should confirm your suspicions, Warrior."

"How?" asked the Ranger.

"Ahhh... Warrior. Gaze into that fine Pearl of yours and think thoughts of this voluptuous temptress who whispers truths out of one side of her pretty mouth and vile lies from the other. And we just may see what she is all about within its glowing deeps."

Within the Ranger's cargo pocket, the Pearl of Fate seemed to grow warm.

Thor reached in... and took it out of the clamshell, holding it before them all.

CHAPTER FORTY-ONE

"THESE WINGED FOLK," SERGEANT THOR HAD asked Socrats back at the Well of Azzim. "How does that go usually?"

"Badly, Ranger. But we get through them Stygians. We have rarely all died there. But the beating we take assaulting the slopes under their damned fire from them short bows they carry aloft... poison arrows that slay slow..." He shook his head. "The Stygians, for that is how they are named, are real bastards to be up against. Ain't no stand-up fight. Just push through and make it to the pool that's a gate. Into the water... out the other side. Within an hour after that, fire giants and hellhounds all over us. Ain't too much longer after that... we all dead, Ranger."

Thor ran through the chain of events in his mind.

"Tell me the layout of the tower," he said. "The pool is in the courtyard. What's in the tower? Can we take it and shoot them from there under cover?"

"You wouldn't want to. That tower is nothing. Musta been something long time ago. Now it's their rookery. Nasty place full of... I've never seen it, but I've smelled it for sure. And it ain't pleasant. That's where they sleep, and it's filled with stinking dry rotten old nests. They don't come out at night, but if attacked... then they will. We've tried that a time or two. No, in the end we go up that road, under shields, and men get hit and they either die, or they're poisoned, sick as dogs, and useless by the time the giants and hounds of hell jump us on the other side o' the gate."

Thor pondered this, brooding like some ancient warlord, fist on his chin. Seeing all the dangers and no easy path through.

He considered shooting them all. His skills were sufficient. But the cost in ammo would be devastating later if Socrats' description of what they faced there was even half true.

The Carl with the ADM munitions was perfect, in a way. But so was an army of strange and fantastic creatures besieging a city a good target for that kind of ordnance. They'd need all he had left in the magic Bag of Holding to punch through.

And there were giants. If anything he had was a giant killer… it was the Carl G.

As the young Rangers say… *Carl G don't care.*

Thor smiled grimly at the thought of lighting up a giant with a Carl.

Socrats yawned. It was getting late.

"But it's the smell of that tower, Ranger. Smells like death that ain't been cleaned out in a thousand years. Birds is dirty, foul things, black-crow-feather men and their harpies… hells, that place smell like death warmed over gone bad three days ago. I'd burn it to the ground just to get the smell out of my nose. I'm serious, Ranger—it's one of the things that stays with me every time through. I can even smell it now, and we ain't anywhere near that ancient tower. Nasty, horrible. Fetid."

Thor looked up.

"Then that's what we'll do… we'll burn it, old man. We'll burn it to the ground before dawn and the scouts will lead the rest through the smoke. We hit the gate and we're gone. If you can't fight them, then keep moving off the *X* and give them something else to think about. So says the Book of Joe."

"Who's… Joe?" asked Socrats.

CHAPTER FORTY-TWO

AT MIDNIGHT, WITH LITTLE SLEEP, AND SOME of that due to Alluria constantly watching him closely from her place on the far side of the fire, Thor rose, got into his rig, grabbed the SAW, exchanged a few words with Sato, and was greeted a few minutes later by Cray the Crawler and the rest of the scouts.

For most of the rest of the night they crept through the badlands that lay before the hill and dark tower upon it. They stayed away from the dusty old road they were expected to march down in the morning.

Some of the scouts were carrying their prepared pots of "Greek fire."

The Spartans simply called this *nape*, telling the Ranger it was an ancient word among their kind for fire that destroyed and could not be quenched.

Thor laughed a little in the darkness.

Nape.

Napalm.

Going wide and far around the hill to its other side, keeping an eye out for the Stygians, the scout platoon made the sheer face of a rock wall that led up to the back side of the thin black tower rising high into the night.

Thankfully, for no calculable reason, there was no moon out this night in this strange land.

And... there was no apparent way up to the tower from this side of the hill. Which was perfect for the expert scouts, and the Ranger.

They started quietly climbing, taking their time, each keeping a count of the minutes that had passed. Using their fantastic version of "paracord."

Meanwhile, with two hours until dawn, the Spartan camp, almost as one in perfect silence, geared up, packed up, and started their soundless march down the road in the pre-dawn dark.

This was the plan, and every Spartan, and the treacherous witch Scylla, knew it. What most didn't know was what would happen next, after the tower. The general chatter about the plan was that the Spartans would march immediately down from the rock cliffs where the gate on the other side of the Plane of Fire lay.

From the gate it was just a few hours' march to the great dusty bowl where the City of Brass lay on a small dune sea among a few rocky ridges of greater mountains.

It was here the main force of Repham's army waited, sieging the City of Brass and the efreeti inside.

But the Ranger had other plans.

And now that he knew the witch was treacherous, he was keeping that change of mission to need-to-know. And very few... needed to know.

But first they had to get through the pool in the ruined old courtyard of the Tower of Fire and Air. And if they could pull that off with little to no casualties...

Then...

Then perhaps their chances were far better going into the battle at the City of Brass against the host of Repham the Slayer.

Thor, Alluria, and Sato had seen within the depths of the Pearl confirmation of their suspicions. Rubbing a large amethyst ball she kept on a silver chain about her shapely neck, as Thor held the Pearl of Fate and concentrated on the comely witch within its pink depths, her mouth moved silently, her eyes gazing into the well-cut large purple gem she'd kept hidden from them all.

"Show me who she talks to," muttered Thor, unsure if that was how the magic item operated.

It responded.

The pink mist within the Pearl swirled, and they were staring into the grim visage of an ashen-skinned giant. His eyes were like sparkling rubies. His dark beard and hair curly. He wore an ancient helmet not unlike those of the Spartans. He had a large nose and cruel features.

Soundlessly within the Pearl of Fate... his lips moved as though speaking to the witch on the other side of the gem.

Treachery and betrayal.

The scouts mounted the cliff in the darkness before dawn and came to the base of the high dark tower. The climbing was far from done though. Timothy and two other scouts, including the platoon sergeant, continued from the base to the top of the tower. They would ignite their "nape" there, preventing the wicked crow-feathered bird-men from flying out the top when the fire started and got going in full conflagration.

The stench of the foul spire was outrageous.

Thor and the other scouts made their way down the sides of the broken old twisting trail that was the road proper leading up to the tower.

Below and not far off, the rest of the Spartan element was staged and ready to move on the signal from a horn one of the scouts carried.

Thor had already distributed the ChemLights. These were the last of the ones that had come with the speedball, and he'd given them to the scouts stationed along the trail who would guide the Spartan main body up through the smoke and chaos while they carried their shields high to protect themselves from arrow fire.

The smoke and flames would give cover. The burning of the nests would confuse the Stygians, or so Thor hoped.

"The Stygia... are an ancient race. Once the air cavalry of the Saur. There was some falling-out with the great pharaoh of Sût himself and they were forced into the east as a curse for their failures," Sato had told him. "But that was long ago and before my time, Warrior. It is said the trinkets and treasures they keep in their nests are more important to them than even their very lives."

We'll see, thought Thor.

Dawn.

The flames inside the tower were already underway, and within less than five minutes the spire was billowing black smoke in inky vomits. Ten minutes later it was a bright Roman candle in the red dawn.

The Stygians swarmed and swooped, calling out madly to one another in their barking crow language. They were incensed, enraged, and panicking.

Already, as great gulfs of black and gray smoke covered the hill and drifted off toward the rest of the wastes, the Spartans hustled forward, mouths and noses covered by wet cloths, laboring under their gear and packs.

There was some fighting.

But the Stygians cared more for their burning nests as had been told, and kept disappearing into the spire at various levels, never to be seen again.

The sound of their crow-calling was like hearing madness itself talking a thousand times over. But the Spartans kept moving up the chem-lit trail in the suffocating heat and caustic foul-smelling smoke.

The Spartan scouts guided them all the way.

Some Stygian warriors came in and thought to fight with beak and claw. They were hacked to death by the Spartans they encountered, and the staccato bark of the super SAW could be heard rebounding through the canyons and off the hill itself as clusters of them who'd thought to make a stand were cut to shreds.

When the last of the Spartans had gone through the gate, Sergeant Thor and Cray the Crawler, the scout platoon sergeant, conferred on the head count and made their way into the courtyard beneath the burning tower.

It was like looking up at a vision of hell. The black tower was all on fire and there was no sound but the crackle of the flames eating everything they could.

It wouldn't be long before all that was left was the skeleton of something unknown that once was.

Sato was knee-deep in the water of the pool in the courtyard.

"Come, Warrior... we wade down into the waters and the world turns over... and then... it is another land. Fantastic and like nothing I have ever seen."

Thor entered the pool... and followed the ancient rock-carved steps down into an aquamarine brilliance that was like the bluest sapphire he'd ever laid eyes on.

Chimes tinkled.

Some unseen bell tolled in deep spaces far from the reality they were violating.

And then... there was a simple... *pop*.

They were through the gate, coming back up through the cool waters...

Coming back up... to the Plane of Fire.

CHAPTER FORTY-THREE

What would happen next would happen quickly. Already events were in motion for the endgame and the attack on the forces of Repham as soon as Sergeant Thor came up from the dripping waters of the crystal-clear pool that was the gate to the Plane of Fire.

Spartans were hustling into formation, tight and crisp. Their armor shining in the brilliant noon-light as though they were ready to parade. Their red-and-blue caps both standing out and blending in with the strange and surreal surroundings.

Sergeants walked the line, inspecting their men one last time as the first sergeant glared at them all through his one remaining eye.

On a large rock, the commander stood, making notes in a small leather book, sketching what he could see. And nearby, the lean soldiers carried the three standards of the platoons.

Devils.

Falcons.

Panthers.

Thor thought back on Eighty-Deuce lifers he'd known in the Before. They would have lived for this moment, hard unit that it was, and they would be proud of what had become of the men who carried on.

The 82nd... outnumbered and well behind enemy lines. Going into battle against impossible odds.

Because that's what they did. And what they'd always done since they were first stood up.

A long, long time ago.

The first thing the Ranger could see was the sky. It was a brilliant burning blue. Almost ultramarine blue. The most expensive color in the world back in the world that was. The Before. And it was huge. It seemed to stretch off into impossible distances and lands that defied imagination.

Lands of raging fires. Lands of boiling majestic stormfronts of cloud.

There were even clouds, high up and far off in the distance, that seemed to have what appeared to be castles, or palaces there.

The rocks of the small draw the pool that was a gate lay in... were deep, and dark, and red. Here on the other side that was the Plane of Fire, it was almost a natural pool, unlike on the other side where it had been more like a fountain with architectural features.

Soft blinding-white sand that was warm surrounded the pool but quickly turned to another color.

The red rock of the mountain that rose away from the draw was the color of burnt cinnamon.

And the air... it was heavy and still. As though it was some vast living thing with a breath and an energy all its own.

Thor, Sato, and the scout platoon sergeant walked forward out of the draw into a vast red desert of loose-packed crimson sand. From here they could see the lands below, for the rocky mountain that sheltered this gate to the Plane of Fire lay along a high ridge of jagged mountains.

The heat shimmered, and far out there they could see active volcanos and rivers of lava coursing through the land like the great rivers of the Ruin. Farther off, and lower down beyond this savage line of volcanos and the great river of fire, were darker, hotter lands that made it seem, from this distance, and this vantage point, as though one were looking into a blazing hot blast furnace.

Giants, tiny at this range, but impossibly tall and made of living fire out there, moved about among the dark and jagged mountains far off.

"It would seem," mused Sato, "that we have come out of the gate into a border area between the regions of fire and air I have heard this place described as. And look!" He pointed down into a bowl where a sea of the crimson-colored sand dunes had gathered, girded by three intersecting ridgelines of burnt-cinnamon rocky hills and smaller peaked mountains. "The City of Brass itself..."

And there it was.

A fantastic thing to behold.

High up, and at this distance...

The City of Brass was like a giant genie's bottle half-buried in the crimson sand dunes down there in the bowl of a small valley lying between the broken ridges. But on its side. It was made of purple glass and filigreed with gold and other colors at its slender waist and fat bottom.

Inside lay a large city made of gleaming brass, turned a strange shade by the rich purple glass of the outer bottle. There were high towers and minarets and fantastic domed palaces therein. And other smaller byzantine labyrinths of streets and alleyways that were mesmerizing from this distance.

The air was so clear here on the plane, and not smoking and dark like it was far off in the distance by the volcanoes like teeth and the great river of fire, that many details of the fantastic city within the immense purple genie's bottle were able to be seen with eyes as sharp as the Ranger sniper's.

Near the open neck and mouth of the incredible bottle were gleaming white and brass guard towers. And before these towers, around a sharp hill, lay a vast and spreading army of creatures that seemed as small as ants at this distance.

But they were not ants. Humanoids and other strange creatures moved busily about.

Among these "ants" moved tall, armored giants.

This was the army of djinn berserkers, led by the fire giant Repham the Slayer. And they had laid siege to the City of Brass, for great were the wonders and magic contained within, and it was the desire of the wicked djinn sultan, *Al-Fasid...*

The Depraved One.

... that he possess it for himself.

Djinn and efreeti are constantly at war on the Plane of Fire.

And it was into this conflict the Spartans would throw themselves now to satisfy the debt of their honor. Even if it meant their slaughter.

Thor stepped forward next to the commander of the Spartans, standing before the assembled platoons, the horses, Alluria, the blind old Spartan who had his weathered old hand on her soft shoulder, and the rapacious witch...

He gave the false orders for what they would do next to relieve the besieged city below.

Sato quietly shifted toward Stormbringer, taking up his rein, and leading the angry warhorse toward the witch, wrapped in her cloak, eyes roving over Sergeant Thor as he deceived her one last time.

CHAPTER FORTY-FOUR

Even as sergeant thor lied to them all about how they would make the attack against Repham's forces, the Ranger was quickly developing a plan from what he'd just seen, and what his conversations with the blind old Spartan had been.

The city was surrounded.

The attack of enemy forces against the city was from three sides, concentrating on the neck of the "bottle."

A steep hill directly in front of the bottle, and not far from the entrance to the city, was topped with what looked like siege engines, and circus-tent-sized command tents and pavilions. Pennants and flags fluttered there, and it was obviously some type of command center for Repham the Slayer.

And so far, they seemed pretty capable at that.

But he betrayed nothing as he told them all how they would now march down through the pass, into the dunes, and within two hours attack the enemy rear as they tried to take the towers to the City of Brass near the open neck of the genie's bottle.

For a brief second, he clocked the witch.

Her eyes were closed and fluttering already as she rubbed the amethyst gem about her neck...

Telling the fire giant general, Repham, all their plans as she was now hearing them.

Time was of the essence.

Now the Spartans would be ambushed, as they always had been, before they reached the rear of the invading force and gave battle. Probably somewhere in the crimson rock pass leading down into the dunes, or in the dunes themselves.

As fast as the fire giants and their hellhounds could move to intercept.

Nearby, Sato waited until the treacherous witch finished her communications, and then, as the orders to march were finished by the Ranger, the thief led the stormy horse forward and bid the witch to mount so she could "save your energy for the powerful magics you will work on our behalf and which will be needed during the coming desperate battle."

She smiled imperiously as though riding above them all were her natural place. And knowingly enjoying the satisfaction that she'd just signed their death warrants, and would be well rewarded for her betrayals.

Alluria deftly removed her dagger from off her shapely hip and was just seconds from sticking the witch when Sato easily had the woman up on the simmering tempest that was Stormbringer and riding sidesaddle.

Alluria gave Sato a hot look as though her vengeance to kill had suddenly been delayed by the thief.

Then, faster than anyone but Thor could notice, for everyone was busy getting ready to march, conducting last-minute gear checks, issuing orders, and adjusting positions, Sato did some unnoticed trick and the hotheaded warhorse reared violently and all at once, then bucked at almost the same moment.

The witch was flung bodily from the warhorse, and Sato appeared to catch and... guide her... even as she came down on a sharp crimson rock half-sunk in the burning sand, breaking her neck.

Instantly.

A moment later... she was dead.

CHAPTER FORTY-FIVE

In the chaos that followed the "accidental" death of the treacherous witch, Thor made for the priest.

John of Towle.

He took the shaking young man aside and put both his great hands on the priest's slender shoulders. The priest had been brought in to see if he could do anything for her... but... nothing could be done. Her neck was broken. Sato had made sure, and no one was the wiser.

"Listen..."

The priest was looking toward the chaos of the dead witch that had been their "luck" for so long. He was practically sick to his stomach, and it looked like he was going to throw up.

"You're going to need to do your thing now..."

The priest wasn't listening to the Ranger sergeant.

Thor shook him once. Rattling the skinnier man.

"Listen, man... you're gonna need to jump us onto that battlefield right where I tell you to put us. Understand? This is our only chance now. Put us down where I want to be, and we can beat Repham... and settle the debt. Then you guys can go home."

The priest started to sweat, going pale.

Now he was looking at the Ranger.

He nodded his head, mumbling something.

He wasn't a coward. He was just afraid. But Thor had never seen the one man among the Spartans who was the least in their warrior culture... shirk to do his part.

Thor wondered if they even knew that about the priest as Thor himself was finally seeing it now. He would do it... for them. Just as he had all along. Even though... he was a man of faith, and books, and prayers, and life, and growing things.

He would do anything for them.

"I'll... try," stammered John of Towle.

Silence.

Thor looked him in the eye. Steady. Deadly. Confident in the priest's faith.

"You will do it, John."

And then Thor reached into his cargo pocket and pulled out the Pearl.

"This is exactly where I want the DZ."

CHAPTER FORTY-SIX

"Problem with them priests..." said the blind old Spartan back at the Well of Azzim when the Ranger had begun to plan all this. "... is they lost their faith a long time ago."

"How so?" asked Thor. Hand on fist. Staring into the fire that night as the late hour wore on and the old man continued to dump all the intel the Ranger could get his hands on.

Like some ancient warlord brooding over his kingdom. The kingdom he'd taken by his own hand, and blade. "They lost their faith. Long time ago. Like I said, when I was young... we jumped, Ranger. Even outnumbered... with their prayers we could land where the enemy least expected us, link up, and start ruining their supply trains, command tents, lines of communication. Plans. That would throw the main body into disarray, and we could get around to them soon enough. But... kill their leaders first, poison their wells next, and cut them off from each other...that's what a jump will do if it's done right. If them priests make their prayers just right... or whatever it is they do... we can ruin them and break their stuff."

The old man sighed fondly for the glory days of breaking the enemy's stuff.

Then he yawned.

It was getting late, and this info was of no value. The good priests were mostly dead, and their prayers hadn't worked for some time anyway.

The last one, the young one, he had no faith.

But... "He means well," sighed the old Spartan. "And he's willing to march with us. That counts for something among us, Ranger. Gotta be willing. Ain't no one forced to be a sky soldier. It's all volunteer back at the Karthian rock. We chose this life... didn't choose us, Ranger. Makes us different than the legs. Better than, even. You understand that? Is that how it is back in the Before where you come from?"

The Ranger understood.

Later he'd ask John of Towle why the "jump prayers" had failed, or no longer worked.

"I can't see... visualize what needs to happen... the result. I was never good at it. The older priests knew that about me. I know the prayer. Know the traditions and ritual. And... I want... so bad... for it to happen..."

The younger man's eyes filled with water and his mouth twisted. But he fought the emotion that was so natural to him.

"I have prayed even when I didn't believe, Ranger. For them. There is no failure in our unit. It is... mine... all my failure. There is no other answer for why my prayers fail and we must go in on foot. And every death, every casualty that could have been prevented had I only had the prayers... the *faith*... those deaths are on me, one called Thor. And every one has made me less and less confirmed in what I have faith in any longer. So much failure... it can do that to a man. It can make him blind when he needs to see."

The Ranger had no answer to this.

One time, some other soldier had been trying to explain religion to him, and what faith was. That man was... one of the best Green Berets he'd ever worked with.

But for Thor... faith and religion... weren't a thing.

He'd killed things other people called gods and had worshipped, even though Thor had seen them bloody and slaughtered on their temple floors.

He didn't know yet. If there was...

He would tell himself sometimes when thoughts like that occurred... he didn't have enough intel yet. But that if he did... then yeah. Obviously, he would believe.

But only if it was the truth. Because that was what mattered to him.

And part of him guessed, on the edges he sought, he'd get close enough to maybe see, and even touch, that truth.

Then... maybe he could believe.

But now, with the faithless, and in his own way faithful, priest, the jumpmaster of the Karthian Spartans who were once the Eighty-Deuce... he didn't have any words he knew that could spark the man to make the right prayer to let them execute on the DZ Thor needed them to take in order to win this battle today.

The clock was burning. And every advantage was needed. Even the ones that weren't available.

Rangers are always... *in it to win it.* No matter how bad it looks.

But that Green Beret had... faith.

Chief Rapp. The detachment medic and doctrine warfare specialist.

"Listen, Ranger..." the larger man had told Thor one time. "Faith is hard. Real hard. Maybe the hardest thing ever. Way harder than selection. But it's simple too. In its own way. Faith, Thor... is the substance of things hoped for. That's all."

Now fire giants and their warlord, surrounded by panting hellhounds, were inbound to intercept and slaughter them all here in the sands of this strange and fantastic land.

If they could jump...

Then the whole game changed on a dime. They could make the enemy react. And if they did that...

... then they were in charge of the whole game.

Thor spoke. He didn't own the words. They weren't his. Didn't even really understand them. But Chief Rapp, a legit operator, lived by them. And if he could use them to help the priest find his way...

Perhaps...

Maybe...

Who knows?

"Faith," rumbled Thor, "is what you hope for."

And sometimes, the voice of the smaj whispered in the Ranger's mind. *Sometimes, Ranger, you gotta give a troop that's havin' a rough go of it, just a little taste of what's comin' after the ruck hump that is life, just so they can keep pickin' 'em up and puttin' 'em down until it's over. Sometimes it's so dark, you don't ever think it'll be light again. But it do come, Sar'nt. Every day. The sun comes up again. Just sometimes they forget that part.*

Thor showed the priest the Pearl, and the DZ he needed the prayer for.

Slowly, John of Towle took the Pearl and stared into it, his lips already practicing the ritual he knew so well.

The Ritual of the JMPI.

Hoping he could get them there.

CHAPTER FORTY-SEVEN

T HOR HAD GIVEN THE COMMANDER THE warning order that the mission was about to change.

"How so? What new development has occurred now that we have lost our battle witch?" said the commander. "How can things possibly get worse?"

"The priest is going to perform a jump. Sir."

"Oh..." said Devil Six.

He was willing to believe.

He knew maps. He was a commander. He understood his men were marching into certain death ahead, down there on the Plane of Fire before the City of Brass.

"What's the plan then?"

"Gather your platoon sergeants and I'll show you what's going to happen once we're on the ground," said Thor, getting his map ready.

Five minutes later, in sight of the kneeling priest who was nearby and mouthing his words silently, the rest of the Karthian Spartans standing around and ready to march, uncertain what was going to happen next...

Hurry up and wait.

Same as it ever was.

Thor sketched out a quick sand table of the battlefield they would soon find themselves on.

"We're going in here..." the Ranger said, marking the hilltop with the siege engines, catapults of some type. And the command tents. Pennants and standards. It was fortified. But they could take it if they landed on it.

"I think the giants, and their hellhounds," continued Sergeant Thor, "are aware of our presence on the plane and are now moving to intercept our line of march to relieve the city. That will pull them away from the battle for a time to react to us. Once we jump in, I have no doubt they'll be back in at us. But by that time, we'll own their hilltop, ruin their siege engines, and have a defense set up to deal with them. We go for the decap. We kill their general no matter what. Until they get back with their general, I expect the rest of their army to turn away from the city and try to retake the hill we're holding."

Thor looked at all of them. Hard eyes and scars stared back at him. The plan was good. The odds were bad.

Real bad.

But... as every Spartan knew in their own Ruin way...

Chicks dig scars, and battles like this were once in a lifetime.

They were 82nd at their core from a long time ago.

The action is the juice.

Always.

Every time.

"So, we hold the hill no matter what. Got that?" Thor asked, making eye contact with every small team leader.

They nodded grimly, overloaded with packs and armor. Ready to get their kill on.

"Yeah," barked the first sergeant. "And we kill 'em all while we're doing it."

CHAPTER FORTY-EIGHT

BEFORE THE RITUAL OF THE JMPI, EVERYTHING grew solemn in the hot sweaty noonday heat on the Plane of Fire. Every Spartan knelt in the red sand as the last acts were begun before the "jump."

The priest made the ritual of dip.

Desperate combat was expected.

Some of the Spartans handed letters to other Spartans as they whispered, "In case I do not survive... tell her I was thinking of her. Okay... you will do that."

Other Spartans took out their medals of Saint Michael, silently whispering words from long ago. Some stared grim-eyed ahead, their thoughts their own, their resolve to do what must be done... clear. Thor noticed they all had dog tags too. Ancient things they'd kept hidden and tied to their belts instead of around their necks. As though they were the truly holy relics they'd carried all along.

Just as the 82nd had once done.

Then the priest made his prayer as the sergeants organized everyone into their sticks. Sticks were the lines paratroopers once formed up in to go out the door. Chalks were their groups. *Sticks* had survived, *chalks* had not, noted the Ranger.

Sato lined up too. And Alluria, the blind Spartan holding her shoulder with one hand, his staff with the other. His spindly chest out. His face grim-set and sometimes smiling as the other Spartans checked each other's gear, and then someone checked his, if only just for form's sake because he possessed nothing.

He was standing with them. His brothers. Listening to all they said. And he was among them, once again, as one of them.

That was all that mattered to the old man.

And even the horses too were organized as they readied for the jump.

Sergeant Thor was uncertain how this would actually go. But he was in.

Then the JMPI, uttered in clear and loud stentorian tones, was performed. The priest raised his arms, indicating they should ready themselves now.

Stand Up.

The Spartans were lined in their sticks now.

Hook Up.

They raised their right arms.

Sound Off!

Everyone called over their shoulder to check each other's gear. When it got to the last man in the stick, he slapped the leg of the person in front of him and yelled "Okay!"

The priest turned as the air behind him began to shimmer and change in some strange way.

He was checking for something. Part of the ritual…

Then he held up one finger and everyone called out, "One minute!" as small magic meteors began to form and dart behind the priest.

Thirty seconds later the priest made the ancient symbol of a 'C' with one hand and every sky soldier shouted, "Thirty seconds!"

Something very strange was indeed happening behind the priest and energy shot from that area and rippled in waves down the sticks of formed Spartans waiting to jump.

"Stand by!" shouted the priest, his eyes true and confident. Believing totally in what would happen next…

And suddenly a door in reality, in existence itself, shimmering and weird, gusting with wind blasting in at them, opened in front of them all on the red sands before the collective sticks of each unit.

It was… amazing.

"Go, go, go!" thundered the priest in a voice he'd never seemed to possess before. The sergeants shouted this too and suddenly they were all running, one hand on the trooper in front of them, running for that open door in reality that had suddenly come into existence as the ritual had completed.

And then they were falling...

Drifting like feathers...

Feather Falling.

Thor heard Alluria yell *"Wheeeeeee!"* from nearby as they drifted down over the battlefield.

The Rangers had done this before when Vandahar had cast a great Feather Fall spell for the Rangers to jump against a necromancer and an army of the dead they were facing back during their early days in the Ruin.

Just like that.

And... a little different now.

Thor saw the whole battlefield. The odds they faced. Below, the small hilltop was coming closer, faster now by the second. He got his eyes on the horizon and readied himself to perform a proper parachute landing fall, even though he didn't have one, just as he'd been taught once, long ago, and had done many times since.

He didn't know if they would need that with the Feather Fall spell. But he would do it anyway.

The hilltop rose toward them...

Closer.

Faster...

CHAPTER FORTY-NINE

On the ground and moving after the jump, all was chaos even though the drop on the hill had been like drifting down light as a feather.

The Goblins of Torment, as the blind old Spartan Socrats had referred to them in the intel debriefs, were actually imps from the Infernal Planes. They were mischievous, diabolical, and everywhere.

They made wicked attacks of spells and mass attacks when they could find a lone Spartan, ripping him to shreds with their needle-sharp teeth.

In some instances they changed into large spiders, or suddenly became bats or rats. They charged the powerfully built Spartans, a mistake, seeking to sink their venomous fangs into the warriors. The Spartans held their ground, large shields out front, and expertly speared the little demonic bastards as they came.

The Spartans had fought imps before in Skeletos when the minor demons had been summoned by the Archmagus of Athenos.

The diabolical siege engines were the imps' jam, and they'd installed them at the offer of great treasures from the looting of the City of Brass for Repham the Slayer. The giant genie bottle that encased the city had been fractured in many places by the catapults, but it hadn't yet broken due to its magical properties. In defense of the siege engines, the malevolent imps cast small magical firebolts at the Spartans as the teams that had linked up after the jump set to hunt them down and clear them off the siege engines in what quickly became a bloody slaughter.

Fire-resistant shields worked just fine against magical firebolts.

The first sergeant commandeered men and immediately had the siege engines under review, reorienting them and soon beginning to fling giant hot stinking rocks that had been heating in massive brass cauldrons, down on the army of djinn berserkers amassed in front of the city below.

The Spartans quickly got the hang of the diabolical catapults, and became more and more effective with each passing launch. Within moments of the first indirect strikes, ragged and disorganized, djinn swordsmen that were part of the main body were turning to react to the threat the Spartans now presented on the hill at the rear of their lines.

Thor, working the super SAW, cleared the front road of the imp guard set to watch there, getting into a firefight of magic fire bolts against death-spitting MK48. The super SAW proved superior, and a few minutes later winged imp bodies savaged by seven-six-two littered the road.

"Maintain the watch here," ordered the commander as he linked up with the Spartans and Thor at the entrance via the main road into the hilltop camp. He was bloody and wickedly cut across the face. "I will recce the rest of the hilltop and get any other approaches blocked off. We have three casualties already. The scout platoon sergeant was killed by imps."

Then the captain was off, checking the perimeter and assaying groups to sectors.

In short order, the hill was secured.

But the first berserkers were coming up the hill to retake it.

CHAPTER FIFTY

An hour later the final Makor assault by djinn had been repelled.

More Spartans were dead.

The SAW was burnt and there was no ammo left anyway.

The road was littered with dead djinn warriors.

Parts of the hilltop command tents were on fire as powerful djinn wizards had thrown fireballs at the camp. After burning the SAW, the barrel going forbidden popsicle because the last push to try and retake the road had numbered hundreds of enemies, Sergeant Thor had sent Sato for *Mjölnir* and the Ranger switched over to sniper engagement.

The djinn were tall. Blue-skinned and dressed in rich flowing silks to display their physiques. They were powerfully built, and the Spartans had to engage them with two to their one.

The chokepoint on the road leading up to the hill, and Sergeant Thor's fire power and the last of his grenades, had controlled the lethal flow despite the djinn swordsmen thrusting their palms out after pointing at their eyes and attempting to cast Evil Eye on their victims.

A curse of bad luck for the immodest or those given to bragging of their deeds.

The Spartans, men of deeds and not words, and their innate humility, repelled these vicious curse attacks as did the holy powers of John of Towle when he took up a position at the road to both hinder the enemy and cure what wounds he could by prayer.

Sato spotted the djinn wizards casting Fireballs on the sands below, and Thor put fifty-cal BMG rounds into them there. Wizard or not, there was no getting up after taking a round with that caliber at that rate of speed.

A clutch of wizards tried to cover inside one of the towers the djinn army had taken near the bottle's entrance to the City of Brass.

Thor switched over to a special AP, armor-piercing, munition for the Barrett and put two rounds that exploded after penetration into the room where they covered.

The wizards were either dead or badly maimed inside the shredded tower now.

One of the Spartans, part of a pair who'd taken the far side of the road on a high red rock to keep watch from, was the first to spot the returning force of fire giants and hellhounds approaching in the distance.

They were running for the battle.

And suddenly the winds along the hilltop picked up and began to howl.

CHAPTER FIFTY-ONE

THE HELLHOUNDS HIT FIRST, LOPING AHEAD of the main body. Down in the crimson dunes before the City of Brass, among the shattered armies, djinn berserkers were rallying around their wizards who'd survived Thor's accurate sniper fire with *Mjölnir*.

Spells and incantations were being cast.

The berserkers were beginning to whirl and howl, their large scimitars gleaming like cutting blades as the day began its descent toward afternoon.

The heat was stifling.

The smell of death heavy in the air.

"Warrior," said Sato. "They come now, and there are too many of them. Would you fade as we have done before? Perhaps we fight our way through the djinns down there, enter the city, and find allies within. Perhaps we die with them later, and not this bloody day… or perhaps we escape by some trickery… and live, Warrior?"

The Ranger grunted.

The commander was missing.

Several Spartans were dead.

The first sergeant had been badly burned by an incoming fireball. It was expected he would die soon.

And that was when the wind began to move over the still and heavy stinking air that had clung to that battlefield for much of the fight.

Thor laughed and turned to Sato.

"The wind is in our hair, my friend. We will settle the debt this day…"

The ground was actually beginning to shake as the fire giants off in the distance closed for the attack.

The djinn below began to scream as though possessed by fiendish spirits from the Infernal Realms.

"And if not… then we'll stack our fair share and then some."

Thor was standing on the high red observation rock. The Spartans who had survived the battle so far had collected on the road and rocks around him.

They were wounded, scarred, and bloody. But they were not down.

"Will you stack with me, my friend?"

The wind tossed Thor's hair as he watched the inky-black hellhounds streaking toward the main road below like otherworldly homing torpedoes of the damned.

Their eyes glowed red, and yes, they breathed fire.

"Will you stack with me, my friend?" said Thor one last time.

Sato looked down at his hands. His arm was bloody. He had only a few knives left.

Then...

"Of course, Warrior. Always."

"Good," rumbled Thor. "Get me the mule."

CHAPTER FIFTY-TWO

THE HELLHOUNDS AS THE CLOSED WERE revealed to be huge hulking dogs with rust-colored fur. They neither bayed nor howled but instead came on like hunting demons smelling blood. Their malicious eyes glowed red, and they left the road at the last second, in packs of four, and streaked up effortlessly through the red rocks along the hill of battle.

The Spartans engaged the ones they could, spearing the fearsome beasts dead and then hacking them to pieces from behind their shields even as the hounds tried to breathe fire on them.

The Spartans were good at this work.

Thor supported these actions with *Mjölnir* and killed several of the hounds menacing the ring of Spartans defending the road. All the while keeping an eye on the six running giants coming in from the dunes. Their flaming weapons dragging drooling strings of black smoke in the shimmering and relentless heat of the day that seemed as though it would never end.

"They approach quickly now, Warrior!" shouted Sato when the fire giants had passed a marker the Ranger had identified for the thief to alert him by.

Thor picked up the Carl and fired, not saying anything. His breathing was ragged and desperate. The air was hot and dry, and they were all more dehydrated than they should have been. But such is the Plane of Fire.

Down below on the road, Corporal Max with the M203 was engaging the screaming mad djinn with targeted fire and grenades from the launcher.

More dead djinn lay on the road in ruined heaps.

But some had gotten through, and Thor either needed to fire fast to pick them up and put them down, on the fly with the booming lightning strike of *Mjölnir*, the Grinder, blasting the guts of these hulking brutes out the back of their bodies as they came up the road, or go at them with tomahawks when the magazine on the anti-materiel rifle went dry and they'd made it as far as his position on the opposite side of the road from the steadfast corporal and the dead Spartans who died near him.

Alluria fired arrows from the rocks above, still near the body of the blind Spartan who'd been bitten by an imp and died from the lethal venom of the thing's bite.

When she'd asked him if she should run and get the priest, he'd said no, "Save it for my boys. I'm finished, girl."

Alluria had shot the imp through the heart. But it was too late.

The wind pulled at her long blond hair as her bow sang. Thor chanced one last protective glance at her and saw she was running low on arrows.

When he fired the Carl, he used an HE round.

He'd had about seven rounds left in the Bag of Holding on the thankless mule when the launcher had been brought forward and off that complaining beast.

Funny that it should survive and so many hadn't.

He'd laid them all out.

The recoilless rifle launcher did its *Whump* and *Crack*, and the round sped down off the hill and into the desert, streaking for the cohort of incoming giants.

One of the giants tried to catch it with a broad shield and was blown to bits instantly.

The rest came on anyway, peppered by shrapnel from the blast.

Sato was engaged with the djinn in knife combat nearby, and he was winning, but just barely. The sound of Corporal Max's gun was now barking out short bursts. On the rocks all around, the remaining Spartans speared and hacked at the hellhounds.

Shouts of *All the Way* and *Until Dawn* rose up with each kill.

But they were tired.

How long could they hold, wondered Thor.

As long as they need to, came the answer.

Or until they fall.

Honor. A debt to be paid.

Thor fired another Carl round, and this one killed two giants in a terrific explosion. There were now just two huge giants with flaming swords held high.

One...

... was Repham the Slayer. The general of the djinn.

He was in the front and running fast. Faster than the Ranger thought possible. Their closing was... imminent.

The firing of the eighty-eight-millimeter rounds had affected Thor's thinking. The dehydration too.

The last two fire giants reached his position, towering over the rocks and troopers all around and ready to deal death with their flaming weapons. Both saw Thor as the imminent danger, to them and their attack.

He had a round in the tube and was ready to fire when a flaming sword the size of a flagpole slammed into the rocks he was using for cover.

He was cut in a dozen places, and flames singed his arms.

He batted them out, rolling...

Fireballs from the djinn wizards streaked onto the road, exploding in terrific thunderclaps.

Thor scrambled, flung the launcher away, and rolled for *Mjölnir* as the fire giant general chased him and swung its unholy blade again, barely missing the Ranger, its heat searing his face in the passing.

Repham towered above the Ranger on his back now, raising the massive two-handed flaming sword made of blackened infernal steel mined from the lowest most loveless depths of hell.

Thor fired *Mjölnir.*

The round went right through Repham's hip, blowing out armor and bone matter and blood spray. The giant waved the flaming sword suddenly weakly, roaring in pain and dropping it, almost tossing it away as the named general of the fire giants stumbled back with disbelief from the Ranger who'd just... impossibly... unthinkably... *shot* it.

The Spartans were going at it with weapons on the other fire giant fighting from the rocks below. All of them stabbing with their spears. Hacking at the brute once he was down and growling murder at them.

Repham backed away, then fell to one knee, blood coming out of his mouth in great gouts.

Thor grabbed the huge flaming sword up from the dirt of the road, a thing that must have easily weighed two hundred pounds, and swung it, whirling his entire body in order to drive its massive burning hellish-dark fiery weight into the general's leg.

Repham howled, from either the sword strike or the arrow that appeared in the giant's glittering angry eye.

A gift from Alluria.

Thor dragged the flaming sword through the dirt once again, picked it up like it was a lance, and pushed it forward out in front of himself as he ran at the giant, driving it right into the hulking war leader's heart with a titanic grunt and a huge heave.

The general screamed in sudden pain afresh, his voice echoing off the rocks and out into the desert wastes all around. Then, enraged, he grabbed Thor with both of his massive bloody mailed fists and tried...

Tried...

Tried to crush the life out of Sergeant Thor.

But the giant was dead already. He just didn't know it yet.

The python's grip released, and Repham fell over onto his back with a terrific crash.

Thor gasped for air...

The corporal's gun was silent.

He could hear the djinn rallying for another screaming mad charge from the dunes below...

"Gotta..." he mumbled to himself. Bell rung from firing the Carl too many times. Well beyond endurances he'd ever pushed, and any wizard he'd ever met in Ranger school, and all the hard training and real-world fighting since...

He got to his hot boots and dragged the flaming sword out of the fire giant war leader's chest, bracing his boot on the thing's stomach to do so.

He stood there breathing heavily.

The djinn were coming now. Another last attack to see if they could win now that the line was so shattered.

Thor stumbled toward Repham's head, raising the flaming sword up high with the last of the strength he possessed...

And...

The Ranger slammed it down on the neck of Repham the Slayer, severing the fire giant's bulbous head.

Defeating a general of the Infernal Planes.

CHAPTER FIFTY-THREE

L IKE SOME BRONZE AGE WARRIOR FROM THE ancient past, Sergeant Thor held the bloody severed head of Repham the Slayer up, standing atop the high crimson rock over the road to the hill as the hordes of djinn berserkers rallied themselves for one last attack.

"And then some!" roared Thor, holding the blood-dripping giant's head, and the Spartans that had survived raised their spears and shouted in victory.

They would stand and defend the rocks... *no matter what happens.*

But the sight broke the army of djinn, and they fled back toward the realms of Air and Wild they came from, cursing the name of the one who had defeated them.

The battle was over.

CHAPTER FIFTY-FOUR

The beautiful efreeti queen and her entourage of red-and-black-skinned guard came out as the battlefield turned to utter silence.

Foes had faded into the vast waste, the dead lying ruined and flapping in the breeze on the bloody sands.

The Spartans had collected their own dead and carried them off the hill on their shields and down to the entrance of the City of Brass.

The captain was dead.

The first sergeant was dead.

Some of the platoon sergeants were dead.

Sergeant Thor and the remaining Spartans stood before the tall and imperious dark-skinned queen and her gleaming bodyguard.

Alluria and Sato too.

All were bloody and hurt to some extent.

Behind them, wrapped in their cloaks, the Spartans who had sacrificed all for honor lay on their shields. Unmoving.

The queen of the efreeti had huge blue eyes. She was dressed in gold silks, and her black-and-red skin was flawless. She spoke in a deep voice.

"You are Spartans?"

Corporal Max, still holding the M203, stepped forward.

"The debt is paid," he rasped. "Now."

She stared around for a long moment, her long slender neck turning her shapely head in utter amazement at all the slaughter and ruin that had been wrought to save her city.

"Yes," she said after a moment. "It is."

Max turned away. He was a man of deeds. Pretty words meant nothing to him. He had to bury his dead. Honor them. Collect their weapons and lead his men home.

The queen spoke once again in that deep otherworldly voice of hers.

"I am not some mere lender in the market. The debt... was not mine to make. Or require. I asked it of you but... would not have required it of you. Yet you are men of your word. No common thing these dark days of treachery and lies. And I must offer a gift. For saving my city. The City of Brass."

Max turned.

One of the platoon sergeants came forward with the captain's bloody cape and even bloodier sword. Draping Max in it as he stood there on the sands before the fantastic city in a bottle. Kneeling and offering the commander's bloody sword.

Max looked at Thor.

"I was the XO," he rasped in his tired voice. "It is our custom that every Six serve as corporal on the line, until it is time for him to lead. That way... we know what our men face when we ask the impossible of them."

He looked around at the dead for a long moment.

"We know..." he whispered.

The stately and beautiful queen walked forward away from the protection of her guards. She reminded Thor of beautiful African women he'd seen modeling in magazines and on TV back in the Before.

She was... stunning. Inhuman almost.

"Name your gift, Spartans. Then come... into my city and refresh yourselves until your next war."

Max cleared his throat.

"We Spartans only wish to go home to our women now. However long it takes. And bury our dead there. The debt is paid. We want to live."

She stared at Max for a long moment, and it was hard to tell if she was insulted... or just... *perplexed*.

Then, slowly, so stately that it was in this you could she was a queen and could never be anything else, she closed her eyes.

The lids of her eyes were painted in gold against her deep dark skin.

And then...

The Spartans around Thor faded from existence. And their dead too.

All that was left around the Ranger, in the wind and silence that followed, were the enemy dead and the ruin on the field.

And Sato. And Alluria. And the two horses.

And the thankless mule.

The queen looked at Thor.

"They have gone back across time... to their home, and their women. The debt is paid."

Then she began to walk back toward the open mouth of the genie bottle that was the City of Brass. She turned, and the wind caught her silks, blowing them wide and away from her tall and slender body.

"Come. Refresh yourselves among our cool fountains. Sleep in our ivory palaces. A great victory has been won. An evil defeated. We must celebrate. For that, too, is life. And to live... is also a part of war."

CHAPTER FIFTY-FIVE

ON A COOL AFTERNOON IN THE CITY OF BRASS, beneath tall ivory towers and in the shadows of fortresses and palaces, the purple light of the outer bottle drenching the city in an otherworldly light that seemed to mark it safe from the brutal environments of the Plane of Fire, as strange creatures and other races seldom seen thronged its quiet-music morning streets, overwhelmed by exotic spices and floral paradises, Sato met Sergeant Thor near a tea house the thief favored.

"We must leave soon, Warrior. But first, before we go any farther in this life... I must confess something to you, and in doing so, Warrior, I hope... you will still count me as your friend after my words have been spoken."

Thor said nothing.

And after a long moment, Sato continued.

"I have deceived you for quite some time. Since the City of Thieves."

"How so?" asked Thor.

"The girl is not... who you would think she is, Warrior."

Thor laughed.

"Kinda figured that out, Sato. She's an operator."

The thief made a face at this word. He didn't understand.

"One of us. A guild member. A thief. A specialist like Well Well in some tradecraft of the guild."

Then the thief smiled wanly even though he'd been so serious and nodded that this was... *partly true.*

He continued.

"Not quite. But... in a way, yes, Warrior. She is... my friend. And she is... the Queen of Thieves. Leader of our guild, and no mean person of little note."

Thor drank some tea. It was peppermint, and it was quite refreshing.

An operator. Certainly.

Ulterior motives. No doubt.

The Queen of Thieves herself...

That was unexpected.

"We have journeyed with you so she could... *steal* the Pearl from you," Sato said. "I am so sorry, my friend. But this was our plan all along. And it has troubled me greatly. But... she is my queen."

To Thor, that was more than unexpected.

That was a shock.

He checked his cargo pocket. He still had the Pearl.

"Tonight," said Sato. "I believe she plans to take it tonight. And then she will leave the city without you."

Thor was silent for a long moment.

"Why?"

Sato looked off into the bustling streets bathed in soft purple light.

"Ahhhh, Warrior... I would have to tell you a very long and sad tale. A tale of a little girl whose father... was once a great thief. Who went to steal a fabled treasure in a faraway city, and how he was captured in a trap deep in a dungeon none have ever returned from.

"I would have to tell you of how his jailer requires an artifact in exchange for his freedom and has made known to the girl... that the Pearl will set her father free. A father... whom she loves.

"I would have to tell you, Warrior, tell you of this and many dangerous things and a very dangerous wizard some call... the Dreaming Sorcerer, who makes his lair in the City of Palms, far to the other side of the Eastern Wastes.

"I would have to tell you... all these things... to explain why we would rob you of the Pearl."

Thor nodded.

Took a sip of his tea.

"I am sorry, Warrior."

"Tonight?" asked Thor.

"Yes."

"Then why tell me, Sato?"

The thief lowered his head in shame.

"She is my liege. I have protected her, raised her, and trained her since she was of eight years. Perhaps I did wrong. It was all I knew, Warrior. All that we of the guild... knew. He was our leader. She was our queen. I tell you these things, Warrior... because you are my friend. And that is greater, I realize now, than the love of kings and queens."

EPILOGUE

In the night she woke him.

"Are you asleep?" she asked.

He hadn't been. He'd been waiting for her to try and steal the Pearl.

"Yes," he said, feigning being groggy with sleep.

She was quiet, sitting up in bed for a long moment and covering her nakedness with the fine silk sheets of the queen's palace.

Then, in the dark, she spoke.

"Tonight... I was going to steal from you."

She was silent. Waiting, perhaps, for him to speak. Or to snore.

He did neither.

He was listening.

"I did not want to. But... it's a long story, Warrior. I have to. But I won't. I will find another way. I won't steal from you."

In the dark he pulled her close, down onto his chest.

She lay there, crying for a while.

Then...

"In the morning... we will do what must be done, Alluria."

She relaxed, and in time she was asleep, snoring lightly on his chest where her hot tears had fallen.

Sergeant Thor lay awake for a long while in the dark, listening to the sleeping palace, the sleeping city.

Thinking of edges...

Thinking of the Dreaming Sorcerer.

THE END

SGT THOR WILL RETURN

IN

THOR THE VICTORIOUS

To our **Kickstarter Backers**! Your support for SGT Thor and Wargate Books helped to make this story possible!

TO OUR GALAXY's EDGE INSIDERS

You've been there from the Land of the Black Sleep to Galaxy's Edge and beyond. Thank you.